Saviour of the Pack

The Other Wolf, Book 3

Heather G. Harris

In remembrance of my darling dog, Oscar.
The best pup in the world.

Chapter 1

I winced as Tristan ripped out a chunk of Greg's fur, exposing red-raw flesh underneath. Theirs was the final fight of our pack tourney, the battle for number two, beta to my alpha. I was *supposed* to be impartial but fuck that; I was inches away from standing up and cheering for Greg. It's not like everyone didn't already know that he was my lover.

Stop toying with him and finish it! growled Esme.

I don't think he's messing about, I disagreed.

Esme snorted. **Greg and his wolf could destroy Tristan in seconds. They choose not to. They give him hope, so the win will be more crushing.**

You sound like you approve.

It is a different way to hunt prey. It is not as good as my way.

What is your way?

Instant death, she said decisively.

Sure but Tristan is a member of our pack. We don't want to kill our pack. It was bad that I sometimes felt I had to spell this out to my wolfish counterpart.

Tristan does not accept us as alpha, she sniffed. **He knelt, but he does not accept us. Not truly. Better a dead dissenter than a live one.**

It's frowned on to kill people just because they don't like you.

You humans frown too much. Who cares what your face does?

Not for the first time, I was speechless. I'm one of a kind, a werewolf who can pipe. Like the Pied Piper, I can talk to animals – all animals, not just rats. My magic means that I can actually *speak* to my resident wolf. Most of the time that's a blessing, but other days the chasm between us is so wide that no bridge could cross it. She's my sister from another mister – a wolf mister – but she is a sister, nonetheless. And, like all siblings, sometimes we squabble but the love is always there.

My breath caught as Tristan's claw snagged Greg's haunches. Greg's wolf let out an ominous growl – not a yip of pain but a *deep* growl. The hammer was about to fall. His eyes flashed gold for a second before returning to their usual shade of blue, then he swung into action.

Now I could see that Esme was right. As Greg pushed into the next gear, Tristan didn't stand a chance. My beta bared his teeth and flashed his deadly fangs, but that was all the warning Tristan got before Greg slammed forcefully into him and sent him skidding across the dewy grass.

My heart was hammering as I watched. The potential for deadly violence was hanging in the air; if Greg lost control of his wolf now, he would rip out Tristan's throat.

As Greg prowled forward, the tension in the field was high. All the spectators seemed to be holding their breath. Tristan got to his feet, ready to go again.

Fool. He should have stayed down, Esme murmured. I didn't disagree.

At the last moment, Greg put on a burst of speed. Tristan did the same and they collided in a clash of claws and fur. 'Come on Greg,' I whispered.

I needn't have worried. In a blur, Greg was gripping Tristan by his throat. Tristan froze – we all did. One wrong move by him, or a tiny slip of Greg's control, and Tristan's lifeblood was going to spill all over the ground.

Then Tristan carefully tucked his tail between his legs and let out the softest whine. *He concedes!* I said jubilantly to Esme.

But will Greg accept it? she asked softly, tension radiating through our bond.

There was a beat that carried on too long before Greg released Tristan's neck. The pack erupted into cheers, and I sank back into my deckchair. That had been so close; Greg had been inches away from finishing Tristan, and Tristan knew it. The question was, would that knowledge make him more tractable, or less?

Tristan gave a few licks to his wounds before crouching and starting the shift back to human. He was a fast shifter relatively speaking, and it took him only about three minutes, but Greg was done in barely a minute. I could have sworn his shift was getting faster, though I didn't know if that were possible.

He stood, naked and unabashed, as a murmur ran through the crowd. His wounds had healed completely during the shift, and there wasn't a mark to be seen. Even I didn't have that kind of recovery. Werewolves heal fast, but that was something else.

Greg pulled on some tracksuit trousers, black of course, and sauntered over. His body was clean; he wasn't even sweating. I smiled at him, 'Good work, second.'

He nodded back, all business. 'It is my pleasure to continue to serve you, Alpha.' The phrase brought all kinds of fun things to mind and I fought a blush. The twitch of his lips suggested I wasn't as good at hiding my thoughts as I'd like.

I stood up and turned to face the assembled pack. 'With the placement of Greg Manners as my second, I now declare the pack tourney complete! Let's celebrate!' A cheer arose. The indomitable Mrs Dawes and her helpers had already started bringing out trays of food for the hungry contestants.

The tourney had started in the dead of night, lit by nothing more than the moon and a few fiery torches. The pack had some sixty-five members, with a few pups that were still too young to call their wolves, and the tourney began with the lowest-ranked. They fought one on one, but at the start of the night we'd had two battles running concurrently, then the winners fought each other. Next there was another bout of four, with the winner of that fighting the last winner.

The early rounds were almost ceremonial in nature. When you were ranked so low in the pack, it didn't really matter if you were sixty-first or sixty-second; there was little reason to let the fur fly and the blood run. Those bouts lasted no more than a token sixty seconds and the vibe was friendly.

Things shifted as the tourney entered the midway point. The atmosphere turned from jovial to tense and anticipatory. The fights became longer and bloodier, and I was glad I didn't have to participate. As alpha, the only time I have to fight is if I'm challenged for leadership; until then, I'm sitting pretty.

There were more than a few surprises in the tourney. The biggest one for me was mild-mannered Mrs Dawes shooting up from forty-one to twenty-two. Seren and Marissa swapped places, moving Seren up to sixth. She had

absolutely *trounced* Marissa, and it still took some adjust-
ment for me to reconcile the moody Goth with the vicious
wolf I'd seen today.

Afterwards, neither woman had looked at the other, and
tension hummed between them. The fight had resolved
nothing. There was definitely some personal beef going on
between them that I wasn't privy to. I hated not knowing
every scrap of gossip, but I'd find out the truth eventually.
I was too nosy not to.

Archie had climbed from twelfth to fifth, a huge
achievement for the nineteen year old. Our resident gar-
dener, David, had moved up from eleventh to eighth. I
saw a few of the single females eying him with interest,
including Seren, who'd broken his heart once before. I
wasn't sure he'd trust her with it a second time.

I wondered if Seren and Marissa were fighting over
David, but one glance at Marissa shot down that theory;
she was looking at David like he'd peed in her favourite
shoes. That was interesting in itself because Marissa was a
smiling assassin. She wore a friendly smile like a mask to
keep all and sundry at bay. I thought she was lonely, and I
made a note to keep a closer eye on her. Alone isn't a nice
place to be, unless it's with a good book and a glass of wine.

Noel, who'd last competed in a pack tourney when he
was high on the drug Boost, had sunk back down the pack
ranks to thirteenth. He was still in the pack's battle core –

but only just. Brian has also suffered a fall from grace, from eighth to twelfth. He looked decidedly pissed off about it.

The unknowns in all this were Finley March and Daniella Hardcrest. When we'd placed our notice with the werewolf council that we were having a pack tourney, we'd received a petition from two separate loners to join us. Loners are few and far between, so to have two petition us was rare. Daniella had slipped in at fourteen and Finley had made number nine.

Having an unknown in our top thirteen didn't sit well with me, but those were the breaks. I hoped we'd get to know each other quickly. I was dying to ask which packs they'd come from, but apparently that was rude with a capital R. Once wolves go lone, their names are struck from their original pack's roster. That seemed a little harsh to me.

Finley and Daniella had both asked to live in the mansion and I'd agreed, allocating them rooms on the ground floor near Archie and Elena. Finley was a chef and Daniella was a nurse, so they both had the capacity to help the pack. So far Finley had kept himself to himself, whereas Daniella seemed a mite friendlier. They eyed each other warily; though they professed not to know each other well, they'd frequented the same circles.

Elena had already adopted them both, whether they wanted her to or not. She was still working through the grief of losing her brother, and I knew she blamed a lot of his loss on him going lone.

Thea Frost was another issue entirely. She was still a guest in the mansion, but we hadn't formally accepted her into our ranks. She was a werewolf that couldn't shift and she'd be a burden on any pack that accepted her. Worse still, she was Beckett Frost's sister and Beckett was alpha-asshole supreme. He wasn't going to let her go easily.

I'd hired our local witch, Amber DeLea, to see if she could concoct a potion to help Thea with her shifting issues, but so far nothing had worked. We had one more potion to try before I'd have no choice but to play my hand.

Thea had watched the pack proceedings glumly. I'd expected her to be pleased when Archie moved up the ranks, but if anything she'd seemed more depressed. Their courtship appeared to have cooled a little since Archie had learned of her shifting problem. He'd admitted to me that he wanted an equal in the relationship – and that included her wolf. If she couldn't run and hunt with him, so many of the joys of pairing with a fellow wolf would be denied to him. I'd noticed him eyeing Daniella – and I'd noticed the despondent Thea noticing, too.

The celebratory feast was going full swing. We were drinking breakfast mimosas and the music was blaring out. The sun was up, and it was warm enough to brush away the April chill. Frankly, I felt on top of the world. Which was how I knew it would all come crashing down on me at any moment.

Chapter 2

Greg and I had gone on a few cloak-and-dagger dates before some choice words from Archie had made it clear that we weren't fooling anyone; the whole pack knew we were an item. It had taken a while for Greg to feel comfortable with public displays of affection, and even now the most he would go to was sitting a little too close to me. Sometimes he'd tolerate a hand on his thigh, but he'd explained that handholding was a no-no because that might delay him reaching for a weapon in an emergency. Let me tell you, dating an ex-soldier/current soldier comes with baggage.

He was totally worth it, though. Behind closed doors he was more than happy to display his affection, and I was absolutely on board with that. Besides, I'm the alpha, the boss, the big cheese, and keeping things clean helped retain my authority – or so Greg insisted. It was this same authority that had me reluctantly retiring from the pack party early. I wanted more mimosas; I wanted to sing to the music and dance on the tables like Seren was doing, albeit I wouldn't be casting sultry looks at David as I did so.

I gave Greg's thigh one last squeeze because I could, then left them to it, Greg included. He deserved to let his hair down, too.

As I mooched back to the mansion, I cast out my magic to find Ares. The unicorn was close, but he was keeping to the shadows of the trees. The pack tourney had brought back his memories of the black tourneys in which he'd been an unwilling combatant. I sent him soothing thoughts and a hint of apology because I should have thought to warn him.

Across the distance between us, I felt him shake his head and give a defiant whinny. He was fine and I was to stop being a worrywart. I got a sense of movement and protection; he was going to patrol our borders whilst the pack was occupied. I sent him my appreciation and gently disengaged our minds.

I'd really been stretching my piping skills. Once, I'd needed to touch my subject to communicate, then I'd needed at least to make eye contact and hum a little song. Now, if I knew the mind I was seeking, I could do it without seeing them. I rarely did that because it used a huge amount of magical energy, but I'd just been for a recharge so I should be good for a week if I was cautious with my piping skills. Shifting to four hardly seemed to drain me at all; it was piping that led to that itching feeling, like an army of ants was crawling underneath my skin. Ugh.

Rosie's café is the local portal, but having discovered that Maxwell, the hall's guardian, was related to me, I'd been driving an extra forty minutes to the next portal. I'd received a few missed calls from Maxwell – he knew something was up, but he didn't know what. Soon, I'd get the balls to tell him. Soon, but not yet. I was still doing my best ostrich impression, burying my head in the sand and singing la-la-la nice and loud.

When I slunk into my office my new fourth, Liam, was sitting at the security console. He had an impressive bruise blooming over his eye from his tussle with Tristan. By tomorrow it would be gone. Werewolf healing is so much better than a regular human's.

'Hey,' I greeted him. 'Did you see the fight between Greg and Tristan?'

'On the screen,' he confirmed. 'It looked vicious, but Greg had it under control.' There was a note of jealousy in his voice. Although Tristan hadn't made Greg so much as sweat, he'd trounced Liam. Liam was young, and his ego was a little bruised.

Liam was too gentle. He didn't want to hurt Tristan, but Tristan was quite happy to hurt him.

'You only lost to Tristan because you didn't want to hurt him.' I voiced Esme's view aloud.

Liam grimaced. 'I used to admire him. We hung out with Mark a lot in the old days, and I thought we were friends.' He hesitated and stopped himself from saying more. He didn't need to; Tristan hated me, and Liam helped me. I was the beef in their friendship burger.

I didn't apologise for it, but I did change the subject. 'Aren't you supposed to be at the party?'

'Someone has to watch things. I promised Greg I'd do it so he can relax for once,' Liam said gruffly.

'That's good of you, Liam.'

'It's no problem, Alpha.'

I sighed internally. I *liked* Liam, I really did, but I had no idea what he thought of me. He'd definitely come to accept me as his alpha, and he was utterly dependable, but we were a long way from being friends. He held my title between us like a shield. I'm a social butterfly: I love people, and I love being loved. Accepting lukewarm companionship is difficult.

'I can watch things for a bit if you want some down time,' I suggested.

He looked at me with barely concealed horror. 'No, thank you, Alpha. It's fine.'

I sat down at my desk. No problem – I had a million things to do. I pulled up my spreadsheet to see what my next planned action was and cross-referenced it with what would save us the most money. We might be a rich pack, but that was no reason to throw money away.

I flicked to tab B on the sheet and saw that my next job was changing the pack's electricity provider. We were being *rinsed*. The fun never ends.

I got off the phone to a green-energy provider. Their energy wasn't the cheapest, but it was *green* and that was important. I'd take the price trade-off if I knew we were being environmentally friendly, making the world a better place one canvas bag at a time. I went back to my spreadsheet and made some handy notes on tab B.

As always when I caught a few minutes to spare, I pulled up my 'witchy suspects' spreadsheet. It was achingly bare. One of the pages had details of local hair and nail salons, I'd already called most of them, but there were a few outliers left.

The black witch who'd been a part of the kidnapping syndicate was still a loose end that irritated me. She was out there somewhere, and our pack – and all of the Other children – were at risk until she was found. I had no doubt she'd recruit some new stooges easily enough and, if Voltaire was to be believed, she had some kidnapped vampyrs chained up somewhere, too. Either that, or they were already ash and dust.

The only clue we had for the black witch was that she had turquoise-painted nails. It was an unusual colour choice because everyone these days was wearing muted colours or glittery, sparkly decoration. She'd probably changed her nail colour by now, but I had to hope one of the salons had painted her nails and could help me. I dialled up a number.

'Lucious Locks and Lashes, Samantha speaking. How can I help?'

'Oh, hi. I'd love to get my sister a surprise gift voucher for her birthday but I can't remember where she goes to get her nails painted. They're always turquoise. Does she come to you?'

'What's her name, please?'

'Er, she does this weird thing where she gives a different name for every appointment. Her husband is really controlling about her spending – it's another reason why I want to give her this voucher.'

'What an asshole,' Samantha commented. 'One sec, let me ask the girls if it rings a bell.' She covered over the phone so her words were muffled, but I easily made out what she was saying. 'Hayley, Jen, have either of you painted turquoise nails recently?'

'Nah.'

'No, not me.'

Samantha came back on the line. 'Not us, sorry. Hope you manage to find the salon. If you don't, give us a bell back and we'll happily paint your sister's nails any colour she likes. And if there's a colour her husband hates, we can absolutely do that.'

I laughed. 'Thanks, Samantha. I'll keep you guys in mind, for sure.' I hung up and hit my head on my desk with a thunk.

There was a knock on the door. 'Come in,' I called from my prone position on the desk.

'I brought you a drink, Alpha,' Mrs Dawes said with a smile. She placed a cup of tea next to my head.

'Thanks Mrs Dawes. You're the best.' I sat up. 'That's very kind of you to think of me in the midst of all this joviality.'

'I saw you slip away. Is everything okay?'

I sighed. 'I'm just doing a few jobs. I'm trying to track down that sneaky black witch. I thought the turquoise nails might be a good lead, but nooooo. None of the salons I've called have been able to help. We'd be in trouble if she had nails like you.' I pointed to Mrs Dawes' flawless French manicure. 'You're so classy.'

'Maybe she does her nails herself.'

'I hope not, or we're totally screwed. Do you paint yours?'

'I do.'

'You've got a steady hand,' I commented. 'Those lines are flawless. When I try and do a French manicure, the white lines are always different thicknesses and a bit wavy.'

'Practice makes perfect.'

'True enough.'

My phone blared and I smiled when I saw who it was. *Bestie calling*, my phone screen informed me. 'Excuse me, Mrs Dawes, I've got to take this.' I swiped to answer and Mrs Dawes withdrew politely and shut my office door. She hadn't brought a drink for Liam; there were perks to being the alpha.

'Hey, Jess!' I said happily.

'Hey, lovely. How are you?'

'I'm good, thanks. We've just finished the pack tourney and everyone is celebrating.'

'Except you,' Jess said perceptively.

I sighed and cast a furtive glance at Liam. Yep, he could totally hear me, and he could probably hear Jess, too. I cleared my throat. 'Liam, take a walk for a few minutes.'

'I'll do a perimeter check,' he promised, and rose from the security console. He shut the heavy door behind him, leaving me in total privacy for the first time that day.

I slumped in my chair again and drew up my legs so I was comfy. 'Greg kept his place as my second,' I confirmed triumphantly.

'Was that ever in doubt?'

'No, I don't think so. He trounced his only challenger. It was a bit touch and go for a minute, and I thought he was going full wolf. His eyes flashed gold and he had his jaws around Tristan's throat...'

'But he held it together?'

'Yes, of course he did.' Pride shone in my voice. 'He smashed it. Everyone will think twice about challenging him again.'

'No doubt that was his intention.'

'Yeah, you're right. He's a smart one, all right. Apparently, it drives his mother wild that he doesn't have a degree, but intelligence is more than a piece of paper. Greg has life experience in spades.'

'I've met his mother. She's scary.'

I groaned. 'Great. Make me even more nervous about meeting her, please.'

'Are you at the meet-the-parents stage?'

'I don't know. I've been thinking about introducing him to my family.'

'Speaking of family – have you spoken to any of the Alessandro clan?'

'No,' I admitted. 'It's on my to-do.'

'Your "never-going-to-do"?'

'No, I *am* going to talk to them.' Even to my own ears, I didn't sound convincing. Jess snorted. 'I am!' I protested. 'Of course I want to meet them and talk to them properly, but I need to know I'm not endangering them first.'

'And now we get around to the reason behind my call,' Jess said smugly.

My breath caught. 'You've found a way into Birkenhead Town Hall?' I asked breathlessly.

'I've found a way into Birkenhead Town Hall. But the window of opportunity is tight.'

'How tight?'

'Tighter than a stripper's ass. We need to do it tonight.'

Fuck. Tonight I'd find out the prophecy and then there would be no hiding from my birth family. No ducking and diving. Could I do it tonight? The pack would be carousing into the small hours. We'd organised a huge barbecue and I'd bought enough wine to run France dry. No one would notice if I slipped off for a few hours. Probably. 'Tonight works for me.'

'Great. It has to be just the two of us. I've bribed one of the security guards, but I promised it would only be us.'

'No problem. I'll leave Greg a note.'

'That will go down well,' she said drily.

'I'll be with you, so how much trouble can we get into?' Jess has all sorts of cool magical powers, not to mention a hellhound called Gato, and a magical dagger called Glimmer. And I had Esme. I'm not a babe in the woods anymore.

'How much trouble could we get into? Hmm. Breaking into the Connection's property to steal a prophecy? Not much trouble at all.' Jess's voice was a shade away from laughter.

Okay, a lot of trouble. 'And you're sure this will work, right?' I asked.

'Sure, no – but I am fairly confident. Why shouldn't it work? When I killed Mrs H, I got her magic including her seer magic. If her prophecy is tuned to her, I see no reason why it shouldn't accept me. We should be able to pick it up, no worries.'

'I love that you're so calm about this.'

'Mrs H is dead, so we're pretty stuck for options.' Jess paused. 'There *is* another option but it's ... complicated.'

'What other option?'

'That's Plan B, and it's need-to-know only.'

'Don't I need to know it?'

'Not yet.'

'Jess,' I whined, 'you're keeping secrets. Didn't we agree not to do that?' I sulked a bit. She knows *everything* about me.

'You know all of *my* secrets,' she replied. 'But this one isn't mine. Anyway, be ready. A car will be at the mansion in ten minutes.'

'What?' I protested, but she had already hung up. 'That's cheating!' I yelled at the dial tone.

Ten minutes didn't give me long. I ran to my room and chucked things haphazardly into my black holdall. What did one wear to a break-in? I threw in some of my pack tracksuits, all horribly black, but for once I didn't care. I was strangely exhilarated – I was going on a heist! I'd never been on one before, but I'd watched a lot of heist movies. That counted, right?

I scrawled a quick note for Greg and left it on my office desk. Glancing at the security console, I saw a car idling outside the gates. Using the intercom, I gave it instructions to stay put and headed out before it drew Liam's attention. When I'd looked at the security cameras, he was at the other side of the grounds, running the perimeter. It was going to be close. As alpha, I probably didn't need to sneak out like a thief in the night, but I didn't want an argument. Sometimes discretion is the better part of valour.

I pushed my arms through the holdall handles like it was a rucksack, and ran down the driveway, enjoying the extra speed that my werewolf muscles gave me. A normal human would take two minutes to run down our drive, but I did it in forty-five seconds.

I was just about to leap over the fence when I caught sight of two wolves loping around the perimeter. I didn't recognise them, so I dropped the holdall and prepared to shift. They saw me looking at them and trotted over. Their body language was friendly, but I didn't trust them.

They are ours, Esme confirmed once she could scent them. **They are pack.**

I don't recognise them.

It is Finley and Daniella.

The former lone wolves had professed not to know each other, yet here they were trotting around together. 'Shift,' I ordered them curtly.

I had to wait a couple of minutes until they were both standing naked before me.

'Alpha,' Daniella greeted me, her tone warm and friendly.

'Daniella, Finley. What are you doing?'

'We wanted to help out. With the tourney in full swing, we thought we'd do a perimeter check.'

'I appreciate the sentiment,' I said finally. 'The tourney has finished now and Liam is performing the perimeter check. If you want to be added to the security roster, please let Manners know.'

'Did he secure beta position again?' Finley asked curiously.

'Of course.' I couldn't help my sense of unease. They might just be trying to help, but why hadn't they told someone where they were going, or asked me or Manners how they could be useful? Instead, they'd slunk off. 'Next time you want to be helpful, please speak with me or Manners and we'll allocate you an appropriate role,' I said firmly.

'Yes, Alpha,' they replied in unison and ducked their heads. They were being creepily compliant.

'Back to the mansion, both of you.' I ordered.

They didn't question me, just turned and walked away. For people who didn't know each other, they seemed awfully comfortable being naked together. Perhaps they were used to it; I was a relatively new werewolf but even I was getting used to the nudity. I was probably being unfairly suspicious.

I'd picked up my holdall and slung it on my back again when I heard a happy whinny and turned to face Ares, who was trotting towards me. My quick getaway wasn't going so well. He came to a stop in front of me, let out a loud harrumph and pawed at the ground with his reptilian claws.

I reached out and touched his mind gently. *I'm just popping out. You guard things here.*

Ares straightened visibly and gave a whicker of agreement. He pranced, lifting his forepaws up with every step like he was a dressage pony, then trotted off, mane sparkling in the sun.

'Alpha?'

Oh shit. My chat with Finley and Daniella had given Liam enough time to find me. My discreet getaway had been an abject failure. That didn't bode well for my sneaky evening heist.

'Oh, hi Liam. I'm just out for … some business. I'll be back tomorrow.'

'Does Greg know you're going?'

'Who is the alpha?' I asked archly.

'You, of course.'

'Right. Well, then, there you go.' I changed the subject quickly. 'I found Finley and Daniella out here patrolling the perimeter together.'

'They must have just started. I didn't see them on the monitors before I left.'

'I find it surprising that they came out here rather than staying at the party and mixing with the rest of the pack. Ask Greg to keep an eye on them for me. I'm off. I won't be long.'

Now that I had an audience, I didn't fancy trying to leap over the fence in case it went embarrassingly wrong so I buzzed for the gate to open and calmly walked to the waiting car. As I slid in the back seat, I instructed the driver, 'Go!'

He turned to me; it was Tom Smith, Emory's right-hand man. 'In a hurry, Alpha?'

'It's a jail break,' I admitted. 'A really shit jail break. Put the pedal to the floor!'

He flashed me a grin and turned back to the road. When he obligingly put his foot to the floor, the wheels spun before the car leapt forward. I turned around, looked out of the rear window and gave Liam a finger wave. His disapproving expression did not waver. Oops.

I stifled a sigh. Maybe I wasn't doing the right thing. I'd wanted to give Greg a break, a nice chilled-out time at the tourney party; he was my boyfriend, and I'd wanted that for him. But as my second, he probably wasn't going to be thrilled about me hopping off.

I was with Tom Smith and going to meet Jess, who has a magical skill set that would rival Dumbledore's. And I had

Esme. I didn't feel like running off was a bad decision, but maybe not communicating it wasn't my wisest choice.

I pulled out my phone and scrolled through my contacts, hesitating a moment before dialling *Sexy Bear*. Greg hadn't loved the nickname I'd given him after one too many 'Doll Faces'.

My phone barely rang before he answered. 'Alpha.' His voice was tight. Ah. He wasn't alone.

'Can you grab some privacy a second?' I waited, hearing the crunch of gravel. He must have been on the drive.

Greg started to talk, and his tone wasn't happy. 'Where are you going?' he demanded without preamble.

'Jess needs a hand. You're all busy, so I thought I'd pop out.'

'You're ... popping out ... to Liverpool,' he asked dubiously.

'Yes! It's only a three-hour journey. No biggie.' Greg wasn't going to buy it for a second; three hours in America or Canada might be a commute, but in the UK it's an arduous journey. Unfortunately, not too long ago I'd been caught out by an enemy bugging my car, so I'd learnt to be wary of divulging sensitive information over the phone or in cars.

'Can't talk too much about it,' I said pointedly. 'But Tom is with me now, and Jess and Gato will be with me soon. I have back-up. I wanted you to party with the pack.'

'I'd rather be with you,' he said unhappily. 'I'm supposed to watch your back.'

'It's tanned, and I scrubbed it with a loofah last night,' I joked. 'It's fine, Greg, really. You do your thing and I'll do mine. Just relax and enjoy yourself for once. I'll speak to you tomorrow. I love you.'

'Love you, Peaches.'

I hung up, put the phone on silent and slid it into my bag. If I didn't see it, then I wasn't missing any calls. Tom met my eyes in the rear-view mirror. 'Manners is going to kick your ass.'

'Yeah,' I agreed balefully. 'Probably. Can we get a McDonald's on the way? An apple pie would really help right now.'

He grinned. 'A final meal. Nice.'

Tom and Greg had worked together for years, so I'd convinced myself that Greg wouldn't be too mad about being left behind. But Tom wasn't letting me pretend anymore, and reality was biting. The prophecy had better be worth it.

Chapter 3

The drive north passed quickly with a spot of karaoke and hitting the drive-through. Tom is the strong, silent type, so mostly I amused myself by imagining the various scenarios in which our plans could go horrendously wrong. I hoped Emory was on standby with bailout money.

Tom parked in front of Jess's house and switched off the engine. I grabbed my bag and hauled ass while he stayed in the car in sentinel mode.

I rang the doorbell and the door swung open. Jess greeted me with a hug. She smiled sweetly at Tom, then pulled me in to the house. 'Brew?' she queried.

'You have to ask?'

Jess put on the kettle, dug out some biscuits and we settled in the living room with our cups of tea. 'So what's the plan?' I asked.

'The less you know the better.'

'Okay. Well, I have black clothes. Do you have camo paint?'

She snorted with laughter. 'Luce, we're not being ninjas. We're just walking into a building and walking out of a building.'

'And stealing a prophecy.'

'Exactly. Simple.'

'I even brought gloves with me,' I complained.

'That's probably sensible. No need to make it easier for the cops than we need to.'

'What time do we rock and roll?'

She grinned. 'Not until dark, Thelma.'

'If I'm Thelma, you're Louise.'

'It is definitely that way round.'

I stuck out my tongue, but it was hard to disagree; if either of us was a loose cannon, it was me.

'Let's put on some *Gilmore Girls* and chat,' Jess suggested.

'You know I'm always up for that. Hey, where's Gato?'

'With Nate, but Nate will be on standby with him later.' She was referring to the vampyr who was inextricably bound to my best friend.

'Standby for what?'

'Plan B.'

I was dressed in jeans and a leather jacket; Jess had vetoed my black tracksuit look because apparently it made me look way too thuggish. I thought it was perfect for skulking, but she disagreed. As she was the professional sneak, being a private investigator and occasional object-acquirer, I agreed to follow her lead.

I went to university in Liverpool but, although I knew the city, I wasn't too familiar with Birkenhead. I knew by its reputation that it was a bit of a rough area, so I was somewhat surprised when we drew up to an area with beautiful sandstone buildings and what I guessed was nineteenth-century architecture. 'I thought Birkenhead was rough,' I commented.

'This is Hamilton Square. It's fancy.'

'No shit. Look at that clock tower. Wait, is that where we're breaking in?'

'Yup. In the Common, it's used to report births and deaths.'

'And in the Other?'

'It stores seers' prophecies.'

'This is the part where you tell me it's guarded by a sphinx,' I half-joked.

She flashed me a grin. 'No, just a few wizard security guards. But I've only bribed the one,

so we have to wait for him.'

It had only just gone 8pm and darkness had fallen, but it wasn't the dead of night. I hadn't

managed to eat much earlier because of nerves, and my tummy gave a loud growl.

We should hunt soon, Esme suggested.

'You want to go for Thai food after?' Jess echoed. 'There's a phenomenal Thai around the corner called Sawasdee.'

'Are you always thinking about food?'

'Not always. Often, though,' she conceded. 'There's our guy. Come on.'

A man in a smart navy uniform was hanging out of a side door. He held it open as we slipped inside. 'You're on your own from here,' he said brusquely. 'But you should have twenty minutes before Mike comes through for a check.' He shut the door and mooched off with his torch, leaving us in darkness.

'You'd think they'd turn on the lights,' I bitched.

'Electricity prices are crazy.'

I thought of the packs' bills and winced. 'No kidding.'

The Town Hall had the type of carpet that made me think of my great auntie's: red and filled with busy patterns. We crept down the shallow stairs and inched past a metal bust of some general dude from Peru. The whole place had a grand feel, so I was pretty disappointed when we reached the basement. It looked like an industrial gym: no whorls or embellishments here. I had a life-changing prophecy stored here, but the room wasn't giving off life-changing vibes. 'They need to get an interior decorator in here,' I muttered.

Jess snorted. 'Focus, Luce.'

'Do you know where we're going?'

'Not exactly, but Nate described it to me. It should be around this corner.'

We turned the corner and I let out a low whistle. 'Now that's more like it.'

The room was lined with bookshelves, but instead of being laden with books they held glowing orbs painted with swirling lights. It cast a glow in the room much like I imagined the aurora borealis must be. 'Awesome,' Jess breathed.

'Yeah – but how the hell do we find mine?'

'Apparently, they are categorised by the seer who gave them. Let's spread out. Shout if you see Lady Harding's name.'

'We only have twenty minutes,' I protested.

'Then spread out fast,' Jess suggested drily.

My heart was pounding but whether it was with the excitement of potentially finding the prophecy or the fear of being discovered, I wasn't sure.

It was a long three minutes before Jess whispered harshly, 'Over here, Lucy!' I fumbled my way to her. Sure enough, she was standing in front of a gold plaque with Mrs H's name on it; behind it were dozens of orbs. Without discussion, we split up again and started to look up and down the shelves. Then I saw it: *Luciana Alessandro*.

'Here!' It came out as a croak.

Jess hastily joined me, and I pointed wordlessly to my name. She reached out to pick up the orb, but her hand froze inches from it. 'What is it?' I asked anxiously.

'I can't get any closer,' she admitted. Her face creased with effort, and her hand shook as she tried to push it closer to the orb, but it wouldn't budge. It slid up and down like she was pressing against a glass pane.

Disappointment welled up in me, acrid and raw. This couldn't be the end. I *needed* this prophecy; my parents had died for it, and I had to know it. 'Maybe you need to summon the magic? You know, call it up?' I suggested.

'I am calling,' Jess said between clenched teeth. 'It isn't answering.'

'Maybe you're calling it from the wrong place. I have to draw the piping magic up from inside somewhere.'

'Where? Your toes? Your knees? Your vag—'

'My tummy. It feels like it comes from my tummy.'

'Not your lady garden?'

'No. That would give a whole new meaning to feminist power. Try drawing it up from your tummy.'

'I'm trying.' Her hand still refused to touch the orb.

'Nothing?'

'Nothing.'

'Fuck.'

'Yeah.'

I reached out, just in case the orb recognised me as the intended recipient of the prophecy. Sometimes magic is smart like that. When my trembling hand was next to Jess's, it stayed there, hovering uselessly no matter how hard I pushed. 'What do we do now?' I asked, letting it drop back down.

'Plan B,' Jess said grimly.

Chapter 4

Jess phoned Nate. 'I need you and Gato. Plan A failed so you're up.' She hung up and turned to me. 'He won't be long.'

'He'd better not be. The clock is ticking.' I was starting to sweat. We didn't have many of those promised twenty minutes left. I'd never been arrested before. What would my mum say?

I stifled a swear word as Nate phased out of the shadows with Gato on a lead, trotting happily by his side. 'How?' I managed to ask.

'It's a public building.' Nate winked. 'I can come and go. Nice to see you, Lucy.'

'And you,' I said.

'I'll leave you to it. Don't get caught, and don't do anything dumb.' He passed over Gato's lead and gave Jess an air kiss before phasing back into the shadows and away.

Jess turned to Gato. 'Take us to the third,' she said urgently. 'To the time you think best.'

Gato gave a bark and a wag as Jess grabbed my hand. 'Hold on tight,' she instructed. Gato leapt towards Jess, touching his snout to her forehead, and the world ... shifted.

'What?' I said inarticulately, and blinked several times. We were in the same basement room, but it was clear from the lighting that we were now in daytime.

'I'll explain in a minute,' Jess murmured. 'Let's get out of here and work out what time Gato has brought us to.' We crept cautiously up the stairs towards the sound of clapping and cheers. 'Someone's getting married. Let's walk out the front door. Hiding in plain sight is always best.'

Jess is the PI, the queen of sneaky, so I was happy to be guided by her. She pulled a packet of cigarettes and a lighter from her bum bag. When we reached the main door, she offered the female door attendant an apologetic look as she waved a ciggy. The woman glanced at us disapprovingly but opened the door.

As we slunk outside, I let out an explosive breath I didn't know I'd been holding. 'But you don't smoke,' I said inanely.

'It's a handy prop. No one will think twice about two wedding guests slinking out for a drag on a fag.'

'I don't know how you do that as part of your job.'

She grinned. 'It's a rush, isn't it?'

'It's terrifying. I love you, but you're nuts,' I muttered.

'To be fair, a lot of sleuthing is incredibly boring. That's why I always love the fun stuff.'

'That was *not* fun. And it was a complete failure. And what the fuck is going on?' The questions exploded out of me.

'You've got a new tattoo, a large triangle on your head,' Jess said. 'You've officially found out about one of the Other realm's biggest and best kept secrets. As with all secrets, you're not allowed to talk about it. As well as the Common and the Other, there's a Third realm. It lets you play with time like it's a Rubik Cube – and now we're in it.'

'A Third realm.' Time travel? Sure, why not? My eyes narrowed. Greg had a big triangle on his head, which meant he'd already known about this secret Third realm. Why was I always the last to learn these things? But I'd only been a part of the Other for a matter of weeks, so maybe it was too soon to be throwing my dummy out of the pram. I looked around at the bright sunlight. 'So *when* the hell are we?'

'Your guess is as good as mine. Gato picked the time.'

'You're genuinely nuts. You let your hellhound pick the era we're in?'

'Oh, don't worry – it's modern day. I spotted electric lights, and that lady over there is wearing jeans. Gato always knows the best time to go to. He's a hellhound – he manages portals like other creatures breathe. Why do you think hellhounds are so desirable?'

We're in a different freaking time, I said to Esme, panicking slightly. *What if we get stuck here?*

She sent me a wave of calm reassurance. **What is time to a wolf?** she asked indifferently. **We are now.**

Greg is then, I pointed out.

Then is when we will go next, she said firmly. Sometimes, her unruffled calm can be irritating.

'Hang on,' I frowned. 'So can anyone use a portal to go to the Third realm?' I asked Jess.

'Technically yes – but in reality, no. The portals are defended by the guardians of the hall, and they make sure they are just used to go to the Common and the Other. If you want to use the Third, you have to petition the Connection and they rarely say yes.'

'But hellhounds can give you access to the Third. Another reason why they are so valuable.'

'Exactly. Come on. Gato knows his stuff, and he'll have brought us to a time when Mrs H is sitting as a Symposium member. We should be able to catch her at St George's Hall in Liverpool.'

Liverpool was only a short train ride from Birkenhead. Jess led us confidently to Hamilton Square train station where we grabbed tickets. The ticket master grinned at Gato, who looked like an ordinary Great Dane to him. He pointed to the sign next to him and chortled: *All dogs must be carried on the escalators.*

Jess rolled her eyes, 'Everyone's a comedian,' she muttered.

We could carry him, Esme said confidently. She was probably right, but a slender blonde lady carrying a 70kg dog was going to cause a bit of a stir. Luckily, there were lifts so we rode down instead and headed by underground to Liverpool.

I still had no idea what time we were in. As we exited the station at Liverpool Lime Street, Jess bought a newspaper and we eagerly scanned the date: 1998. 'Huh, we've not long been born. That's a sentence I didn't think I'd say,' I muttered.

'Yeah, we're both babies. Interesting. Let's go.'

Jess led the way to St George's Hall and took me confidently through security. She calmly said that we had an appointment with Seer Harding to discuss hellhound ownership; other than a cursory check, we were let in with no questions asked. Things were obviously more chilled in the nineties.

'Have you been here before?' I asked.

'Once or twice. I met Stone here and, after that Roscoe. If I remember rightly, Mrs H's office is on this floor. Walk like we belong,' she instructed.

We strolled down a short corridor until we reached the end door. Jess knocked.

'Enter.' Mrs H was sitting behind a pale, wooden desk. She lived next door to Jess when we were kids, and I'd seen her frequently. She was dressed in pastel blue and as neat and well-presented as I remembered – only this time, her skin was purple. Bright, lurid purple.

'Holy hell,' I blurted. 'You're purple.'

Jess sent me a look that suggested I wasn't being cool. 'I forgot she'd be purple,' I explained lamely.

'You knew she was a seer,' Jess pointed out.

Mrs H was smiling. 'Do I know you two ladies?'

'In the future,' Jess explained, tapping the third triangle on her head.

Mrs H raised a neatly plucked eyebrow. 'Ah, well then. And this is your portal-hopping hellhound, I presume?'

'That's the one.'

'Funny, he looks an awful like...'

'Isaac. Yes, he's the same dog, just a bit older.'

'Well now. Colour me intrigued. How can I help you...?'

'Jessica, Jessica Sharp.'

Mrs H studied her. 'Yes,' she said finally, 'I do believe you are. I held you last week whilst Mary was getting her shopping out of her car. You look like her – Mary. So, you're my neighbour, all grown up. What can I do for you?'

'This is my friend, Lucy. You made a prophecy about her when she was born.'

'Did I?'

'Luciana Alessandro.'

Mrs H froze. 'Ah. Then I did make a prophecy, no doubt about that.'

'Will you come with us to Birkenhead Town Hall to retrieve it?'

'There's no need. I remember it quite well. As it happens, I haven't registered it yet, so couldn't future me help you?' She studied Jess's face. 'Ah. No future me, then.' She sighed. 'That's a bit young to pop my clogs, isn't it? I'd best update my will,' she muttered to herself. 'Never mind. The prophecy.' She closed her eyes and recited,

'*Born to fire*
Wolf torn
Bridge the chasm
End the forlorn
Curse be lifted
Wolves be whole
Destroy the order
Pay the toll
A Queen Alpha
Past before seen
Reverse what was

And shouldn't have been.'

Jess was busy writing it all down. I didn't need to; it was burned indelibly into my memory.

Mrs H studied me. 'I remember you, too. You were a fire elemental. But that's not your energy now – your aura is wolf. I suppose the prophecy has already begun.'

'Can you delay registering it?' I asked. If three years were all I could get with my parents, I'd take them happily. I could make memories during those years; keep something of them with me. There were mind healers; memories could be retrieved – but not if they'd never been made in the first place.

'I can, but no more than three years.'

'Please, give me that.'

Mrs H leaned forward. 'I'm sorry for what it has brought you.'

'How do you know what it's caused?' I asked, a shade aggressively.

'I don't. But you wouldn't ask for the delay if it didn't cause you trouble. Besides, the phrase "King or Queen Alpha" hasn't been used for centuries. You're in for a rocky ride, Luciana.' She wasn't wrong.

We stood to leave; the less time we spent in the wrong time, the better. 'Don't go yet,' she ordered. She turned to Jess, 'You're a wizard. Clear my mind of this discussion. I don't want to know about my death.'

'If you get cleared, you won't remember to delay registering my prophecy,' I objected.

Mrs H pulled out a notebook and scrawled something in it. 'There. I won't know why, but I'll do it. Sadly, this isn't the first time I've found cryptic notes from myself.'

Jess hesitated. 'I'm a wizard and an empath. I can use the IR, but I haven't had training. I wouldn't want to try and wipe a specific memory and accidentally wipe out your whole self.'

The Intention and Release – the IR – is how wizards use magic; they gather their intention and then they release it with a word or a gesture. It could be a fine surgical tool or a blunt instrument depending on how it was wielded.

Gato barked and slunk next to me, pushing his back against my hand. I reached inwards to my piping skills and stretched out my mind.

Jess's dad, George Sharp, spoke to me. *Tell Mrs H to summon me. I'll clear her mind.*

Are you sure?

Yes. I remember doing it, he said confidently.

'Um, Mrs H, call George Sharp. He'll clear you.'

Lady Seer Harding reached out a manicured hand and dialled a number on her desk's landline telephone. 'Bring me Inspector Sharp,' she ordered. A few moments later, there was a firm knock at the door. 'Come!' she called.

George Sharp entered. Jess was my best friend in all the world, and I'd half-lived at George and Mary's house when

I was a teenager. It was odd to see him striding in just a few years older than I was. He froze when he saw Jess and Gato. His eyes narrowed and he glared at the hellhound. 'Isaac, what are you doing in the Third realm?'

'He's helping me, Dad.' Jess stepped forward and hugged her father tightly.

His eyes softened and he hugged her back. 'All right, kiddo?'

She nodded into the crook of his neck. 'I wish you'd hinted at your plans last time we met out of time.' She glared a little.

'I've only just started making the plans,' he admitted curiously, looking towards Gato.

'Enough,' Mrs H said. 'You're both flirting with disaster. Treat time with the respect she deserves. George, I need you to wipe the last thirty minutes from my mind. And you three, you need to go. Isaac, take them back.'

I thought about protesting. My birth parents were alive in this time, but my great-great-etc-grandfather, Alessandro, had told me they were travelling around Europe. We wouldn't be able to find them in time. Disappointment welled up in me. It was grossly unfair.

'We'll leave you,' Jess agreed. 'We don't want to be in St George's Hall when we're sent back. Who knows whose office we'd pop back into?' It was a good point. And I really didn't want to spend any time in the Connection's jail.

Jess gave her dad one last hug, and we hustled out of there. I slung my arm around her shoulder. 'You okay?'

She sighed. 'Yeah. But every time I do this, I think I really shouldn't mess with the Third. The temptation is always there, to pop back and see my parents for a cup of tea and a chat. But you remember Leo Harfen?'

'The elf? Sure.'

'He dabbled in the Third too much, and now he scarcely knows what time he's in. Magic always takes its toll one way or another.' She shook her head. 'More importantly, are you okay, Alpha Queen?'

'I don't know what any of it means,' I huffed.

'It means you're going to be a big deal. And someone didn't like that.'

No shit. They didn't like it enough to try and kill me and my whole family. And I was going to find out who that fucker was and exact my revenge.

Chapter 5

Jess and I headed back to Birkenhead, where hopefully Tom was waiting patiently for us. We took the train back to Hamilton Square and strolled back to the Town Hall. It was disconcerting that it was still daytime, and my internal clock was going haywire.

Once we were safely there, we ducked down a side street. Jess turned to Gato. 'Okay, pup, send us back.' I held her hand as Gato leapt at her, touching his snout to her forehead.

I blinked and we lurched back to night-time. 'That is so weird,' I muttered.

'You get used to it.'

'How often have you mucked about with time?'

'Not too often. But Gato portals me back and forth to the Common and the Other all the time, and it feels just the same.'

'That must be handy,' I commented.

She slid me an assessing look. 'You can use him tonight if you want – it will help you avoid Maxwell a while longer.'

I decided not to touch that and changed the subject, 'Tom was parked over there, right?' I pointed.

Jess snorted; I was being transparent. She led the way and we found the car parked right where we'd left it. We popped Gato in the boot and climbed in the back.

'How did it go?' Tom asked curiously.

'Yes, ladies, how did it go?' asked Greg from the front passenger seat.

'Greg! What are you doing here?' I exclaimed.

'That was exactly what I was wondering,' he said flatly.

I winced. 'I called, and I left a note...'

'The call was vague, and the note said fuck all as to why you'd tear out of the mansion like a bat out of hell.' His tone was decidedly grouchy.

'Notes can be intercepted,' I pointed out. 'You knew I was safe with Jess and Tom. Besides, you were enjoying the party. You deserved some downtime.'

'What I deserve, is a girlfriend who won't sneak off without me,' he said grumpily.

'I wasn't sneaking off as your *girlfriend;* I was sneaking off as your alpha. Besides, you found me. All's well that ends well. We can talk more about it later. Alone.'

'We can, and we will.' That sounded ominous; I was going to be told off again. I didn't feel like I'd been too reckless; I'd had Jess with me, and Tom was on standby, and all we'd done was break into a building then do a spot of time travelling. Nothing to write home about.

'And look, we've got matching tattoos.' I pointed to the new triangle adorning my forehead.

'So I see.' He pressed his lips together in disapproval. Maybe he wasn't a fan of time travel.

Jess cleared her throat. 'You want to come back to my place?' she asked. 'You can both crash and recharge.'

'Or I can drive you home, if you prefer,' Tom offered.

I really wanted to accept Jess's offer. We hadn't had a sleepover in ages, and a bottle of wine and some dancing really seemed like a good idea. But duty was calling, loudly and incessantly. I sighed. 'We'd better head back. If you don't mind driving us, Tom, that would be great.'

Greg interrupted before Tom could reply. 'As you said, we all need some downtime. Let's stay the night at Jess's and leave early in the morning.'

'I can grab you a loaner car to drive back with,' Tom offered.

I smiled. 'Twist my arm, why don't you? Okay, we'll stay. If that's okay.'

If they try and twist your arm, I will rip theirs off, Esme growled in warning.

It's just a saying, I explained hastily. *It means they're trying to persuade me to do something I already want to do.*

If you already want to do it, then just do it. She subsided, turned three times and settled down in my head.

'Of course it's alright, otherwise I wouldn't have offered,' Jess harrumphed.

Tom drove us to Jess's house. 'No Emory?' I asked as we walked in.

'No, he's off saving the world. That's why I picked tonight to break into the Town Hall.'

Greg's eyes narrowed; he was still annoyed. Jess looked between us and clearly had the same thought. 'I'll rustle up some dinner. You guys make yourselves comfy in the guest room. I'll holler when the food is ready, but I expect it will be an hour at least.'

'You're going to cook?' I asked, surprised.

'No.' She grinned. 'But I'll order us some epic takeout and get some white wine chilling.'

'Perfect. Thai?'

'I'm all over it,' she promised.

Gato trotted after Jess, and Greg and I headed up to the spare room. The double bed was made up and there were fresh towels set out: Jess had been prepared, just in case. She's a regular girl scout.

I sat down and turned to Greg. 'I'm sorry I slipped away. This was something I needed to do by myself.'

'You weren't by yourself, you were with Jinx.' Jinx is Jess's nickname. Most people call her Jinx, but to me she'll always be my best friend who I grew up with: little Jess Sharp.

I tilted my head. 'Are you jealous?' I asked, surprised.

He shifted uncomfortably and sat next to me. 'You should know that *I'll* always have your back.' He didn't quite look at me.

I stood and stepped in between his legs, then tilted his head up so he met my eyes. 'Hey, I do know that. But I thought you'd enjoy the party and I'd be back before you noticed I'd gone.'

'I always notice when you're gone,' he admitted softly. Gone was the blank face he wore for so much of the day; instead there was a vulnerability in his eyes that I rarely got to see.

I smiled, leaned down and kissed him gently. Greg might not be the most loquacious when it comes to talking about his feelings, but I knew without a shadow of a doubt that he loved me. I didn't need him to wax lyrical about it; I just needed him to feel it. And show it through his actions on a few choice occasions, which he did over and over again. Like following me halfway up the country to see if I was all right.

'Now that we've fought, how about we step right along to the making up part?' I suggested, leaning down to kiss his lips again. This time, I felt them curve up against mine.

'You come up with the best ideas,' he murmured.

'That's why I'm the boss.' I winked. He laughed and reached for me.

I hoped the takeout had a long lead-time.

We showered hastily and headed downstairs for some food; we'd been longer than intended. Delicious scents wafted on the air, curling in my tummy and making my mouth water. I was starving; breaking and entering sure helps you work up an appetite.

Jess was waiting patiently in her living room with the TV on a music channel and turned up loud. She gave me a knowing smirk when Greg and I walked in holding hands. 'You both look ... happier.'

'Showers are so restorative,' I said blandly.

'Sure,' Jess grinned. 'And amazing sex helps too.'

Greg offered her a look of pure male pride and I felt my skin warm. He knew what he was doing all right, and I wondered how soundproof Jess's guest room really was.

By the music blaring out, I'd guess not very. My blush deepened.

Jess turned down the volume a little and led us next door to the dining room. 'Grab a seat, and I'll bring the food. It's keeping warm in the oven.'

'You should have started without us.'

She waved that away. 'I love sharing a meal with friends – it's one of life's simple pleasures.' As we sat down, she ferried in the food from the kitchen and placed the hot dishes onto mats. We started to dig in.

'Is Gato okay to send us both to Common for a recharge later?' Greg asked. 'It'll save us a job.'

'I'm sure he won't mind. We might as well get you started now. We can leave Esme here so she can join in on girls' night for a bit longer.' Jess whistled Gato over and he happily sent Greg to the Common realm so his magical batteries could be recharged.

Thanks, I piped to the hellhound and got a swamp of love in response. I gave him a full body hug and he licked me, then trotted off to lie down in the sitting room.

Jess watched him with concern. 'Gato just hasn't been the same since...' She trailed off and made a visible effort to brighten up. 'Come on, let's eat. It smells delicious.' She wasn't wrong.

We ploughed in with gusto. Jess had ordered my staple of beef massaman, with a side of sticky rice, as well as some starters for us all to share. She unscrewed the top from a bottle of white wine. 'Technically, we should drink beer with Thai food.'

'I'm just not a beer girl,' I admitted, taking a happy sip of my sauvignon blanc.

'Me neither. That's why we're having wine.'

An hour later Greg excused himself, ostensibly for an early night, but I knew it was really to give me and Jess some much-needed time together. He was the best.

The wine was flowing and we'd started singing. I *knew* I was going to regret it tomorrow, but tonight I was doing my best to let my hair down.

Esme was in a similar mood. **Can we kill something?** she asked optimistically.

Probably not. I paused. *Unless we get attacked, in which case, kill away.*

'Don't try and keep up with me,' I warned Jess as I did a shot of Jaeger.

Her competitive hackles rose. 'Why not?'

'Because I'm a werewolf, you muppet. It takes a whole lot more booze for me to get tipsy – but tonight I'm working on it. There are no emergencies on the horizon, so I can just have fun.'

Jess grimaced. 'Way to summon an emergency.'

'Don't be ridiculous. It'll be fine.'

An hour later *everything* was fine. Gato looked at me reproachfully when he finally sent me to Common for a re-charge, but being canned helped deal with the loss of Esme as she was torn away from me.

Jess helped me up the stairs as we giggled our way to bed. 'Shhh!' she whispered loudly as we fell into the banister again. 'You're going to wake up Manners.'

'Greg will be happy to be woken up. I'm frisky when I'm tipsy.'

'Haven't you frisked enough already? Besides, I think we're way past tipsy. I think we may be shitfaced. I know, because I can't feel my face.'

I felt my own face. Nothing. 'Huh. You may be right.'

The spare-room door opened. 'She's definitely right,' Greg said, looking out at us, both amused and exasperated. He was wearing only his boxers.

'Nice,' Jess said, giving me a thumbs up.

I beamed, 'I know, right? He's sexy and clever and super loyal.'

'And he's cut!'

'Yup, his muscles have muscles.'

'I also have ears,' Greg said drily. 'Good night, Jinx. Get yourself a pint of water and some paracetamol before bed.'

Jess gave him a fake salute. 'Aye aye, sir.'

'Smartass. March yourself to bed.' Jess started marching but promptly fell into the wall. 'Gato!' Greg called down. 'Get yourself up here.'

As the hellhound lumbered up, Greg raised an eyebrow. 'Do you really think you should have let Jinx get that

drunk?' Unrepentant, Gato gave a wag. 'Whatever,' Greg
muttered. 'But I'm not clearing up any sick.'

'You would,' I contradicted, winding my arms around
his neck. 'You love me. You'd totally clear up my vomit.'

'Let's not test that theory. Come on, Calamity Jane, let's
pour you into bed.'

'Yee-haw!'

'Christ.'

I pried my eyes open and waited for the head-pounding
to come. Nothing. I sat up, and the world didn't swirl
ominously. Hey, no hangover! I dressed quickly and slunk
downstairs.

'Hey, Gato!' I hugged him and he gave me several wags
in return, before pushing his snout to my forehead and
sending me careening into the Other. Esme and I were
reunited with a jolt, and it felt like heaven to be back with
her. Joy washed over me; everything was right in my world
again.

Hey Esme! I'm not even hungover! I crowed.

You deserve to be sick, Esme grumped. **You made our
limbs flail.**

We were somewhere safe. It was fine, I protested.

It is never fine to be that much out of control. It made our head spin and our tummy lurch. I was working hard to clear out the poison, and you kept pouring it in.

If you'd let me get my drink on, I wouldn't have had to work so hard! Next time, just let me get drunk.

No. It is ridiculous.

It's tradition.

Is it? she asked suspiciously. **You seem to have a lot of traditions.**

It's a human thing. We collect traditions. I stopped myself from saying 'like wolves collect fleas', as that was a sure way to start a fight with my resident wolf.

Jess was making breakfast when I walked into the kitchen and I happily inhaled the scent of slightly burnt bacon. 'I'm hoping it will cure me or kill me,' she whispered.

'Uh-oh. Are you hungover?'

'Are you not?'

I shook my head smugly and her eyes narrowed. 'That is so *not* fair. You drank way more than me!'

'I did say not to try and keep up.'

'You know I'm competitive,' she complained.

'Let's get some bacon and OJ in you, and the world will be a better place.'

'And tea.'

'Obviously tea,' I agreed, putting the kettle on. Jess was shaking slightly, and I felt bad for her. I should be feeling just as rough.

She took a call from Tom. 'Tom will drop a car off for you soon.'

'Cool. I'm not in a hurry.'

'Has Gato sent you back to the Other yet?'

'Yeah, he did it first thing.'

'I'm surprised and impressed that we managed to send you both to the Common for a recharge in the first place,' she admitted.

'We sent Greg before we started drinking,' I pointed out.

'Oh, did we? It's all a bit hazy.' She looked at her phone and winced. 'I sent Emory a lot of text messages last night. A *lot*.'

I grinned. 'Sexy ones or I-love-you ones?'

'Yes.'

'Which?'

'Both. I was wrecked. Why do I always think it's a good idea? Note to self, drinking is always a bad idea. I am *never* drinking again.'

'We always say that.'

'I mean it this time.'

'We always say that, too.' I laughed. 'Anyway, the tea is working. Your shakes have stopped.'

'Great. If you could just stop the gnomes from jack-hammering inside my skull, that would be perfect.'

'Dwarves,' Greg corrected as he sauntered in. We looked at him blankly. 'It's the dwarves that live in caves and dig up stuff.'

'What do gnomes do?' Jess asked.

'Protect gardens,' I joked.

'Gnomes are real,' Greg said.

'As in real gnomes, not plastic garden gnomes?' I asked incredulously.

'Real gnomes,' Greg confirmed.

I sighed. 'Even with all my extracurricular reading in Lord Samuel's library, I still didn't know gnomes were a thing.'

'Yup. They're friendly with the dryads, so you weren't too far off base when you said they protect gardens. They hate man-made structures.'

There was a beep outside. Tom had drawn up in a sexy car. Another black car was idling at the kerb – Tom's ride back. He chucked the keys to Greg who caught them easily. 'Emory says enjoy it, but don't get caught speeding.'

'As if I would,' Greg said lightly, but he was grinning mischievously.

Tom flashed him a grin. 'Uh-huh. It's just like old times.'

'Maybe I should come with you,' Jess said eyeing the car. Though I had no idea what it was, it was obviously car porn to the three of them.

'Emory is hoping to get home tonight,' Tom told her.

'In which case, there is no way you're coming with us,' Greg said. 'Emory would have my guts for garters.'

Why would Jess's mate want to wear his guts? That would smell and attract a lot of flies, Esme interjected.

No. I stifled a giggle. *It's a saying.*

I felt her huff. She didn't like our sayings.

Jess sighed. 'I haven't driven a Maserati Levante before.'

'I'll let you know how amazing it is,' Greg said sweetly.

'Jerk.' She stuck out her tongue at him.

Tom rolled his eyes at the banter, gave Greg a man-hug then motored off with another of his brethren colleagues. It was time for us to say farewell, something that I hated.

Greg and I headed back inside to pack our bags. When we returned, I chucked my duffel bag into the back of the sumptuous SUV and turned to my best friend. She was looking as forlorn as I felt, and we pulled each other into a massive hug. I managed to fight the tears that wanted to come; Jess is like a sister to me, and I hate saying goodbye without knowing when I'll see her again.

She read my mind. 'I'll visit soon,' she promised.

'You'd better. This trip counts as my visit to you, so now you owe me one.'

'Seems fair.' She drew back and looked at me seriously. 'Go and speak to Maxwell. Enough hiding, Lucy. You waited your whole life to find your biological family. Now you know that they didn't abandon you – they loved you.

It's time to face the music. Put on your big girl pants. Maxwell doesn't deserve you swerving him for no reason.'

She was right, but suddenly I had a huge lump in my throat. I finally gave voice to my fears. 'But what if they *don't* love me?' I whispered, my voice cracking.

She hugged me again. 'Oh Luce, how can they not? You need to do this, and the sooner the better. Roscoe mentioned to me that you've stopped going to Rosie's. Maxwell thinks that it's because of them withholding information during Jason's kidnapping, and he feels awful. He doesn't deserve that.'

No, my cousin didn't deserve that. Dammit, it was time to woman up. 'I love you, Jess,' I said.

'I love you, too. I'm only a phone call away.'

I climbed into the car. Greg was already behind the wheel, giving me space to say my goodbyes. 'You okay?' he asked, tracing a stray tear that had slipped down my cheek.

'Yeah. Jess was just giving me some home truths.'

'She doesn't often pull her punches.'

'No, but she's right. I've been avoiding Maxwell and my birth family. I've wanted to know about them my whole life – and now that the opportunity is here, I'm being a coward.'

'It's not cowardly to be uncertain or fearful. Meeting them is a big thing. You'll get to it in your own time.' He started the engine and laced our fingers together on the gear stick so we could hold hands while he drove. It steadied me.

I gave his fingers one last squeeze before disentangling them from mine and pulling out my phone. I hesitated, thinking about my options, then decided to ring my great-great-etc-grandfather. He deserved more than a text message. Even so, I was secretly relieved when my call went to voicemail. 'I got the prophecy. Call me,' I said, and hung up. The best voice messages are short and sweet; besides, my vampyr relation had struck me as a fellow who would appreciate brevity.

I kept turning the prophecy over in my head. Maybe it wasn't so mysterious; after all, I'd been born a fire elemental and made into a werewolf. The bit that gave me pause was the Queen Alpha part. Was 'Queen' used simply to denote that I was a female alpha, or did it mean more? And which curse was I supposed to end? There was only one that came to mind: the gargoyles. They were former werewolves twisted and cursed by the witches, but I knew fuck all about ending curses.

What do you think about the prophecy? I asked Esme.

Curses are bad. If we can end one, we should. It was a simplistic view, but hard to disagree with.

But how?

I have no idea, she admitted. **But we'll find out.**

I loved her confidence. With my head spinning, I decided it was time to take a nap; sleep always helps me gain some perspective. I settled against the headrest and in minutes I was out. I woke when I heard Greg say, 'Shit, this doesn't look good.'

Adrenalin thrummed through me at the abrupt awakening. 'What doesn't look good?' I asked, sitting up and dabbing away a small dribble of drool from the corner of my mouth.

'There's something going on at the mansion.' Greg's tone was grim.

Through the windshield, I saw a bunch of people gathered outside. People were visibly upset, clinging to each other. Cassie was crying.

I sighed. I had spoken too soon, and by doing so I'd summoned an emergency. Fuck.

Chapter 6

Greg and I pulled up and immediately piled out of Emory's beautiful car. 'What's going on?' I called out.

'Alpha!' Liam said with relief. 'There was an attack.'

'Don't be so melodramatic,' Seren snapped. 'It was bull-shit. No one was even hurt.'

'Ares was hurt!' he protested.

'None of the wolves were hurt,' Seren amended.

'At least three unknown wolves encroaching on our lands is not bullshit,' Finley added. The former loner looked stressed.

David disagreed vociferously with Seren. 'They attacked Ares and they pissed on our front door! They're claiming our lands as theirs, and attacking that which is under our protection.' I had never seen him do more than make sad doe eyes at her, so it was a welcome change. 'A territorial dispute isn't bullshit,' he went on. 'It's war. Good thing Finley, Liam and Daniella came upon them when they did. Who knows what else they had planned?'

We will destroy them! Esme snarled furiously.

'What they did was quite enough,' Marissa growled. 'They hurt Ares!'

'Everyone calm down,' Greg ordered over the hubbub. 'Was anyone other than Ares hurt?' His gaze swept over the assembled wolves, but they all shook their heads.

'Ares was hurt,' Marissa cried. 'Why is no one bothered that Ares was hurt?'

'Of course we're bothered,' David disagreed. 'Mrs Dawes is already seeing to him.'

'Where is he?' I asked urgently. I scanned the crowd for Ares, but I couldn't see the unicorn that I'd grown so fond of. A coppery tang hung in the air, and a patch of the gravel was slick with blood. My stomach lurched; that was a *lot* of blood.

'He's in the rear courtyard by the servants' entrance,' David told me.

I reached out my mind to Ares' and found him in such pain and chaos that I instinctively shrank away. It was hard to reach out again knowing the jarring agony that I'd feel, but he deserved some comfort.

I didn't hesitate in shifting to four – bye-bye clothes – and let Esme take us to Ares as fast as she could. My wolf was furious; someone had dared encroach on *our* land and hurt *our* Ares. She wanted retribution.

Later, I urged. *Let's check on Ares first.*

I felt her agree. The attackers were gone, so ensuring the safety of our pack was paramount. All that blood... Ares would need a healer. We rounded the corner and saw him lying on the ground, bleeding badly. Mrs Dawes had her hair tied back and was swiftly painting some runes on him.

'Thank goodness Amber left you some of her gunk,' I said as I shifted back to two legs.

Mrs Dawes gave a visible start. 'Alpha! Thank goodness you're back.'

Ares' wounds were beginning to close. I gave Mrs Dawes a swift hug, nakedness be damned. 'You're amazing! How did you know to do that?'

Mrs Dawes hesitated. 'Did you know Amelia Jane?'

I shook my head. 'No, not really. I've heard of her. She was a witch. She died a little while ago.' She'd also deliberately fudged Jess's security runes so my best friend could be attacked. It later transpired that the poor girl had been blackmailed into doing it.

'I was friends with Amelia Jane and she showed me a few healing runes – just in case. But I only recently acquired some healing potions. It seemed – prudent, what with all the recent problems we've been having.'

Good old Mrs Dawes; eminently practical and always prepared. 'You should have mentioned it earlier. Think of all of Amber's invoices I could have avoided,' I joked.

Mrs Dawes smiled tightly. 'It's forbidden to teach non-witches the runes of power. It's so easy to do them wrongly, and if that happens it can drain all our power rather than take it from the realm around us. I only risked it with Ares because we called Amber and none of the witches could get here in under twenty minutes. I didn't want to lose him – unicorns are so wonderful and rare. Saving him was worth the risk.' Her gaze was openly affectionate when she looked at Ares, and she gave him a gentle, reassuring pat.

'The risk – as in you could get extinguished?'

Mrs Dawes nodded solemnly. 'Exactly.'

'If it's as dangerous as you say, why did Amelia Jane show you some runes?' I asked.

'As I said, we were friends. She didn't want me dying just because a witch couldn't get to me in time.'

I gave her a warm smile, but it didn't seem like a likely scenario. We shifters are tough, and it would take a hell of a lot of damage to put us at death's door. Archie's ruined torso flashed into my mind, and I forcibly pushed the upsetting image away. Yes, it could happen.

Ares gave a happy whicker to draw our attention back to him. There was a huge pool of blood on the concrete floor, and he rocked back and forth briefly before finding his feet. He stood carefully and took a few steps before he threw his head back and whinnied his triumph.

He gave Mrs Dawes an enthusiastic head nuzzle and pushed her back a few feet. She gave a happy laugh. 'All right now, Ares.'

As he pranced around us happily, I said, 'I'm glad you're feeling better, my friend. What happened?' I reached out my mind to his.

Instantly I was assaulted by anger, then images flashed through my mind so quickly I could hardly process them. Ares patrolling the perimeter of the mansion and finding strange wolves at our door; Ares rearing and smashing down his lethal, claw-like feet in warning, only to be attacked not by three wolves, as Liam had said, but by seven.

Ares had found the three ahead of him, but hadn't noticed the four slinking up behind him. They had attacked and ripped his flesh with teeth and claws while he had screamed. He had whirled to face the attack and the wolves had fled from his fury, but the damage had been done. The smell of other non-pack wolves was all round, and a coppery tang of blood scented the air – Ares' blood. Finley, Daniella and Liam had found him first and raised the alarm.

My mind disentangled from his with difficulty. 'You're alright now,' I said aloud. 'We'll find the ones that did this to you.' I touched my mind to his and let him feel my determination, my need for retribution.

Esme and I wouldn't let this stand; we *couldn't* let this stand. We wouldn't survive as alpha for long if we let it be known that other wolves could come onto our territory and attack the creatures under our protection.

'You can pipe,' Mrs Dawes said with wonder.

'Yeah, I can. It's not much of a secret, and a good few of the wolves know about it, but for now I would ask that you keep it to yourself. Discretion is the name of the game.'

'Mum's the word,' Mrs Dawes promised.

'Thank you.'

'I'll clear up the blood here.' She pointed to the gory pool in the courtyard.

'Thank you. What would I do without you?'

'Let's hope we don't have to find out,' Mrs Dawes said with a wink. She pulled out her hair bobble and let her usual bob fall back into place.

Ares and I walked back to the main entrance of the mansion. Tension was still high, but it ratcheted down a level as soon as everyone noticed the unicorn. Those in wolf form came closer to him, nuzzling against his legs and letting out soft whines. Ares raised his head higher, prouder, then did a fancy little dance, picking up his legs in an elaborate dressage-style trot.

Channelling my inner Winston Churchill, I turned to address the gathered wolves. 'Our land has been encroached upon, our Ares attacked and wounded. This will not be borne. We will find the aggressors, and we will take them to task for daring to attack the Home Counties pack.'

Those who had shifted into wolf form threw their heads back and howled at my promise of retribution. Now all I had to do was deliver. Easy.

'For now, we institute a constant patrol of our grounds. Greg will set up a schedule, and shifts of four wolves will guard the mansion at any one time. It's going to be busy for the next few days, so brace yourselves.'

I probably sounded a bit grimmer than I intended, but I had the words of the prophecy ringing in my ears. I was supposed to be Queen Alpha, and I was sick and tired of people seeing my niceness as vulnerability. What did I have to do to make the Other realm realise that I wasn't to be messed with? I wasn't sure – but I knew that I would do it. This sort of attack wouldn't have happened under Lord Samuel's reign, and I was damned if it would happen again under mine.

My phone rang; it was my mum calling. It wasn't the best timing, but I'd missed three of her recent calls so I swiped to accept and headed for the privacy of my office. I shut the door behind me. I usually had an open-door policy, but Mum didn't know that I was a werewolf, and I didn't want one of the pack hearing me describe them like they were regular humans.

'Hey, Mum. I'm sorry, this isn't the best time.'

She gave an exasperated sigh. 'Lucy, it hasn't been the best time for ages. I haven't seen you in weeks – your dad and I are getting worried. You haven't been the same since you were ill.'

'Since I almost died,' I corrected. I'm not one to pussy-foot around.

'Yes, since you almost died. I almost lost you, Lucy. You're here and you're safe, but I feel like I'm still losing you.'

I felt a pang of regret and my voice softened. 'I'm sorry, Ma. I didn't mean to make things difficult. I'm still finding my feet, you know?'

'I know, love, but it's a mum's job to help you find them.'

'I'm an adult now. I'm supposed to find them myself.'

'No matter how old you get, you'll always be my darling daughter. I help strangers all day long, so let me help you,' she pleaded. Mum's a nurse and a tough old broad; it was rare for her to wear her emotions on her sleeve.

I hesitated, but she deserved to know the truth – or what I could tell her of the truth. 'I found my birth parents.'

There was a pause, no more than a beat or two, before she replied, 'Lucy, that's wonderful! I'm so happy for you.'

'Thanks, Ma. You're always so supportive, and I know this must be difficult for you. Trying to find my birth parents doesn't diminish in any way, shape or form what you and Dad have done for me all these years. You know that, right? You're my parents, and you always will be. I just want some questions answered.'

'Of course you do, darling. That's human nature.'

I wished I could tell her that my nature was fifty percent wolf these days, but the Verdict forbade me from breaking the secrecy that kept the Other realm hidden.

'So, tell me about them,' Mum said.

'They're dead.'

She gasped, and her distress vibrated down the phone. 'Oh, Lucy. Oh, darling, I'm so sorry.'

Tears welled up in my eyes and my heart ached. I was so lucky to have my mum, so privileged to have been loved by her and Dad and Ben. Mourning these strangers who had birthed me felt like a betrayal of the family that had raised me.

'My name was Luciana, and I think they loved me.'

'Darling, of course they loved you. How could they not? How did they pass?'

'I don't know the full details,' I admitted. I didn't want to tell her that they'd been murdered, because she would worry about me even more. She'd worry that this digging would put me in the crosshairs of the killer.

I hoped that it would. It was time to start rocking the boat. *Come for me, you fucker. I'll be ready.*

We'll be ready, Esme whispered.

Mum let me turn the conversation away from the topic of my dead parents. Before we hung up, I promised that I would visit soon. 'Soon': a term vague enough that I could make sure it wasn't forsworn.

Chapter 7

There was a gentle knock at the office door and I recognised the rhythm straightaway. 'Come in,' I called to Greg.

He sauntered in with a welcoming smile, which faded as he studied my face. 'Hey, are you alright?'

'I'm fine. I was just having a chat with my mum. I told her about my birth parents being dead. It's all quite awkward and awful – I worry that looking into my birth parents might make them feel that I don't consider them my real parents.'

Greg shook his head. 'The love you feel for your family is obvious. I doubt they'll think for one moment that you don't love them just because you're investigating your past. It's something you have to do. They'll get that.'

'Yeah, I guess.' I changed the subject. 'What do you think about the attack on Ares?'

'I think it's a declaration of war,' he said grimly, confirming my worst fears.

I sighed. 'I thought you were going to say that. But if they're declaring war, where's the gauntlet? How do I know which pack is declaring war on me?'

'We'll have to review the security footage, but there's one that comes to mind.'

I knew who he was thinking of. I didn't want to jump to conclusions, but not long ago Beckett Frost had dumped a dead body at the mansion with a message that we would be next. 'Frost,' I murmured.

'Frost,' he agreed.

'It seems like a weird move to go from threats in a dead guy's mouth to peeing on our door.'

'They could have been interrupted before they finished what they started. Or maybe Ares was the real target all along. Unicorns are quite rare – and a docile, tractable one is rarer still.'

I thought of Ares' red eyes and clawed feet. 'I'm not sure I'd call him docile.'

'For a unicorn, he's positively chilled. He treats us like we're his herd. It's a bit off, to be honest – I've never seen it before. But back to the attack. Maybe some of the wolves who came in will have distinguishing features that we can use to track them down. Archie and Liam know a lot of the local wolves, so perhaps they can identify them. And

Thea and Elena might be able to help if the wolves were sent from Frost.'

'It feels like a long shot. Elena hasn't been part of Frost's pack for years, and Thea was isolated because of her inability to shift. I doubt either of them can reliably identify our attackers, even if they *are* Frost's wolves.'

'Maybe, but it's our only play until we receive another message.'

I sighed again. 'Why can't we all just get along like one big happy wolf pack?'

'The Other creatures would take issue with that. If the werewolves were united, they'd pose a significant risk to the status quo. At the moment, we're fairly low on the ladder of Other creatures. That's why they leave us alone.'

'Except we're not being left alone, are we? We're being attacked. Again. This is really starting to piss me off.'

Greg smiled. 'You're new to the throne. Challenges are par for the course.'

We are ready for any challenger, Esme growled.

I don't feel so ready, but I do feel pissed off.

Anger helps.

Anger leads to hate, and hate leads to the dark side, I quipped.

The dark side of what?

Never mind. Remind me to make you watch Star Wars *when this is all over.*

There was a quiet, timid knock at the door, and I raised an eyebrow at Greg. I was pretty sure I knew who it was. Sure enough, he opened the door to Thea Frost. He stood back, his arms crossed over his chest in intimidation mode.

I guessed my role was good cop, so I gave her a welcoming smile. 'Come on in, Thea.'

She tucked a thin strand of red hair behind her ear before reluctantly coming forward and sitting in the chair opposite me. She didn't return my smile. 'I thought I could do this, but I can't.' She drew her legs up and wrapped her arms around them.

'Do what?' I asked, keeping my tone friendly even as my gut lurched. I'd always been wary of Thea, and I suspected I was about to learn why.

'I was sent here by Beckett. I'm supposed to be undermining you,' she admitted. 'And when Beckett Frost and his wolves come next time, I'm supposed to open the mansion to his pack.'

Chapter 8

Thea looked small and nervous. When she met my eyes, everything in her being pleaded with me to understand, to believe her.

'I don't want to help Beckett, not anymore. I'm not sure I ever really did, but he's the worst kind of bully and I didn't feel I had any option. Now I've had several weeks somewhere else, I've seen what a real pack should be like. You're friends. You like each other. Even your pack tourney to determine positions was polite. If that tourney had taken place in the Devon pack, Greg would have ripped Tristan's throat out, no questions asked, no hesitation. It would have been expected. Hell, otherwise Greg would have been punished for being so soft.'

'How can you possibly keep a strong pack going if everyone keeps killing each other?' I asked, exasperated. It was that kind of attitude that had kept werewolves stuck as second-class citizens in the Other realm.

'I'm not sure that Beckett cares about logic. He forces his wolves to breed regularly – he's playing the long game, raising an army of fanatical pups. And he kidnaps any lone wolves he finds, and keeps them in Devon until they stay willingly. He's the king of Stockholm syndrome. He can always find new wolves, and if he can't find someone new, he turns someone.'

'That's against council policy,' I pointed out.

She laughed a shade hysterically. 'He doesn't give a shit about the council's policies. He teaches the old stories, he turns wolves, he kills his own wolves. The Devon pack is nothing like the Home Counties pack.' She met my eyes, defiance showing for the first time. 'I want to petition to join the Home Counties pack for real this time. I'll do everything I can to help you and the pack stay safe from Beckett.'

'Even if that means killing him? He's your brother.'

'We're related by blood, nothing more, and family should be more than that. I was always weak in my parents' eyes. They discarded me like I was the runt of the litter, and I was happy to be left alone.'

'When did your wolf stop answering your call?'

'A few years ago. I think she hates me. Beckett was making us do things, horrible things. I didn't want to do them anymore.'

'Why should we believe you?' Greg asked, his stance still belligerent.

'Why would I tell you that I'm still working for Beckett if I wasn't planning on betraying him?'

'It could be a double bluff.'

She sighed. 'It's not. I don't know how to persuade you that I'm telling the truth, but I am. I don't want to be part of the Devon pack – hell, I don't really want to be part of any pack. My wolf won't answer my call, so although I call myself a werewolf I scarcely am one these days. If Beckett would let me, maybe I could just go to the Common realm and stay there.'

'Beckett wouldn't let you do that?'

'No. Think of the shame of it – his sister, nothing more than a commoner. As it is, I'm sequestered from most of the pack. Beckett doesn't want them learning about our shame, that I can't shift.'

'What happened the day your wolf refused to answer your call?' I asked.

Thea looked down; for a moment I thought she was going to refuse to answer. Finally, she said, 'Beckett told me to kill one of our wolves that had brought disgrace to our pack by going lone. I tracked him to London and picked him up at a bar. We had a few drinks together, and I persuaded him to meet me upstairs in a private room. Fool that he was, he'd always liked me. I didn't want to kill him, but orders were orders. I went into the bathroom and tried to shift – it always took me quite a while and that was another source of family embarrassment – but this time my wolf didn't answer. No matter how much I begged her, she wouldn't take over. I've never heard of a wolf doing that before – they're always eager to take the reins. So I made my excuses and I left. As it turned out, he ended up dead, but at least it wasn't by my hand.'

'You're talking about Elena's brother, aren't you? Jackson?'

'Yes. I was Elena's friend once upon a time, and I used to hang out with Jackson as well. Killing him ... I expect it was another of Beckett's tests. He loves his bloody tests,' she said bitterly. 'But I failed. I was a disappointment, a second-class citizen in my own pack. If it hadn't been for Beckett's protection, the other wolves would have killed me.'

I studied her. 'I think your wolf was protecting you. She didn't answer your call because it was the only way to keep you safe. Otherwise, you'd have compromised something essential within you by killing Jackson.'

'She's just a wolf,' Thea said bitterly. 'You give her too much credit.'

'You give her too little.' I shook my head and looked at her sadly. I couldn't imagine being so dismissive of Esme.

Greg met my eyes and his warning was clear; he knew what I wanted to do and he thought it was a bad idea. But I was frustrated, done with hiding, with cowering and being attacked. Not using all the weapons in my arsenal wasn't doing me any favours.

'I'm a piper,' I informed Thea calmly.

Greg sighed audibly as Thea frowned at me in confusion. 'How is that possible? You were Common.'

'That doesn't matter. What matters is that I can speak to your wolf. Will you let me try?'

'Knock yourself out,' she said a shade aggressively.

I reached inside myself to draw up that well of magic within me. I reached out towards Thea, but skimmed past her mind and reached another. *Hello. I am Lucy, the Alpha of this pack,* I said.

I felt an alien mind connect to mine, but she didn't reply.

I can help you, I persevered.

Nothing can help us, Thea's wolf responded.

If you let me, I can.

Nothing can help us, she repeated, and I felt her turn away. She was still connected to me but she was ignoring me. I could have forced the issue, tried to take control of her, but that didn't sit right with me.

I let the connection break, and met Thea's wide eyes. 'I'm sorry. I couldn't persuade your wolf to let you shift again. Amber DeLea has one more potion that she'd like to try on you, but if that doesn't work I'll try to speak to your wolf again. She wasn't in the mood to talk with me today, but maybe we'll have better luck another time.'

Thea nodded, but hope had gone out of her like a snuffed flame. My heart ached for her. She'd been through so much, and I knew what it felt like to be a fish out of water.

I reached out impulsively and touched her arm. 'You can join the Home Counties pack. Wolf or not, I accept your petition.'

Thea sobbed and fell into my arms. 'Thank you,' she murmured over and over again. I hugged her until her tears dried up.

As she regained her composure, I gave her one final squeeze and stepped away. 'I know this is hard for you, but I believe that you won't help Beckett. However, I need to find out a little more, if you can talk to me now.'

Thea unfolded her legs, sat up straight and leaned forward. She was pulling herself upright with a strength that had previously been missing. 'What do you need to know?'

'The wolves that attacked Ares – they were Beckett's?'

'I wasn't told about his plans, but I can review the security footage and identify any wolves that are his. I was removed from a lot of the pack gatherings so my shame wouldn't be revealed, but I spied when I could. An attack like this is certainly his MO.'

'When was he planning to attack the mansion?'

'I don't know exactly. Soon.'

'Is he going to let you know when?'

'He was supposed to – if he believed I was still working for him.' She hesitated unhappily, 'I didn't send in my last two reports when I was supposed to, so he'll know that I'm compromised. I'm not sure if Rob's dead body was for me or for you.'

Inwardly, I cursed that she had let the reports slip; if she'd kept up with them, I'd have had a double agent. Dammit. I did my best to appear calm. She'd been trying to help, though the effect had probably been quite the opposite. I flicked a look to Greg and saw that the same thoughts were running through his mind. He sent me a slight grimace.

'Never mind,' I said.

'I'm sorry. I'm useless.' Her strength seemed to dwindle and her body hunched in on itself.

'Hey! You're not useless. Someone else on our team is always a win, and you're welcome to join us.'

Greg uncrossed his arm. 'You've given us a heads-up and pointed to potential attackers. That's more than we had before you talked to us, so thank you for that. Don't beat yourself up about what could have been.'

I sent him a grateful smile.

'What should I do?' Thea asked.

'Greg will let you review the footage to confirm the wolves were Frost's. Other than that, nothing for now. Leave it with us.' I exchanged another glance with Greg. We'd come up with a plan.

She hesitated by the door. 'Do you have to tell the others?'

By 'others', I assumed she meant Archie. I considered the question carefully, but there was really no reason to tell the others that she'd been working with Frost. After all, we'd suspected it all along; to have that suspicion confirmed didn't change anything, other than perhaps affecting Archie's opinion of Thea, which I found I didn't want to do.

'No, I don't see much need to tell them. For now, just go about your business as normal. Tell them that you've been accepted into the pack. This moment won't come again, so relax and enjoy it. This pack is kind and caring and it takes care of its members.'

She smiled radiantly, and I saw the person that she could be with a lot of TLC. I was determined to see that person again; it wasn't her fault she'd been raised by a bunch of thugs.

Thea left me alone with Greg. I crossed the distance between us, stepped into his arms and basked in his hug for a moment. 'Well, that wasn't much of a surprise,' I said finally.

'No, it's no surprise that Beckett Frost is gunning for us. Ace was last seen here, and although we may have managed to convince the council that we didn't have anything to do with his disappearance, Beckett probably has his suspicions. There were a few coincidences that I doubt he would let slide...'

'So what do we do now?'

'The same as we were doing before. We prepare for war. At least this time we know who we're facing.' He gave me a long kiss. 'We're going to be okay, but things might get messy for a while.'

'I can do messy,' I said with determination.

'I don't doubt it. You're gutsy and strong, and you'll see the pack through this. Now, I'm going to set up a temporary roster and do a sweep of the property to identify any holes in our security.'

'Sounds like a plan. I'll speak to Amber and see what can be done with Thea's wolf.' I cleared my throat. 'I don't know what you'll think about this, and feel free to say no, but I was thinking ... why don't I speak with *your* wolf? I can connect you guys like Esme and me, at least temporarily—'

'Yes.'

I blinked. 'Do you need time to think about it?'

'No. My wolf and I shouldn't be separate – we don't *want* to be separate. I can tell. We try to be on the same page, we can feel each other, more than any other wolf I've spoken to – except for you.'

'You were made a werewolf by Glimmer,' I said slowly. 'Jess told me everyone made by Glimmer is never exactly like the others of their species.'

'I don't need to recharge as much,' Greg admitted. 'I've never felt the itching, and my wolf and I are close to each other. He's ... it's like he's got my back. I don't know how, but since I've had him with me I've sometimes *felt* danger before I've seen it.'

'He's seen it and warned you.'

'Yeah, that's my guess. So yes, please. Link us.'

I reached out with my magic. Because it was Greg, and because I could, I touched his muscled forearm, idly stroking up and down as I trailed my magic around and through him. And to his wolf. He was right: his wolf was much nearer to the surface than anyone else's I'd piped so far.

I brushed against him. *Hello,* I said.

Hello, Lucy. His tone was warm, and I was buffeted with his easy affection for me, for us.

Have you got a name? I asked curiously.

I'd like to be known as Red.

I'm nosey and I was curious why he wanted that name, but if he'd wanted me to know he would have added an explanation. I reined in my curiosity with some effort. *Well, Red, would you like me to bond you and Greg together? I don't know how permanent it will be.*

Please, Lucy. His tone was almost a whine.

Of course.

I reached out to Greg and Red simultaneously, clumsily drawing a bond around them. Then, once they were

linked, I removed myself from the equation. A soft smile
curved Greg's lips and he turned to me, his eyes blazing.
'Thank you, Lucy. We both thank you. This is – as it
should be.'

He pulled me into his arms and kissed me, and I lost myself in the moment. Finally Greg drew back, regret dusting
his face. 'To be continued,' he murmured against my lips.

I nodded breathlessly. 'Soon.'

'Duty calls. I've got to sort the roster and do a sweep. You
need to call Amber.'

I blinked, grateful for the reminder to shift my brain into
gear again. 'Right. We've got this.'

'Damn right.'

Greg left and I dialled Amber. She answered on the third
ring. 'What is it, Lucy? I'm busy.'

'You're always busy,' I pointed out sassily.

'I'm extra-busy,' she huffed impatiently. 'There's been a
fire.'

'Oh no! Is everyone okay?' Amber had taken me to
a coven once. I'd expected a dank cottage, somewhere
with cats and spiderwebs; instead, we'd gone to a high-rise
building where each witch had an apartment. There were
communal areas, too. It had been nice, but not at all
witchy.

'Fine,' she grumbled. 'Except for the witch who caused
it. At least, she won't be fine by the time I'm done with
her,' Amber muttered ominously.

I winced with sympathy for the poor witch. 'Oops. What did she do?' I imagined a cauldron fire or something equally bizarre.

'She left her crystal ball in the lounge window.'

'So?'

'So, crystal ball plus sun equals fire. One of the first things you learn as a trainee is to keep your crystal ball covered except for when you're using it.'

'Ah. I have to admit I'm surprised. I've never seen you witches use crystal balls.'

'You haven't learned all of our secrets, Lucy.'

I sighed. 'Not more secrets,' I grumbled.

Amber laughed a little. 'There are always more secrets in this realm.'

'Why you'd want to be a leader of it is beyond me.'

'I could do a lot of good from within the symposium. Whether people like it or not, the Connection is here to stay. The best way to bring about a positive outcome for my people is to manipulate it from within.'

'Even your promotions are coldly calculating,' I noted.

'What's wrong with that?'

'Nothing, of course. You do you.' I returned to my reason for calling. 'Anyway, I was ringing to ask for your help.'

'When do you do anything else?'

'You're always so busy, I doubt you'd appreciate it if I called for a chat.'

'You'd be surprised.' She said it so quietly that I almost missed it. Then she barked, 'What can I do for you, Alpha?' Had I hurt her feelings?

'Um, the thing with Thea Frost. You were hoping to make one last potion that might help?'

'Yes, of course. It should be ready later today. I'll drop it around.'

'Cool. Maybe you could come in for a glass of wine or a chat or something?' I offered lamely. We might be in the middle of a war, but a girl should always make time for her friends.

'Maybe,' she answered coolly and hung up.

I'm not sure she wants to be friends, Esme said dubiously.

She's sending mixed messages, I agreed. *Treat them mean, keep them keen.*

Esme sniffed. **Treat them mean, and they'll leave. As they should.** She thought it was a ridiculous concept.

There was a knock on the door and Mrs Dawes popped her head around the frame with a ready smile. 'Sorry to interrupt, Alpha, but there are some guests here to see you.'

'Sure, show them in.'

'I should say that one of them is a vampyr.'

Of course; a vampyr can't be invited in even once, or they have a standing invitation and all the witches' runes in the world can't keep them out. 'Which vampyr is it?' I asked.

'Alessandro.'

I wasn't surprised but I worked to keep my face blank and uninterested. 'Thank you. I'll see him outside.'

Alessandro wasn't in sight, though his black limo was. As I approached, his driver left the vehicle and held open the door for me. As during my great-great-etc-grandfather's last visit, I didn't want to get in, but I needed this chat.

My heart all but stopped as I prepared to climb into the car and saw that the limo was occupied not just by Alessandro, but by Maxwell as well. He was looking at me with open wonder on his face. 'Luciana,' he breathed in awe.

I glared at Alessandro. 'You couldn't even let me tell him what I am to him?'

'I gave you a chance but you did nothing with it. This is no time to be pussyfooting around. Someone killed your parents for the prophecy that you've just heard. Tell me.'

The car's engine started, and we lurched off. 'Are you kidnapping me?' I groused.

'Are you not coming willingly?' Alessandro raised an eyebrow. 'We have much to discuss, Luciana.'

'Stop calling me that, both of you. Whatever I was, I'm Lucy now. Just Lucy.'

'There's nothing "just" about you,' Maxwell objected. 'You're my baby cousin. I cried at your funeral – and here you are. You're a miracle, Lucy, my miracle. I always felt a kinship with you, and all this time we were more than just friends. My *cousin*.'

'Your cousin who had her elemental magic extinguished, her memory wiped, and was placed for adoption with a Common family,' I pointed out. 'All through the machinations of one decrepit, deceitful vampyr.'

'Careful, Alpha,' Alessandro growled.

'Or you'll what?' I asked, raising my chin defiantly. 'Steal my magic and remove me from my family? Oh, wait...'

'I kept you safe. I kept you alive.'

'You took my magic from me!' I shouted. 'I've always felt drawn to fire. I've always felt happiest watching it dancing in a grate. Now I learn it should have been mine to call.'

'Regardless, you're still in the Other.'

'No thanks to you. And I still don't have fire in my arsenal.'

Alessandro blithely ignored me. 'What did the prophecy say?' he asked firmly.

I glared for a long moment and honestly considered keeping it from him.

He is your elder. Esme's tone was heavy with disapproval. **He deserves your respect.**

Respect is earned.

He saved your life.

So he says. What proof do we have?

You live and breathe, and your parents do not.

Hurt and grief washed over me.

I said something wrong, didn't I? Esme sounded distraught.

It's okay.

I'm sorry. I never mean to hurt you.

Nor I you. It's okay. We're *okay.* I gave her a mental hug.

Let's tell him the prophecy and see what he has to say, she suggested in a milder tone.

Who? I said, deliberately being obtuse.

Your great great-great-grandfather.

My loser-loser-loser grandfather, I quipped pettily. *Fine. I'll tell him.*

I met Alessandro's eyes. 'I'll tell you.' My phone rang. 'In a second,' I amended. I swiped to accept the call. It was Greg. 'Hey.'

'Have you been kidnapped?' he asked without preamble.

'No, I'm good. I'm with Alessandro and Maxwell.'

'Do you need me?'

'Always, but the pack needs you more. Keep doing your thing. Make us impenetrable.' In a less serious moment, Greg would have made a dirty joke but this moment was tense and his response, when it came, was business-like. 'Roger that. Keep safe.' He hung up. No declarations of love. He must have been with Liam.

Alessandro was studying me. 'It is important to you, the mansion?'

'Obviously.'

'Very good. I will help you, and you will tell me the prophecy.' He paused, then continued. 'Your homestead has a significant security issue.'

'What?'

'It is owned by a company.'

'Yeah, so?'

'So, it is not classed as a residence but as a commercial property. Any vampyr can phase into it whenever they like.'

Fuck.

Chapter 9

'If any vampyr can phase into the mansion, then why haven't you?' I asked my grandfather suspiciously.

'That would be impolite,' he replied in a slightly shocked tone, like being rude was the greatest of all evils. I guess when you bite someone and drink their blood to survive; you need to find something else to be the new low.

A thought occurred to me. 'Does Wokeshire know this?'

Alessandro smiled. There was nothing friendly about it. 'Undoubtedly.'

'Wonderful.'

I didn't want this information to be overheard by a werewolf's sensitive hearing, so I dropped Greg a text, all in capitals so he'd know I was freaking out. WE HAVE A PROBLEM. THE MANSION IS OWNED BY A COMPANY SO VAMPYRS CAN JUST PHASE IN.

GET IT TRANSFERRED INTO MY NAME. PRON-
TO. GREASE PALMS.

I got a response almost right away: FUCK. *I'm on it.*

'How long does it take to transfer property?' I asked.

Maxwell grimaced. 'Weeks.'

I glared at Alessandro. 'You couldn't have told me this
sooner?'

'It might have been to my advantage to leave this particular hole in your security. Calm yourself. No vampyr will
attack you. I have put you under my protection.'

'Not that I don't appreciate the effort, but you're only
one vampyr – and you're clanless. How seriously are they
going to take you?'

'Very seriously, unless they wish to be chargrilled,' he
said drily, like setting his enemies on fire was a foregone
conclusion. Yikes.

'Grandad, you're a real piece of work, you know that?
And it's all well and good putting *me* under your protection, but what about my pack? I'm their alpha.'

'As you are the alpha, if you let serious harm come
to your pack, they would kill you. Consequently, I have
placed the whole pack under my protection.'

'So my pack wouldn't kill me for incompetence?'

'Indeed. Now, I helped you. Tell me the prophecy.'

There was no doubt that his help had patched a serious
security problem, so I did kind of owe him, though I'd
have felt happier if he'd told me much sooner. However,

we Barretts pays our debts – actually, we try not to incur debts in the first place.

Reluctantly I recited the prophecy for him.

'Born to fire
Wolf torn
Bridge the chasm
End the forlorn
Curse be lifted
Wolves be whole
Destroy the order
Pay the toll
A Queen Alpha
Past before seen
Reverse what was
And shouldn't have been.

'Are you happy now?' I snarked.

'Yes.' His voice conveyed no emotion whatsoever. If he *was* happy, I couldn't tell. He continued, 'You were destined to be a wolf. I was right to remove your magic.'

I opened my mouth to argue then closed it with a clack. Hard to argue with destiny. 'Where are we going?' I asked, changing the subject uncomfortably.

'It's time for a family reunion.' Maxwell smiled. 'We're overdue.'

I wasn't prepared for this. 'I'm not dressed to meet my family,' I said inanely. 'I'm wearing jeans.'

'Nobody will care that you're wearing jeans. You've come back from the dead.'

'That's no reason to look ghastly,' I said haughtily. 'Cleanliness is next to godliness and all that.'

'You don't look ghastly – though maybe ghostly. You're very pale. You take after Maria.'

I gave a small smile. 'What was she like?'

Maxwell considered the question carefully. 'She was fun and kind, always ready with a smile. I was eight when she died, so I don't remember her as well as I wish, but I loved her. She was my favourite auntie. She always hugged me when she saw me, and she whispered that she loved me when we said goodbye. My dad's a bit old school and he isn't terribly good at vocalising his emotions, so I always loved how open she was with me.'

There was a lump in my throat that I couldn't swallow, and my eyes were suddenly blurry. 'That's nice,' I managed. 'Thank you for sharing that with me.'

Maxwell manoeuvred around the limo to sit next to me and slung an arm around my shoulders. 'I hope you're prepared for plenty of stories. Everyone is so excited. Jason has been peacocking around, since he's already met his cousin.'

I grinned at that. The last time I'd seen Jason, he'd been kidnapped by a witch, an incubus, an ogre and a griffin. He'd held up admirably well and helped the other children cope. I'd been impressed, and I hadn't even known that we were related. 'He's a tough kid.'

Maxwell smiled, pride shining out of every pore. 'Yeah, he did okay.'

The car stopped moving and I swallowed my apprehension. I was finally meeting my birth family; this was the moment I'd been waiting for most of my life. Admittedly, it wasn't quite like I'd imagined because in the scenarios I'd dreamed of as a child, none of them had my birth parents dead and gone.

Of course I'd thought about meeting my parents. When I was young, I'd imagined them either as near-royalty or drug addicts; I hadn't really contemplated anything in between. I pretended that they'd had to give me away as a result of some complex political intrigue. When I was older and more cynical and bitter, I'd imagined that they'd sold me for cash for their next fix. Neither extreme was true: they'd been ordinary, save for a bit of fire-elemental magic, and they'd loved me. They'd left me not through choice but because they'd died.

I turned to Alessandro. 'Who killed them? You must have investigated their deaths.'

Pain flared in Alessandro's eyes, there and gone in an instant. 'Of course I looked into it,' he growled.

'We suspected they were killed by an earth-elemental family, but we never found proof,' Maxwell explained. 'The Connection told us they were killed by an assassin, but the griffins swore that it wasn't a contract they'd taken.'

'It wasn't the griffins,' Alessandro confirmed. 'I tracked down the assassin eventually. It was a dryad.'

'A *dryad*?' I asked incredulously.

Maxwell frowned at his grandfather. 'You should have told the family that.'

'Why? What does it change? They were killed by an assassin. You knew that much.'

'You know Mama has been holding a grudge against the griffins.'

'The griffins deserve her ire, whether they killed Maria and Luca or not. They mustn't be trusted.'

'The dryad,' I interrupted. 'What did you find out from him? You must have asked who had hired him?'

Alessandro gave me a flat look. 'Obviously. And much as I threatened to burn down his entire forest, he refused to tell me anything. He said he had a geas upon him, which he couldn't break, for fear of death. I believed him.'

I snorted. 'He told you nicely, and you just accepted his word?'

'No,' he disagreed levelly. 'I tortured him with the living flare, but he stuck to his story. Believe me, he would have told me who had hired him if he'd been able. The living flare breaks us all eventually.'

Yeesh. The living flare is an horrific curse a fire elemental can inflict that makes their victims feel like their skin is crackling and burning and smoke is filling their lungs. They can live on indefinitely through the pain. Jess had told me that Benedict used it like a party trick, and heart attacks were common under the strain of the curse.

Torture was wrong – I knew it was wrong – but I was struggling to work up any sympathy for the bastard that had killed my parents.

He killed your parents, your elders. He deserves to be ripped limb from limb, Esme growled. I didn't disagree.

'What was his name? The dryad.'

Alessandro paused; for a long moment, I thought he wasn't going to tell me. 'Orion Baker.'

'And after you'd tortured Orion, what then?'

'The trail went cold. I gave the Connection the information I had obtained, but they did nothing.'

'What about this old earth-elemental family then? Could they have hired Orion?'

'They denied it,' Maxwell said.

'Of course they did. Surely you didn't just accept their word?'

'We had no choice,' Alessandro said firmly. 'We weren't in a position to challenge them.'

'And now?'

He smiled grimly. 'Now we are getting strong enough to let them burn.'

'If we prove they're responsible,' Maxwell interjected. 'I'm not going to war without evidence.'

'That's your boyfriend speaking,' Alessandro growled.

'Do you see Roscoe here? That's me speaking, Grandfather.'

'You've become his marionette,' Alessandro grouched. It was clearly an argument they'd had many times.

'Roscoe may occasionally have his fingers in my ass, but I'm not his puppet. I assure you he doesn't control what comes out of my mouth, just what goes in it.' Maxwell gave his grandfather a decidedly cheeky wink.

I didn't realise that a vampyr could blush, but Alessandro's skin reddened. I snickered.

'Enough,' Alessandro said. 'The family have been waiting long enough.'

'The car has only just stopped,' I pointed out.

'I'm not talking about now.'

The limo had stopped outside Alessandro's, the family restaurant. I had a whole collection of rabid butterflies in my tummy; I knew Maxwell, and I'd met Jason and his mother Alyssa, but everyone else was an unknown.

'Don't be nervous.' Maxwell gave my shoulders another squeeze. 'They're just so happy you're alive. Now is the time to ask for any family heirlooms you've got your eyes on,' he joked. 'For one day only, they'd give you the moon if they could.'

The driver opened the door. 'Thank you, Harley.' Maxwell beamed at him. Despite the grisly nature of our discussion, my cousin had all the excitement of a puppy dog at the prospect of introducing me to our family.

We climbed out of the limo and I checked over my clothes in the window of the restaurant.

We are presentable, Esme said.

You always say that.

I have learned that you are more comfortable if we are wearing clothes. You are wearing clothes, so it is fine.

I didn't have it in me to point out that being presentable was more than just being clothed. I was wearing washed-out jeans and a T-shirt that read: *Four out of the five voices in my head think you're an idiot. The other one is trying to work out where to bury your body.* It had been a gift from Greg, and I liked it because it showed he was getting to know Esme as well as me. But maybe it wasn't the best outfit for meeting my birth family.

It was early, so the restaurant was closed though the lights were on. Maxwell strode forward and opened the door, holding it wide for me. No more hiding. I walked through to meet the rest of my family for the first time. It was a surreal moment, and I'd never wished so hard for my make-up, or Greg, or something else to hide behind.

They will love you, Esme whispered encouragingly. **Be brave.**

Her words did the trick. Straightening my spine, I fixed a smile on my face and strode forward. They were all sitting in a booth together. Jason looked up and gave me a smile. 'Hey, cous.'

'Hey, Jason. How are you doing?'

'I'm good. I haven't been kidnapped lately, so things are looking up.'

'My grandbaby,' a woman whispered. Her hair was heavily streaked with silver, and her face was worn and tired, though there were laughter lines under her eyes. She was dressed in a beautiful loose dress. That was all I noticed before she barrelled into me, pulled me into her arms and sobbed, 'Luci! My Luci!'

Sending Maxwell a panicked look, I hugged her and awkwardly patted her back.

'She's your *nonna*, Helena. Your grandmother. She was Luca's mama,' Maxwell said, his voice laden with emotion.

Helena pulled back and made an effort to stop crying. She wiped her eyes. 'I'm sorry, my child. I don't mean to overwhelm you, but I'm so happy to see you.'

I smiled. 'I'm pretty thrilled to meet you.'

Her smile dimmed. 'You don't remember me?'

Alessandro cleared his throat. 'When she was extinguished, her mind was cleared.'

Helena glared at Alessandro. 'I will never forgive you for taking her away from us, Grandfather.'

'You do not have to forgive me because it was the right thing to do. She is alive because of it. The prophecy tells me I was correct to do what I did.'

'You've heard that damned prophecy?' A greying man stepped forward. He was tall and thin, unbowed with age. He gave me a half smile. 'Hello, Luciana,' he greeted me in a warm baritone voice. 'I'm Riccardo, your *nonno* – grandad – but you can call me whatever you're comfortable with.'

'It's very nice to meet you, Riccardo,' I managed. Maybe other terms would come with time.

'You look so like Maria,' another woman said. 'But I see Luca too in the shape of your eyes, your nose. Hello, Luciana. I'm Maxwell's mama, your Aunty Emily.'

After that, it all got a bit overwhelming as I met Niccolo, Maxwell's father, and Edward and Bianca, Maxwell's siblings. They all clustered around me, taking turns to exclaim how nice it was to see me and how much like Luca and Maria I looked. As the noise in the room rose, it became a bit much. They're not kidding when they say that Italian families are loud.

Esme crooned in my head, trying to soothe me. Chaos didn't faze her; puppies were often loud and unruly.

'Yo!' Jason shouted. 'You're freaking Lucy out. Give her some space before she wolfs out on us.' The room fell silent instantly.

'I won't wolf out,' I promised awkwardly. 'My wolf is lovely. Her name is Esme, and she is very pleased to meet you all.'

'Esme is a lovely name,' Helena said loudly. 'Even if it is French,' she muttered. In the silence of the room, we all heard her quite clearly.

'Mama!' Alyssa chastised. 'I'm so sorry, Lucy.'

Jason snickered.

'It's fine. Esme and I are not offended,' I said. 'I once had a lovely holiday in France.'

'And have you been to Italia?' Helena asked hopefully.

'No, I haven't. Sorry,' I admitted. Her face fell. 'But I'd love to go one day,' I hastened to add.

The older woman brightened. '*Si*! We will take you. We can visit my sister in Val Camonica.'

'Take her when the Badalisc comes,' Jason suggested. 'You can take me too. You promised!' He turned to me. 'The Badalisc is a goat-snake creature with horns and glowing eyes.' He mimed having horns. 'It comes down to the village for two days and they have this awesome festival where everyone's naughty behaviour is read out. My mum says it's the funniest thing.'

'It's only funny when it's not your secrets being blathered about,' Riccardo complained. 'Talking of secrets, would you feel comfortable telling us the prophecy? We lost Luca and Maria because of it, so I'd be grateful to hear it. Perhaps it will give us some peace.'

Helena swatted him. 'We don't know for sure that it was the prophecy that caused their deaths.'

'Their deaths were too close to the prophecy being registered for it to be anything else,' Riccardo disagreed. It was clearly a familiar argument.

'I don't want to know the damned prophecy,' Helena said bitterly. 'It cost us too much.'

'I'm sorry,' I said into the silence. I looked down at the floor and swallowed past the sudden rock in my throat.

'Tsch. It is not your fault, my child.' Helena gave me a squeeze. 'You couldn't stop it any more than you could stop breathing. It is what it is.'

'Tell us the prophecy,' Jason chimed in. 'I want to know!'

'I'm not sure I should go bandying it about,' I confessed. 'Mum and Dad may have died because of it, and I don't want to be responsible for any more deaths.' I thought of James, my incubus ex-boyfriend whom I'd killed, and Ace who had also died at Esme's claws. 'Except for my enemies,' I amended.

Jason snorted. 'Yeah, she's real good at ripping into her enemies. You should have seen her bring that prick down.'

'Language, Jason!' his mum snapped.

'You might as well tell us the prophecy. The more people who know it, the less dangerous it becomes,' Maxwell pointed out. 'Our enemies would have to kill us all to silence it.'

'I don't want to paint a target on all of your backs,' I objected.

'For good or ill, we will stand by you. Ignorance could do more harm than good,' Alyssa said. 'Please. Tell us. We deserve to know.'

I bit my thumb, conflicted, but Alessandro took the decision out of my hands and calmly recited the whole thing. I was glad he'd taken the choice of sharing the prophecy away from me because whatever followed, I wouldn't be wholly culpable. I met his eyes across the room and nodded, then saw the acceptance of my thanks in his eyes.

'What curse is it talking about?' Jason asked.

I hesitated, thinking about my answer before I spoke. 'There were some wolves a few hundred years ago. They got too dangerous, and the witches cursed them and turned them into gargoyles. That's the only curse that I know of, the only one that makes sense. But I don't know how to lift a curse that was made hundreds of years ago. Apparently, I need the blood of one of the witches who delivered it – but that's impossible.'

'Only if you think of time as a linear thing,' commented Riccardo.

'And if you don't have access to a portal,' Maxwell said with a wink.

I suddenly felt incredibly stupid. Of course: the fire elementals guarded the portal, and they were the guardians of the hall. I could use the portal to go back in time.

'Wouldn't you get in trouble if the Connection found out that I'd used your portal to access the Third realm?'

'Definitely, but some things are worth getting into trouble for. Besides, they'd have to find out first,' Emily pointed out. 'I wasn't planning on telling them. Anyone else?' They all shook their heads.

'Hang on, I've got another option,' I said as I thought of Gato.

I pulled out my phone and dialled Jess, but my call went straight to voicemail. I hung up and dialled again, and then again. Each time, it was the same thing: Jess was somewhere in deepest darkest Wales, in a place with no signal. I could wait for her to become available and meet me somewhere with Gato, or I could use Maxwell's portal.

'You're sure you won't get in trouble?' I asked.

Alessandro stood. 'It will be fine. Come, Lucy, I will accompany you.'

'To the hall?'

'To the past.'

Chapter 10

I rang Greg to explain that my absence was going to be longer than planned. I expected him to argue about my planned jaunt to the past, but all he said was a heartfelt 'be safe'. He didn't make jokes about affecting the time continuum, which I appreciated because I was nervous as hell already. I asked him to man the fort in my absence, and we rang off before I could beg him to come with me. I always felt better with him by my side.

I turned off my phone; there was no point taking it to Victorian times where – or when – there were no satellites to provide a signal. We piled into Alessandro's limo and motored off to Rosie's. We all just about fit into the limo; now I realised why he kept it on retainer. With such a big family, it was handy to roll in one car. Carpooling, rich-vampyr style.

Alyssa had rustled up a plain black dress that she thought wouldn't attract too much attention in Victorian times. She wasn't kidding: the thing was really ugly. I grumpily threw it on, and half-hoped I'd have cause to do a swift transformation so that the f-ugly dress could be sent into the ether forever.

Alessandro phased into the shadows to fetch something, and Maxwell made us all a coffee while we waited. Grandfather didn't take too long; suddenly he reappeared dressed in an archaic suit. 'Did you just happen to have that in your wardrobe?' I asked. 'Because hoarding isn't healthy behaviour. Except for dragons, I guess,' I amended.

He gave me a flat look. 'Let's get this over with,' he said grimly.

'Not looking forward to the experience?'

'The food is terrible in Victorian times,' he responded drily.

'Not the finest vintage blood?' I quipped.

He didn't reply. 'Hold my hand,' he instructed. 'I'll step into the portal first to determine the time we go to.'

'And how do you pick the time?' I asked curiously.

'I know it.'

'How?'

'You'll see.' He took my hand and together we strode through the back room of Rosie's. He took the lead as we walked back out again, hands still held.

Someone was in the anteroom, slumped in a wooden chair, feet crossed at the ankle, muddy boots on the table. It was evening and the room was lit by candles. The floor was tiled and swept clean. It certainly wasn't the Rosie's I knew.

'That's not very hygienic,' I commented, pointing to the chap's feet.

'Shit!' the person exclaimed and whirled round.

My jaw dropped. It was Alessandro. Huh.

'Hello, Alessandro,' the vampyr greeted his younger self.

'Oh fuck,' young Alessandro whimpered. 'Papa is going to kill me. Both of us in the Third realm? There's not supposed to be two of us at once! Which one of us is going to pay the price? Elizabeth won't believe this.'

'Both of us will pay – one way or another. Calm down, it's already been done. And Papa doesn't find out about the Third realm, and you can't tell Elizabeth either.'

Tension washed out of young Alessandro's shoulders. 'Thank goodness for small mercies. Our wife isn't going to forgive me the omission if she finds out.'

'She won't find out,' Alessandro promised. His poker face was good, but something in the tightness of his hands betrayed emotions he was trying to hide. I felt sorry for him; his wife must have surely died decades ago in his memories.

I looked between the two versions. Old Alessandro had lines around his eyes and silver in his hair. He was a vampyr so he could control whatever age he wished to appear as, and today he was in the mood for silver foxing. 'I can't call you both Alessandro,' I said. 'It's going to get confusing fast.'

'Call me Ali,' the younger Alessandro suggested. 'My friends do.'

'And call you Sandro?' I suggested to the older one, tongue in cheek.

'No.'

'Do your friends not call you that?'

'I don't have friends.'

Ali sighed. 'Great. Something to look forward to. I'm going to get old and grumpy and friendless.' He peered at Alessandro. 'I still look pretty good though, so that's something. I bet the ladies still love me.'

Alessandro winked.

'Ew, that's gross, Grandfather,' I muttered.

'You're my *granddaughter*? How far back have you travelled?' Ali asked, wide eyed.

'Don't answer that,' Alessandro ordered sharply.

I rolled my eyes. 'Obviously not.'

Esme, are you okay? I reached out to her.

Yes. I am ready, she assured me, but she sounded concerned, subdued. She was hiding something from me, and I could feel it like a knot in my muscles, achy and irritating.

Ready for what? I asked, and hoped that the time had come for honesty.

Anything, she replied. She felt tense, like a coiled spring.

Ali was speaking again. 'If you won't tell me how far you've travelled, can you tell me what you're here for?'

'She needs to see the local alpha,' Alessandro said.

'John? Why can't you just say John?'

'I couldn't remember his name,' Alessandro admitted, though it rang false to me. But why would he lie?

'Great, I go senile too,' Ali sighed.

Alessandro reached out and gave his young self a swipe around the head. 'Respect your elders.'

'Self-respect *is* important,' I agreed sagely.

Alessandro glared at me. 'Are you quite done?'

'Probably not, but I'll let you know.'

'This is so strange. Maybe I drank too much,' Ali muttered, looking at his cup.

'I can hit you again if it will help,' Alessandro offered.

'No, that's okay.' Ali rubbed his head with a doleful expression. 'We had best get going if you want to see John. I'll get Maxwell to take over here.'

'Maxwell?' I said, surprised.

'My brother. It's a family name,' Alessandro explained.

'Well, that's not confusing at all.' For a moment I'd thought that my cousin was hiding some hereto unknown immortality.

'Pull the carriage around first, and let Lucy and I get in before you summon Maxwell.'

'Obviously.' Ali rolled his eyes. 'I didn't realise I was so annoying. I don't need you to teach me to suck eggs.'

Alessandro's gaze grew flinty. 'Watch yourself, boy. You have a lot to learn.'

'Quoting Papa now, are you? I've really gone to the dogs.'

'You have no idea,' Alessandro said drily.

We followed Ali out of what would one day become Rosie's and waited out front until he came around the front of the building with a horse-drawn carriage. I was impressed: it was all shiny black with gold lettering, clearly a symbol of the wealth that the Alessandros had in bucketloads. The surprise came when I looked at what was pulling the carriage: a unicorn, complete with blood-red eyes and clawed feet. I bet that was another symbol of wealth, one exclusive to the Other realm.

I reached out with my mind and encountered Ares. To say I was shocked was an understatement. 'Ares?' I said aloud as I sent him a wave of affection and greeting. The unicorn studied me, head tilted, fixing me with crimson eyes that promised blood if I made one wrong move. *I'm so happy to see you.* I felt curiosity roll back. *May I stroke you?* I felt his assent.

I stroked his pristine, luminescent fur and felt a tug of horror at the thought of all that he would go through. The Ares I knew had a coat marred by a myriad of scars.

'You're a piper?' Ali asked in surprise.

'Yeah. Go figure.'

'I've never heard of anyone being a piper *and* an elemental.'

'I'm not an elemental. Not anymore. I was extinguished.'

Ali gasped, genuinely shocked. He looked at me with horror, like I had confessed to bathing in the blood of children as part of my skincare regime.

'And that,' Alessandro said drolly, 'is the reason that I arranged for you to be extinguished.' His tone was a trifle smug, and I could easily imagine him doing a mic drop.

'What?' I said in confusion.

'When the time came, I recalled this conversation. I knew you survived and somehow found your way back to the Other realm again.'

'You're saying that being extinguished was my fault?' I asked incredulously.

'In part,' Alessandro agreed. 'If you'd kept your mouth shut, it probably wouldn't have even occurred to me. It's not exactly a go-to solution.'

I opened my mouth and closed it sharply. Fuck. He had a point. 'Perhaps I'd better try and not say too much from now on.'

Alessandro grinned unexpectedly. 'Silence isn't really in your skill set.'

'It's nice that you agree that I have a skill set.'

'If we're done chattering,' Ali interjected, 'I'll get Maxwell and we can get this tawdry mess on the road. The sooner we send you two back to your proper time, the better.' Under his breath he muttered, 'And the less you can fuck things up.'

I gave Ares one last affectionate pat; he was still eyeing me cautiously, but there was also a flicker of interest. We weren't besties yet, but he was warming to me. I climbed into the shiny obsidian carriage that was hooked up to him. Ali disappeared for a few moments, then hopped back into the driver's seat.

The mansion was only a couple of miles from Rosie's, but it took us over half an hour by horse-drawn carriage. Ye olde times were more boring than I'd expected, and the ride was bumpy as hell. God bless whoever eventually invented proper suspension; my ass thanked them.

'When did they invent suspension?' I complained after a particularly vicious bump.

'You're in the *crème de la crème* of carriages. This is as good as the suspension gets in this era,' Alessandro said. 'I hope you're ready.'

'For what?'

'Anything.'

Always, Esme said firmly.

'Apparently we are,' I confirmed. I kept my self-doubt to myself. No need to spread it around; that shit was contagious.

'The mansion is privately owned in these times, so I'll have to stay inside the carriage. Once you're inside, you're on your own.'

I was never on my own because I always had Esme. 'This isn't my first rodeo,' I said calmly. It was probably my *second* rodeo. Who knew you were supposed to learn everything by the second rodeo? But then, there was always a steep learning curve in the Other.

'Let's hope it's not your last,' Alessandro said grimly.

'Are you always this upbeat, Grandfather?'

'Life has taught me to expect disappointment.'

'I bet you're the life and soul of a party.'

'It is questionable whether I have a soul,' he retorted.

We came to a stop in front of the mansion. It felt weird to see my home and know that it wasn't my home, at least not yet. The place *gleamed*; it had clearly not long been built. *My* mansion had been kissed by the ravages of time – some peeling paint here, some knocks on the wood there.

For all it was the same building, it was nothing like home because it wasn't filled with the wolves that I knew. There was no Liam, Seren, Marissa or Mrs Dawes; worst of all, there was no Greg. I was strolling into a pack full of unknowns. I hoped the current alpha was similar in outlook to Lord Samuel rather than the malicious Frosts of the Devon pack. I had no time for alpha ass-holes.

Alessandro told Ali to escort me to the front entrance, but I noted that he didn't explain why he was staying in the carriage. If Ali could go in the mansion, evidently he was still human, and he had no idea about his vampyric future, poor lug.

Ali drew himself up and knocked proudly on the familiar wooden door. It was opened by someone dressed in butler regalia. 'Alessandro Alessandro to see the Lord Alpha,' he proclaimed loudly.

I suppressed a snigger, his name was Alessandro Alessandro? No wonder he just used the one.

The butler shut the door a moment whilst he conferred with the Lord Alpha as to whether we would be allowed access.

'Alessandro Alessandro?' I couldn't resist teasing.

'My mother was high on opiates after my birth,' Ali sighed.

I laughed out loud – until Esme murmured, **Be ready.** Her gentle instruction wiped away my smile. She was right; we needed to get our game face on.

'Do you know what to expect?' Ali asked.

'The unexpected,' I said, my tone a shade grimmer than I'd intended.

The butler returned. 'You may enter,' he intoned.

We followed him into the wolf's lair.

Chapter 11

I entered my own living room alone, leaving Ali to cool his heels in the hall. As I walked in, I did a double take. My fresh yellow walls had been replaced with heavy wooden cladding. Oof. The yellow was a good change. There weren't as many bookcases, making the room seem significantly larger. Looking around, I noticed that the alpha was not alone.

'Bastion?' I blurted in confusion. The taciturn griffin raised an eyebrow at me, curiosity dancing across his face. His younger face. He hadn't mastered that impenetrable mask yet. 'Erm, your reputation precedes you,' I claimed hastily, trying to cover my error.

Even in Victorian times, Bastion was dressed in black and radiated danger. Dammit, it was hard to remember that this wasn't *my* Bastion; he didn't know me from Eve. 'It's so nice to meet you,' I continued, flailing.

It would be best if you were silent, Esme advised.

You're not wrong, I agreed. *I just wasn't prepared to see Bastion here.*

Silent in all ways. He can hear us converse.

Shit: I had forgotten that Bastion was a coaxer, and as such he had an ability to converse that transcended words.

I followed Esme's advice and shut my trap, but it was a little too late. I saw Bastion's eyes fix on the large triangle on my forehead, the symbol of the temporal realm, and his eyes narrowed. Major oops.

I turned my attention to the other man in the room: the alpha werewolf. He was taking my measure as I took his. He had a broad strong frame, dark wiry hair, a manicured beard, and a warmth in his eyes that took me by surprise. Something about him set me at ease.

'Hello, Alpha,' I greeted him. 'I'm Lucy Barrett.'

'My honour to meet you, Lucy Barrett. You are here because Alessandro Alessandro has vouched for you and confirmed that you bring urgent business to my door.' He touched his hand to his heart and gave a slight bow. 'My name is John Dufresne. Let us discuss this "urgent business".' The French accent took me by surprise because Ali had just called him John, which sounded distinctly English.

'My honour to meet you, John Dufresne,' I parroted back, giving him a slightly deeper bow than the one he'd given me.

My honour to meet you Lucy Barrett, said an alien voice in my mind. **I am known as Swift.**

What? While I floundered, Esme took the reins. **My honour to meet you Swift. I am known as Esme.**

Well met, Esme. You have travelled far but I cannot hear the Great Pack within you. How is that possible?

Esme hesitated. **There is a curse.**

We know of it, but it should not affect you – your eyes are not golden.

I joined Lucy after the curse had been cast.

And as a result you have been riven from the pack? Swift said, sounding both astonished and horrified.

Yes, Esme admitted.

For how long?

It is but a handful of moons since I joined with Lucy.

The loss must pain you, Swift whispered.

I still recall the Great Pack's warmth, she admitted. **It preserves me. One day, it will call me home.**

But the silence...

Lucy helps fill the void.

John spoke aloud. 'All of the golden eyes have gone mad from the silence.'

How could he speak to both Swift and Esme? Was he a piper, too? I'd never met another werewolf who could speak to their wolf like I could. I frowned. 'How did you hear the conversation between Esme and Swift?'

He frowned at me. 'That is normal.' His head tilted as he studied me. 'I hear through my wolf, Swift, through our joining and—' He stopped abruptly.

At my obvious bewilderment, he tried again. 'I am connected to Swift. He is a wolf and Esme is a wolf, so he can talk with her. Through my connection to Swift, I can hear what is said.' I nodded my understanding and John continued. 'The golden-eyed ones have started to change. Their skin has started to harden and grey. They have growths upon their backs.'

They were talking of the cursed wolves, the first ones that were being changed into gargoyles – the first gargoyles to exist. I suspected that the growths on their backs would form wings eventually. 'Don't let them go into the sunlight,' I blurted before I could think better of it.

'Why not?'

'They will turn to stone – though apparently they do shift back. Eventually. But it's still an unpleasant experience.'

John's eyes narrowed at me. 'And how do you know this?'

'I've spoken with a gargoyle.'

Hope lit up John's eyes. 'Do you know how to undo the curse?'

I shook my head helplessly. 'But I know a witch who will be able to.' Amber was the most competent person I'd ever met, witch or not; I had no doubt she could break the curse if she had the right materials to hand.

John's gaze grew distant. He stared into the grate for a moment that was long enough to become awkward. I opened my mouth to start the conversation again, but Bastion held up a hand, 'He and Swift are consulting with the Great Pack,' Bastion explained softly.

The Great Pack? I huffed, 'If this pack is so great, why don't I know about it?'

'Your wolf is new to you, and the witches' curse is still in effect. We hope to lift it.'

I sat down heavily. They didn't lift it – they couldn't; it was still effective in my time, some two hundred years in the future. 'What *is* the Great Pack?' I asked. John's brief comment had left much to be desired.

'I cannot tell you without risking the witches' geas,' Bastion responded. 'That is why Dufresne also hesitates to speak of it. Neither is it my place to say.'

'It is mine,' John confirmed, his eyes now focused on me again. 'If anyone should speak of it, it should be me. I have consulted at length with the Great Pack. They are of the view that you should be told of its existence, so I will explain matters to you.' His jaw clenched. 'And I will accept the consequences of breaking the geas.'

I swallowed hard, suddenly feeling nervous. I didn't want anything horrendous to happen to the alpha just to give me knowledge. 'Is there not another way?' I asked. 'If Esme was to tell me...'

'She would be ripped from you. It is why she has said nothing to you before. If you know a witch that can break the curse, then you must bear this burden. Bastion has delivered one of the witches who laid the curse to us. To break it, you will need her blood, or that of one of her sisters who was present when the curse was cast. I will entrust you with the blood and you will break the curse.'

I opened my mouth to tell them that I was from the Third realm, from a time not yet made, but then I closed it again. Who knew what would happen if I told them the truth about when I was from? I'd already caused myself to become extinguished – kind of.

As if he could read my thoughts, John smiled. 'You have the third triangle upon your head, Lucy Barrett. We are not ignorant of that meaning. You will break the curse whenever it is meant to be broken. Swear that to us, and Swift and I will gladly sacrifice ourselves for the wolves that come after us. We are pack, and this rift cannot be maintained. For the good of all, we will risk the wrath of the geas.'

I nodded. My mouth was dry, and I licked suddenly parched lips. I could feel Esme's relief that finally I would hear her greatest secret, and no longer would the growing distance stretch out between us. I was also eager for it to end.

John started. 'All men are born, and all wolves start their lives in the Great Pack. The Great Pack exists in the moon's shadow and in the hunting night. Every wolf, whether in England, France or the Americas, is joined by the Great Pack. It connects us all, strengthens us. What one wolf can know, all wolves can know. We may live shorter life spans compared to the vampyrs, dragons and trolls, but our strength is the Great Pack. Together we are stronger.'

I frowned. 'What are you saying? That the wolves have some sort of ... hive mind?'

'We are not bees.' John sounded affronted. 'We are the Great Pack; one pack that unites us across distances greater than any man could travel. Knowledge is power. Together we are a force to be reckoned with.'

When I'd joined the werewolves, I'd been surprised by how little respect they were afforded within the Other community. There were many other more powerful creatures. The Great Pack could really level the playing field.

What one pack knows, all packs could know... So, for example, we could learn about vampyr politics across the world and apply that to our own local vampyr clan so we weren't constantly on the back foot. The prospect of the knowledge of hundreds, even thousands, of minds joined together made me positively dizzy. At heart, I'm a geeky academic; I checked that I wasn't drooling at the possibility of all that knowledge at my fingertips.

'It is through the Great Pack that the humans and the wolves can communicate. That link is how I can speak to Swift. But that bastard curse has separated all the golden-eyed ones from the Great Pack, and now they cannot shift back to human form. Our new pups, when they called to their wolf for the first time, can't speak with them, and they must battle with their wolf not to become golden-eyed – feral. It is wrong. There shouldn't be a struggle between us and our wolves.

'The witches' curse hasn't just affected the golden-eyed, as they intended, but all of us that live now, and all of us that will come in the future. The new wolves cannot speak to their humans or to the Great Pack. They are disconnected. It is wrong,' he repeated, the distress in his voice ringing out.

I understood. If the curse could be broken and the rift between the humans and their wolves could be healed, all werewolves would be able to speak to their wolves. There would be none of this wrestling for dominance, no risk of going feral. It would change everything.

Bastion clasped John sympathetically on the shoulder. 'The geas will come for you, Reynard.'

'I am ready.'

'Wait!' I cried. 'What? Reynard?'

'My birth name.' Dufresne waved a hand dismissively. 'I adopted John when I moved here, a proper English name.'

I stared at him with horror. I knew Reynard, he was my ally – and in the twenty-first century, he was gargoyle. Surely there couldn't be two local Reynards?

By breaking the geas, Dufresne had called the curse down on himself. Even as I watched, his skin grew paler. 'Reynard!' I whispered, reaching for him.

'It is all right, Lucy Barrett,' he said calmly. But it wasn't all right, not by a long shot. He was turning into a gargoyle, and it was my fault. Was the meagre knowledge he'd imparted worth it? It didn't seem like it; nothing could be worth it.

We accept what is to come for the greater good of the pack. Swift's voice filled my mind. Despite his words, I felt his apprehension; he might have accepted it, but he was still scared. I could feel his fear like slimy tar upon my skin.

I watched in horror as John collapsed to the floor. A scream was ripped from him as he started to shrink, then there was an awful crunching noise and thankfully he passed out.

This was no slow transformation, like the cursed golden-eyed wolves had experienced; this was fast and hard and painful, a punishment for breaking the geas. There was no pleasure in the change, like I experienced when I shifted from human to wolf.

John's fine shirt ripped as wings sprouted from his back. His mouth was still open from his screaming, and I watched in disbelief as his teeth sharpened until they looked like a shark's. Finally, the transformation stopped and he lay, passed out in his ripped finery. His features had twisted into those of the grey-skinned Reynard that I knew.

Now I knew why I had trusted John the moment I'd laid eyes on him, despite his position as an alpha werewolf. Some part of me had recognised him as my friend, Reynard the gargoyle.

His scent, Esme murmured. **It's the same. That's why we trusted him.**

I suddenly recalled my first meeting with Reynard as I crouched naked under a children's climbing frame.

He blinked, his yellow eyes flashing in the night. 'Well now. It's good to see you again. That's a lightning-fast shift, wolfie darling. I haven't seen one that fast in a few decades.'

I blinked in confusion. 'Have we met before?'

He smiled, his maw full of sharp spikey teeth, which felt less than friendly. 'My mistake.'

Cheeky, sneaky gargoyle! Dammit, *Back to the Future* should teach everyone not to mess with time. How I regretted walking through that damned portal. I'd cost my friend the rest of his wolfish life, and damned him to immortality as a gargoyle.

Chapter 12

'I'll summon his second,' Bastion said grimly.

I barely registered what he said. I had run to Reynard when he fell, and I was still cradling his head in my lap. 'You do that,' I muttered, distracted.

I picked up Reynard and carried him carefully to the sofa that one day I would be transformed upon. The sofa on which I would lay a beaten and bloody Reynard in the distant future. Then I knelt on the floor next to it so that I could keep a close eye on my friend.

The door opened and another man walked in. He took in the scene immediately, but his expression barely changed. Maybe it was from him that Bastion would eventually learn the art of the poker face. 'What has happened to our alpha?' he demanded.

'I'm sorry, I didn't mean to,' I said helplessly.

'You are responsible for his transformation?'

'Yes,' I admitted. I waited for condemnation to spew forth, but instead he regarded me carefully.

'Then you are now our alpha.' He said it evenly, but the hairs on my neck rose. Danger, danger, Will Robinson.

'What? No, I'm sorry, I can't be. I literally can't be.' My mind was blank. I'd travelled from a different time; I couldn't stay here to be their alpha. I was their pack's alpha in the future, not now. 'I have to go. I can't stay here.'

'Perhaps not, but you have disposed of our alpha and so you take his position.'

'I *can't* be alpha. You can be the alpha instead.'

'It doesn't work like that. I either have to kill you, or you must remain my alpha.' There was a hint of aggression in his body language, and I got the feeling he was favouring the first option. I felt Esme prepare herself in response. She was a hair's breadth away from seizing control, ready for violence.

Bastion interrupted our tense conversation. 'What about a stewardship?'

The second raised his eyebrow. 'It has been some time since we have had a stewardship.'

'Then you're about due a new one, aren't you?' Bastion stated calmly. 'John chose to take this path because Lucy says she can break the curse. She needs the witch's blood to do what needs to be done.'

That seemed to give pause to John's second. He turned and met my eyes, searching for the truth. 'Can you break this curse?'

'Not me personally, but I know a witch who can.' Probably.

'My son has been cursed. His eyes are golden and he doesn't answer my call. He doesn't know me. I must keep him caged like a feral beast. Swear to me that you will break the curse, and I'll agree to take up stewardship here.'

'How does a stewardship work?'

'You appoint me as your steward and I run the pack in your stead. It's normally done for a short period of absence if the alpha has to leave for some reason, but the pack will accept it. I am respected.'

'Fine. I swear that I will do everything in my power to break the curse. What's your name?'

'Isiah Samuel.'

'Fuck.' I looked at the blond man before me, the ancestor of a man I would kill one day. It was a total mindfuck. Note to self, do not fuck with time or time will fuck with you. Isiah Samuel raised an eyebrow at my expletive, and I shook my head. It wasn't something I could explain. I didn't want to destroy the timeline any more than I already had.

I straightened my shoulders and lifted my head high. 'Get me the blood of the witch and I will do everything I can to break this damned curse.'

'Very well. And I, or my line, will hold the pack for you as stewards until such time as you return.' His gaze lingered on the large triangle on my head.

'Done,' I agreed aloud.

'And done.'

'Witnessed,' Bastion called.

I felt magic settle upon me like a hug that was too hard and fast, but it was over before I missed a breath. 'What was that?'

'A magical oath.'

'And what will happen if either of us forswear it?'

'Death,' Isiah Samuel said simply.

Great.

On the sofa, Reynard started to stir. His eyes flicked open; they were golden. 'Hey,' I greeted him. 'How do you feel?'

'Lost. I am lost, you whelping wench. Swift. Where is Swift?' He swallowed hard and pushed himself up. 'I cannot feel Swift.' He examined his greying hands. 'What manner of fecking beast have I become? What am I without my sodding Swift?' His hands were shaking.

'A gargoyle,' I said softly, feeling awful.

I remembered Swift's fear all too clearly. He hadn't survived the transformation, and the curse had ripped him away. A sob threatened to escape me. I reached my mind out to Esme's and we clung to each other in desperation.

The thought of being separated from her – it was too much to bear.

We will not be separated, she promised firmly.

Never, I agreed.

'A gargoyle?' Reynard said. 'So I must keep to the shagging shadows, or I become a stony fuck. I'm cursed like the Common tales of a vampyr but without the speed and strength. Bloody marvellous.'

'Yes, but at least you haven't got a hankering for blood,' I offered weakly.

'That's the silver lining in the sodding cloud, for sure.'

'Oh, and you'll probably find that you're vegetarian now as well.'

'I fucking hate vegetables,' Reynard snapped.

'Well, you can always *try* meat,' I said dubiously. 'But every gargoyle I've ever met has been a vegetarian.'

'And have there been many gargoyles in your past, my bitey pup?'

A vision flashed before me, a memory of poor Hamlet smashed to pieces on my lawn. 'A few.' In my past, in my future, in my present; time was a ball of string that a rambunctious kitten had played with.

'Samuel,' Reynard said to his second. 'I can't lead the pack now.'

'Indeed, you have no wolf. I can't sense Swift.' Samuel's tone was cool and factual; there was no emotional reaction to the loss of his boss. He studied Reynard like an exhibit at the zoo, something alien and otherworldly.

'Swift's gone. How could he be gone?' Reynard's eyes sharpened and he turned to me. 'Technically I became cursed because of you, so that makes you the new alpha. You lucky cu—'

'Yes, we've discussed that already,' I interjected hastily. 'Samuel is going to assume stewardship whilst I ... resolve the curse.'

Reynard's eyes flicked to the large triangle on my fore-head. 'However long that may bloody well take.'

'Indeed.'

'We had better get you the witch bitch's blood then.'

'About that – have you got a syringe? Or...?' I asked hesitantly.

'Do you mean to ask whether the witch will be living at the end of the bloodletting?'

'That's exactly what I'm asking.'

'She'll live, though she may wish she hadn't. Samuel, see to it.'

'You are not the alpha now, Reynard. You can't give me orders.' Samuel's tone was a tad smug; there was a history here that I was ignorant of.

'I *am* giving you orders, though,' the gargoyle snapped. Fetch me the witch's blood, and make sure you leave her alive. I don't want her to die.'

'Why not? She should die. She has cursed us all.'

'She is one of a great number of witches who cursed us. It serves no purpose to swat each fly.'

'Perhaps, but you do not leave an enemy alive at your back,' Samuel growled.

I thought of James and I wavered. But no: we couldn't go around killing everyone. 'We do not know if she is an enemy,' I reminded them. 'She may simply be obeying her coven leader's orders. She may be a soldier, nothing more.'

'I will keep her alive, and I will ascertain her motivation,' Samuel said, begrudgingly. 'If she is merely a soldier, I will simply imprison her.' It was obvious that if she were not merely a soldier, he would kill her.

I knew that he was right. James had taught me a valuable lesson about leaving someone alive who is your enemy. Only the strong survived in the Other realm, and I intended to survive, no matter which time I was in.

Chapter 13

Samuel had given me a leather satchel for the terrifyingly large flask of blood. Despite his reassurances, I couldn't help worrying about the fate of the witch confined in the cell. He had smugly told me that he'd used a knife to slice along the witch's forearm, to ensure he got enough blood for me. He promised that the cut wasn't mortal, but I wasn't sure I believed him. He might be my second, my steward, but I didn't trust him – not like I had instantly trusted Reynard.

Watching from the shadows, Bastion gave me a slow nod. The tension dropped from my shoulders. *Bastion will make sure the witch lives,* I said to Esme in relief.

Indeed, Esme agreed. **Until we meet again, Bastion,** she called to him.

He inclined his head, his eyes still watching us, curious and deadly. I gave him a bright smile and a finger wave. He pushed himself up from the recesses of the room and escorted us outside. 'Have a care, Lucy Barrett. These are dangerous times.'

'They only get worse,' I muttered unthinkingly.

I was still carrying the sickeningly warm glass flask, secured with a cork like a fine vintage wine. Maybe this was how the poshest of vampyrs rolled in these times. I put the flask away and secured the satchel's buckles. It wouldn't be the done thing to carry about a flask of blood for any Common human to see.

Bastion put a warning hand on my arm as I went to climb into the coach. 'There's a vampyr in there,' he warned.

'I know. He's with me.'

'Interesting company you keep.'

I smiled. 'Only the finest of companions for me.' I patted him familiarly on the cheek and his eyes narrowed at my impudence. Oops. Not *my* Bastion. I snatched my hand back like it had been burnt. 'Stay safe, Bastion.'

He did not respond but watched me coolly and silently as I climbed into the coach with all the elegance of a drunken gazelle. I pulled the satchel onto my lap; fancifully, I felt like I could feel the warmth of the blood even through the thick leather.

Ali clicked to Ares like he was a horse, but Ares stood stubbornly still. Ali swore. 'Move, you stubborn, slim-line rhinoceros!'

Ares' head swung round and he threw a malevolent gaze at Ali.

'Fine.' Ali sighed. 'I'll feed you the left-over pig carcass later.' At that, Ares whinnied in delight and started moving.

I waved cheerfully at Bastion as the carriage moved off. He watched us leave, face implacable. There you go, there was the poker face I knew and loved. When he was gone from my sight, I sat back on the cushioned seat.

'Did you succeed?' Alessandro asked. He was trying to act cool but there was a tension in him that was surprising, like he was invested in the outcome.

I was tired and Reynard's transformation was weighing heavily on me, so I simply nodded and turned to stare out of the window. Ali was at the front of the coach in the driving seat; he had taken one look at my face and left the questions for later. Good. They could wait two hundred years or so.

I rested my head against the window frame and stared out into the night. The moon was full and round, and it cast enough light for me to make out the familiar terrain as we passed by. The motion of the stagecoach rocked me, lulling me gently into an exhausted sleep.

I was a hair's breadth from dropping into Morpheus's arms when a howl rent the air. It was far too close and Ares whickered in warning. I reached out and touched his mind. Through his eyes, I saw not just one wolf approaching us but many, far too many. 'Fuck,' I said aloud. 'Stop the coach!' I called to Ali.

'We should try and outrun them!' he called back.

'No, stop,' I instructed.

He swore but reluctantly obeyed, and the coach ground to a halt. Ominous growls filled the air; it looked like I was meeting my new pack now, whether I wanted to or not.

I shoved the bag of blood at Alessandro. Giving a bag of blood to a vampyr felt like a bad move, but I didn't have any option. If I had it with me when I shifted, it would disappear to hang out with my forever-lost favourite jeans. If I left it rolling around in the carriage, anyone could take it. So, I gave it to my grandfather and hoped to hell he didn't get peckish.

I leapt out of the carriage, not wasting time by removing my dress. More clothes to join the missing collection. As I shifted, I handed control to Esme. Our transformation was lightning fast and in a blink we were on four legs. We padded around to the front of the stagecoach and waited for the challenge that was surely coming.

It wasn't the wolves that I'd expected. These ones had golden eyes. It was the cursed ones.

I reached my mind out to theirs but I sensed no human presence, and the wolfish counterparts' minds were immersed in chaos and rage. I pulled back hastily before that edge of madness took a hold of me. I had no idea if the curse was contagious, but I wasn't about to check. With these feral wolves there would be no discussions, no chance to persuade them that an attack wasn't the right way forward. I had no weapons left in my arsenal, save for Esme.

WE ARE ALPHA, she snarled. **Attack us at your peril.**

That seemed to give some of the wolves pause, but the two at the front were bold and cocky and ignored our growled instruction. Their golden eyes shone with violence as they attacked in concert. Esme didn't wait for them to bring the attack to us; instead, she tore towards the front-runner, slamming into its body and throwing it to the ground. She had no time to rip into its flesh before she turned to face the second attacker who was already at our side, ready to bite and claw.

This was no tourney. Esme went for the second wolf's throat, but the wolf twisted at the last second and she bit its shoulder instead. As she ripped out a chunk of fur and flesh, it howled in pain. Then the first wolf was back on his feet and at our hind legs. It grabbed Esme's back left leg and dragged her back. She lost her footing temporarily.

Esme rolled, ripping her leg out of its mouth – the cuts might bother us later, but not now. Then she flung herself back onto her feet and snarled viciously. Alpha or no, we were dangerously outnumbered – and the other golden-eyed wolves realised it. They started to slink forward to join the attack. No matter how strong and fast Esme was, if they all joined in we were done for.

A huge ball of fire erupted into the wolves, and they danced back to avoid being singed. Alessandro and Ali were standing on either side of Ares and the stagecoach, balls of fire gathered in their hands. The wolves were quick and the lumbering fireballs were easy to avoid, but they kept them busy and I was grateful for that.

Esme focused on the two attacking wolves and started to rip into them with abandon. I heard the sound of wood crunching, but this was no time to be distracted. We had tunnel vision as we focused on our attackers.

A third wolf escaped from being pinned down by the fireballs and joined the two attackers. Things were getting dicey.

I didn't want to kill the golden-eyed wolves because it wasn't their fault that they were cursed, but Esme had no such compunction. She knew it was them or us, and she was determined that we would be the ones left standing. I didn't have time to argue, and she had the reins.

The third wolf dashed towards us, but before it could attack it was met with a whinny and a clash of clawed feet:

Ares had ripped himself free from the Stagecoach and was fighting by our side. He reared up and smashed into the third wolf, ripping into its delicate side, spilling guts and blood onto the floor.

'Enough!' called a human voice from the edge of the forest. Samuel emerged, flanked by another twenty wolves with normal eyes. They spread out to encircle the golden-eyed ones. The cursed wolves recognised their packmates and began to stand down.

The wolf on the floor whimpered pathetically and Samuel crossed over to it. 'It's all right,' he soothed. 'We'll get you healed.'

It will die if they do not move fast, Esme said.

Samuel seemed to realise the same thing. 'Get the horse that's tied up by the cabin. Quickly!' he ordered one of his pack.

I watched in astonishment as the wolf shifted into human form as fast as I did. The naked man ran off and we stood in tense silence. Was it a coincidence that we'd been attacked and the pack wolves had come to the rescue, or had Samuel orchestrated the whole thing?

'The witch influenced the golden ones to attack their packmates. They escaped, and we tracked them here,' Samuel offered in explanation. I wished I had Jess's truth-telling abilities to have the buzz of a truth or a lie, but I didn't so I decided to take his words at face value.

Esme didn't bat an eyelid. She stayed on four legs, battle ready. Edgy.

The man came back, riding the horse bareback. 'Attach him to the coach,' Samuel ordered. He cleared his throat as he turned to me. 'Ah, can we borrow the coach, Alpha?'

It wasn't our coach, so I turned to Ali. He nodded. Samuel strode forward, picked up the injured wolf and laid him carefully on the stagecoach floor before climbing in next to him. Was it his son? 'Go!' he shouted.

The coach trundled off, achingly slowly, and I wondered if the wolf would make it.

We watched tensely as Samuel's pack followed, carefully encircling the golden-eyed wolves. The two that had attacked me were bleeding and limping, and I felt a grim satisfaction in that.

You held back, I murmured to Esme.

You didn't want them dead.

Thank you.

We are a team.

Always.

I touched Ares' mind to thank him for his help; I wasn't sure what would have happened without his intercession. An image arose in response of the two Alessandros on his back. We were still some distance from the portal. *Thank you, that's a good idea.*

I shifted back into human form and told them, 'Get on Ares, and we'll run to the portal.'

Back on four legs, Esme started to trot. Our senses stretched out, watching and waiting for more enemies to come. She smelled a hidden troll, but it made no move towards us so we kept going; it left us alone and we returned the favour.

We just needed to make it to the portal, then I could be home again with Greg and my pack, for whom I suddenly felt a true longing. I was even missing Tristan's argumentative face. Whatever our problems, I appreciated now that he had never been as difficult as he could have been, and he'd never attacked me despite having many opportunities. He may not like me but, unlike Samuel, he respected me.

Finally we arrived back to Rosie's – or whatever the hell it was called in Victorian times. Ali slid off Ares' back and I shifted back into human.

'It doesn't feel right to keep you, after you saved our bacon,' Ali said to the unicorn. 'Go on. Go where you will.'

Ares snorted in reply and nuzzled his head against me. I hugged him. 'Go. Be careful.' The warning was empty; I knew what he would face, and I regretted it with every fibre of my being. He didn't deserve to be someone's brutal circus act.

The unicorn trotted off without a backward glance and Ali sighed. 'And how am I going to explain to Father about losing the stagecoach and the unicorn?' he asked his older self, who was standing next to him.

'You're not,' Alessandro said calmly. 'You're going to be otherwise occupied.' Then, in a flurry of movement almost too quick to follow, Alessandro leapt towards his young self, teeth bared. Before Ali could react, Alessandro's fangs were buried in his neck.

'Woah!' I shouted, 'What the hell? Grandfather, stop!' I used every inch of my extra strength to pull him off, but as I ripped Alessandro off, Ali collapsed to the floor with blood pouring from his neck. Shit. Maybe tearing Alessandro away had been a bad idea.

Ali's desperate eyes met mine.

He's dying, Esme said, regret tinging her voice. **You know what must happen.**

I did, but that didn't mean I had to like it.

'Too late to save his mortal life, Luciana,' Alessandro said grimly. 'It must be done.'

'Why?' I demanded shrilly as I moved to Ali's side. I put my hands to his ruined neck, desperately trying to staunch the overwhelming flow of warm blood. As its coppery tang drifted in the air, I was dimly aware of Esme's sudden blood lust, the urge to rip into the warm body before us. I chastened her and the feeling subsided – but it didn't go completely. Wolf problems.

'Why?' Alessandro said. 'Because it is how I turn. I remember it vividly. It's not the kind of thing you forget. I have started the process and you must finish it.'

Ali's eyes were still trained on me, wide and panicked. He tried to speak but nothing came out. He mouthed '*Elizabeth*' to me. His wife – he wanted me to tell his wife. I felt sick.

'You must give him your blood, or he will die,' Alessandro continued coldly.

'If I give him blood, he will become a vampyr.'

'Yes,' Alessandro said patiently. 'Like me. And then he can protect the family from the shadows, as I have done for two centuries.' He produced a knife from his boot. 'Cut your wrist yourself, or if you prefer I can open a vein for you.' What a gentleman. What a choice.

I took the knife with shaking hands. 'We could give him the witch's blood!' I suggested, suddenly remembering the large flask that we carried.

'And then how will you break the curse? Besides, the blood needs to be yours. After you were extinguished, you were made Other again by Glimmer. Your blood will enable Ali to retain his fire-elemental abilities. And believe me, he'll need them.'

I had no choice, Alessandro stood before me and he was a vampyr, so clearly I'd done it; I'd given my blood to a dying Ali way back in the past. I was NEVER time travelling again; it was one constant mindfuck.

I let Esme control our hands because I simply didn't have it in me to slice into our flesh. She didn't hesitate. I didn't cry out as the knife bit, although tears welled. I offered my bleeding arm to Ali and he battled a moment before he reached for it weakly. He was fading fast. I brought my bleeding limb to his mouth; his choice had been made, as had mine.

He drank from me until I felt dizzy.

'Enough,' Alessandro said finally and knelt beside us in the gory mess. He drew my forearm towards him and licked at the wound, sealing it shut. In a minute it was gone, not even a mark left to show what we'd gone through.

Although Ali had passed out, the wound on his neck had closed over. Alessandro picked him up and carried him away, taking him to I didn't know where. He returned a moment later carrying something dark in his hands.

'Get dressed.' He chucked the bundle at me. Another black dress. I hastily pulled it on; I didn't want to think about who he'd stolen it from. Still, I dressed; no one wants to be naked in front of their grandfather, at least not in their twenties. It's kind of cute when you're three. 'Come on,' he called impatiently.

Fully dressed, I stood up straight. 'I'm not talking to you,' I muttered immaturely.

'That does not matter.'

'It matters to me.'

'Yet you still appear to be talking to me. Oh, how I rejoice.'

'You're an asshole. You know that, right?' Alessandro ignored me and summoned a large ball of fire in his hands. 'What are you doing?' I asked.

As I watched, he de-aged before my eyes. His grey hairs turned black and the lines on his face melted away until Ali's youthful face stared back. But it wasn't quite Ali; something about the change had burned away any imperfections, leaving him with a symmetrical face that was eerily like his younger one but not quite the same.

'The fireball will ruin Maxwell's night vision so he can't see us properly. He'll see the fireball and assume we're friendly fire elementals. It will give us the moment we need.'

I'd forgotten that his brother had taken over guarding the portal: Maxwell. Everything was coming eerily full circle. I stayed behind Alessandro as he opened the front door and strode confidently in.

'Ali?' Maxwell called out.

'Yes,' Alessandro called back, then moved with vampyric speed, zooming into the room and hitting his brother over the head with a chair so hard that it split.

Maxwell slumped to the floor, unconscious. Alessandro knelt next to him, checking his pulse. 'Sorry, brother,' he murmured so softly that I wouldn't have heard it but for my extra-sharp werewolf hearing.

'Come on, Luciana,' he said as he stood up.

'Don't call me that.' I said stubbornly. 'It's Lucy now, just Lucy.'

'There is nothing *just* about you. You will break the curse and become Queen Alpha. I have further information for you which may help. Your friend, Emory,' he sneered the word 'friend', 'is king of more than the dragons. He is the ruler of a great many creatures including your gargoyles. It is why he is called the Prime Elite. The elite part means he also rules over other species.'

'How did I not know this?'

'It is a secret, closely guarded by a geas – so naturally everyone knows except the Connection. Still, that's not saying much. The Connection still doesn't know about the existence of mermaids,' he snorted.

'Aren't you worried about falling foul of the geas?'

'I have other concerns. Right now, I want you to fulfil your destiny, break the curse and become Queen Alpha.'

'And why would you want that? You're a vampyr, a sworn enemy of the werewolves.'

'And why do you think I have stayed clanless? You are *family*, Lucy. Nothing is more important than that. Remember that. Do what you must, but don't forget your family. Promise me.' He'd gone full intense-creepy.

'I promise,' I said finally, because family had always been everything to me, too. But I didn't intend to change who I was; the fact that the Alessandros now joined the Barretts altered nothing. Family *was* important; family was everything.

'Take this.' He passed me the satchel containing the flask of blood.

'You carry it.'

'No, it is your burden.'

I rolled my eyes at his dramatics, but I took the bag. He took my other hand. 'Everything I've done, I've done for you and the family.' He leaned into me and kissed my forehead. 'Be well, Lucy – my granddaughter. I'm proud of you.'

Before I could respond, he tugged us both into the portal, even as I panicked that his words felt entirely too much like a goodbye.

Chapter 14

I was disorientated when we strode out of the portal into a brightly lit room. It was reminiscent of the room I'd just been in, but gone was the stone flooring and wooden cladding, and in its place was a warm and trendy café. It was enough to make my head spin.

Nor were we alone. The café was full, despite the closed sign that now hung over the door. Liam was sitting with Alyssa, Jason and Emily. Riccardo and Helena were with Maxwell. Niccolo was pacing.

My hand was still clutched in Alessandro's. I turned to face him, searching for any signs of impending death but there were none. I felt revitalised, rejuvenated. So much energy was pouring through me that I felt almost edgy with it. 'I'm buzzing,' I commented.

'It's the Third,' Alessandro explained. 'It's like a recharge in Common but on steroids.'

'You seem fine as well.' His goodbyes had made me feel like his demise was imminent.

He looked faintly surprised. 'I shouldn't be. Using the Third always takes a toll. It can affect your memory if you use it too much. But to meet yourself, let alone affect your own path ... there is a price to pay.'

'And you thought it would be death?'

'Yes. I've heard it takes your most precious thing from you. What could be more prized than life?'

'You're a vampyr. You're already dead.'

He frowned. 'A technicality. It should have taken something.' His eyes widened in sudden panic and he held out his hands, palms up. Nothing happened. He swore loudly and viciously.

'Grandfather!' Alyssa chastened, holding her hands over Jason's ears.

Jason sniggered. 'Too late Mum,' he said loudly. 'That was shutting the barn door after the horse had bolted.'

I get that one. Esme's deadpan comment nearly provoked me into gales of inappropriate laughter, but luckily I held it in.

Jason turned to his grandfather. 'You seem to be swearing at yourself, in which case some of those things are really quite derogatory to your own mother.'

'My fire,' Alessandro spat out. 'It's gone. I've been extinguished!'

'Well, that's karma for you,' I said aloud before I could censor the words. I winced as they left my mouth; talk about kicking someone when they're down.

'It's not just karma,' he said grimly. 'It's a death sentence. I wasn't wrong. The Third realm is killing me, just a lot slower than I expected.'

'Hold up, why is it a death sentence?' Maybe I'd got my drama-queen tendencies from my grandfather.

'I'm deliberately clanless so as to ensure that my sole focus can be you ingrates. My fire has kept me safe from attacks – we vampyrs fear fire because we're walking corpses and we go up like tinder. There's no getting us to a healer if we're faced with flames. Once the vampyrs realise I don't have my fire to protect me, I'll be dead by the end of the night.'

'Well, I won't tell anyone,' I asserted. The rest of the room murmured agreement, including Liam.

'It's only a matter of time,' Alessandro sighed, defeated.

'All life is only a matter of time,' I pointed out. 'Carry a lighter in your pocket.'

'Or a flamethrower,' Jason suggested helpfully.

'I don't think they come pocket size,' I quipped.

'Shame.'

'Enough,' Alessandro said. 'We did what needed to be done and I will pay the price. I'm going to retire. I need my rest.'

'You've been retired for centuries. You're ancient!' Jason said cheekily.

'Only a couple of hundred years old actually,' I interjected helpfully. 'In vampyr terms he's a spring chicken.'

'I'm glad you're all having fun at my expense. Good night, family,' Alessandro said grumpily, and headed for the front door where his chauffeur was waiting.

'Good night, Grandfather,' the room chorused.

'So what went down?' Jason asked. 'You've been gone an entire day. More and more of us camped out here the longer you were away.' He gestured to the assembled Alessandros.

'What?' What was the point of a third magical realm that controlled time if I'd lost an entire day by stumbling around in it?

Liam cleared his throat. 'That's why I'm here, Alpha. Greg is holding the fort in your absence but has requested you return to the mansion as soon as possible. The small hiccup you discovered is still an issue.'

My mind went blank. What small hiccup was he talking about?

The fact that the vampyrs can attack us at any time, Esme explained.

Ah, that hiccup.

I turned to my family. 'I've got to go. I'm sorry to leave you in a lurch like this, but suffice to say the objective has been achieved.' I stood up to leave before suddenly thinking better of it. 'Actually, I could do with some elemental backup. Are there any local elementals that you can spare? Fire elementals,' I added, thinking of the vampyrs' fear of fire.

'We'll all come,' Helena asserted. 'You can fill us in on all the details of your trip later on.'

'Okay,' I agreed readily enough. 'That would be great. We have guest quarters – it would be a good idea if you could pack a bag for a day or two. I'm not sure how long I'll need your help.' I thought suddenly of the portal. 'You'll have enough men, won't you? To guard the portal?'

Maxwell nodded confidently. 'Easily. We've grown in strength and in numbers, and we have a significant workforce to call on. Do you think we'll need more than the family at the mansion?'

I didn't want to ask for even more of my newly discovered family, but the answer was probably yes. 'Any you can spare,' I said finally. 'Just for a couple of days. There's a risk that some vampyrs may attack the mansion, but by then the danger should be largely eliminated. We haven't had any direct threats so I'm probably worrying over nothing, but I'd rather be safe than sorry.'

'I'm on it, Cous,' Maxwell replied, giving me a wink. Cous: it was nice to have some extra family. I'd have to ring my mum and fill her in soon, though of course I'd skip through the whole time-travel bit. I wouldn't want to fall foul of the Verdict; Alessandro had lost his fire due to breaking a geas. The Verdict wasn't something to toy with.

'Great, thank you. See you all back at the mansion.' Liam followed me out of Rosie's, and I waited until we were in the car before asking him the burning question. 'So give me the skinny. What's really going on at home?'

Liam grimaced. 'Somehow Tristan found out about you transferring the deeds of the mansion into your own name. He's spreading it about that you're using the pack for your own financial gain.'

'You have *got* to be kidding me. With the mansion in a company's name, we're vulnerable to attack from vampyrs. It's that simple.'

'Sure, but we got the witches to rune up the mansion, didn't we? So we do have *some* protection.'

Something in me eased. How could I have forgotten about that? 'Yes, that's true. But all we need is a stray witch to sneak in and counter the runes, then we could find ourselves slaughtered in our sleep,' I pointed out.

'A witch would have to sneak into the grounds and get round all of our security cameras,' Liam said. 'That's not what I think,' he added hastily. 'I'm just playing devil's advocate.'

'You're right, of course, but leaving it in the name of a company doesn't seem wise. Especially as we know there's a black witch out there that's taken an interest in us.'

'The one that kidnapped the kids?'

'Yeah – and she got away scot-free. We still have no idea who she is. In fact, I'd better ring Amber and see if she's got anything on that.'

I dialled the one witch I trusted. 'Hey, Amber, how are you?'

'Is this a social call?'

'Erm, not really.'

She sighed. 'Of course not. How can I help you, Alpha?'

'Look, Amber, we'll go for drinks when all of this has calmed down, I promise.'

'It's never over. It's never "calmed down". But sure. How can I help?' she repeated.

I felt bad for her; she wasn't wrong, but we still needed to deal with business first. 'A few things. Have you got any further in identifying our black witch?'

'All I know for sure is that everyone from my coven has an alibi. Some of them are shaky, but there are no standout suspects. I need to do more digging.'

'Call Jess,' I suggested. 'She can dig faster than you, and we haven't got much time.' Having a truth seeker inter-view people made it a hell of a lot more effective. 'For now, the black witch will have to wait because there are more pressing matters. Did you get anything further to help Thea?'

'No. I can't find a potion, other than those we've already tried with and failed. I'm sorry.' Her frustration was evident in her voice; she hated to fail. I could relate.

'No problem, I have other plans in the works. On a separate note, do you remember you said I need blood from one of the curse casters to break a curse?'

'Obviously.'

'Right. I have some blood, and I need a curse breaking.'

'Curse breaking is pricey,' Amber cautioned.

I rolled my eyes; everything involving the witches was pricey. 'Yeah, yeah. Can you do it?'

'I can do my best. When do you want me?'

'As soon as possible.'

'Tonight?'

'Yes.' It was 6pm now, and dark had fallen.

'I have a few things I need to prepare.' She sighed. 'If you want it done tonight, I'll come over at 10pm.'

'Great. See you later. And Amber?'

'Yes?'

'I *am* serious about that drink.'

'Me too,' she said and hung up. Amber wanted a friend; I could relate to that, too.

She's lonely, Esme said.

I guess so. She's the boss, too, and it's tough being boss.

I don't mind it.

I smirked. *You love it.*

Someone has to be in control, so why not us? she said with aplomb.

Why not indeed?

'Amber will be over tonight,' I said to Liam.

He slid me a sideways glance. 'To break a curse? On whom?'

'Eyes on the road!' I ordered, sidestepping his question.

I sent a text message to Reynard. *Can you come to the mansion? Tonight at 10? Bring some of your trusted gargoyles with you.*

I looked into the rear-view mirror. 'Is that car following us? It's been on our tail the whole way since Rosie's.'

Liam flushed. 'I hadn't noticed,' he admitted. I didn't blame him, though I knew Greg would have noticed.

'Okay,' I instructed, 'let's test out that theory. Hang a left here.'

Liam obeyed, quickly turning the wheel so we pulled into a sharp left-hand turn. The car behind us came too. Fuck. 'He's still behind us.' I licked my lips, my mouth suddenly dry. 'That could be coincidental.'

'A helluva coincidence,' Liam disagreed.

'I agree, but we need to be sure. Take the right coming up in a hundred yards.' I'd grown up in this area and I knew the roads like the backs of my hands. The one led to a private road affectionately known as Millionaire's Row. The houses were all huge and had pools or tennis courts.

Once, I had dreamed of owning my own accountancy firm and having a house on Millionaire's Row; now I was a werewolf and I had a mansion. Life is funny sometimes.

We took the right. The car behind us followed. I bit my thumb and contemplated our next move. 'Stop the car,' I said to Liam.

'What?'

'Stop the car! Let's see who these jokers are. Get your phone ready, zoom in and take some pictures while I distract them.'

'Alpha, I advise against—'

'You can advise all you want – I'm not having someone follow me. This isn't James Bond. This isn't acceptable.'

Liam obediently pulled the car to the kerb and stopped. I waited to see what the other driver would do; would they keep on driving? Were they even trying to pretend not to follow us?

It slowed to a stop.

I hesitated for a second. 'Stay here, keep the engine running and be prepared to leave in a hurry,' I instructed Liam. Throwing caution to the wind, I opened my door and climbed out. Arms folded, I leaned on our car boot. Whoever they were, they could come to me.

The passenger seat of our pursuer's car opened and a familiar face emerged. I struggled to keep my face neutral. Why was Krieg, High King of the Ogres, following me?

'High King Krieg,' I greeted him, touching my hand to my heart. I gave a bow, but only a little one. I didn't need anything from him. He'd owed my mother a favour but, rather than truly help me, he'd chucked me a few crumbs of information and called it a day. Obviously, I didn't know what kind of favour he owed her for; maybe she'd just held the door for him in passing, or maybe she'd saved the life of his only child. Unless Krieg felt like telling me, I would never know.

'Alpha Lucy Barrett,' he said.

'You're following me.'

'I wished to speak with you.'

'Have you heard of a phone?'

'Phones can be tapped,' Krieg said dismissively. 'This way nobody will know the substance of our discussion.'

'And what do we need to discuss that requires so much secrecy? Are you about to profess your undying love for me?' I quipped.

'You're impertinent.' He frowned at me. 'I could kill you for a comment like that, but it wouldn't serve my purpose.'

'And what is that?'

'I wish to dispose of an enemy without getting my hands dirty.'

I tried not to show my surprise. 'You may not have gotten the memo but I'm a werewolf, not a griffin.'

'We have a mutual enemy,' Krieg told me.

'So that makes us friends?'

'Not even close,' he retorted. 'But I will use you as my tool to dispose of him.'

I resisted the urge to comment on his tool, and decided to bite instead. 'Who?'

'Beckett Frost.'

I sighed. Of course. Beckett Frost had been gunning for me since I'd killed his brother, Ace. 'You're not telling me anything I don't already know.'

'He had his wolves attack your unicorn. He's working with the black witch, and she needed unicorn blood.'

Now that *was* news. 'How do you know this?' I demanded.

'My source is irrelevant.'

'I need to know it's trustworthy.'

'If I say it is, then it is.'

I ignored that and thought about the attack on Ares. Finley and Daniella had been at the scene afterwards, and maybe it was unfair to suspect their motivations, but I knew Frost used lone wolves to supplement his pack – or at least that's what Thea had said. Could either of them have collected blood from Ares after the attack? Surely someone would have mentioned it if the attacking wolves had been carrying a flask? No, Ares' blood must have been taken afterwards.

'Frost is coming for you,' Krieg said.

That wasn't exactly new information considering he'd dumped a corpse at our gates with a note attached stating that he was coming for us. We might be on his to-do list; however, he didn't seem in a hurry to attack and I didn't intend us living our lives in constant fear. We'd be wary and sensible, but I wasn't putting our lives on hold just because Beckett Frost had a bee in his bonnet.

I studied the ogre. 'And you're warning me why?'

He flashed me a sudden grin. 'Because I want you to win. Kill him for me, there's a good lapdog.' He winked and strode back to his car. Asshole.

I slid back into the seat next to Liam. 'Let's go,' I ordered. The car leapt forward – and promptly juddered and stalled.

'Sorry.' Liam reddened and restarted the engine.

'We're not in a hurry,' I said, but I made a mental note not to entrust him with a get-away car in the future. Not that I hoped to need one again. 'Let's go home.' We drove the rest of the way in silence.

Liam dialled in the code on our keypad and the wrought-metal gates swung open. The wheels crunched on the gravel driveway as we drove up to the door. I swung out of the car. A trip to the past and a car chase were my limit. I *really* wanted to see Greg.

I took the front stairs two at a time and hauled open the heavy front door. For once there was no sign of Mrs Dawes, and I smirked because I'd beaten her to it. I ran into my office and there was Greg – alone, thank God. 'Hey!' I all but threw myself into his arms.

'Hey, sweetheart.' He kissed me. 'Don't take this the wrong way but what on earth are you wearing?'

I snorted. 'It's a long story. Don't you like it?' I batted my eyelashes.

He grinned. 'To be honest, I could totally get behind it. You look all … Victorian and prudish. Makes me wonder what it would take to peel you out of it.'

'Not a whole lot,' I murmured, kissing him. His hand skirted up my thigh and encountered nothing. I was completely naked under the dress. 'I had to shift,' I explained. 'I lost my clothing.'

That was enough to pour figurative cold water all over him. 'Are you okay? What happened?'

I had a sudden urge to wash away the memories of the last twelve hours, especially the look of fear in Ali's eyes. I would see that in my nightmares for some time to come. 'I'll explain later.'

I didn't want talk. I wanted action. I wanted something to erase the blood that should still be on my skin. It was gone, though, lost between the realms somehow. 'For now, let's christen my desk,' I suggested, leaning in for a kiss.

He pulled back, assessing me. 'You're alright?'

'Yes,' I insisted. 'Fine. I just want to have sex. Now.'

'Sex is a normal urge after a disaster,' he reassured me, but his tone of voice was too knowing. He'd been a soldier half his life; he knew first hand about post-disaster coitus. I wondered if he had consoled himself with *fucking Mindy,* then pushed the thought of her out of my mind.

The last laugh was mine. Greg was mine, and I wasn't letting him go.

Chapter 15

After we'd dressed again and I'd explained my adventures, Greg told me about his. They were largely desk-based; he'd been pulling strings all day, speaking to solicitors to get the papers drawn up as quickly as possible and delivered here. He dug out the transfer form, which I signed and he witnessed.

'I'll get it couriered to the Land Registry tonight,' he said. 'I've got someone waiting to action it tomorrow.'

'Fingers crossed this is the last night we're vulnerable.'

'We've got the runes,' he pointed out.

'Yeah, I'd forgotten about those. That's something – but we can't forget there's a black witch running around. One who needs unicorn blood, apparently.'

'She's probably planning to kidnap more children to do who knows what.'

'Exactly.'

'She's still on my to-do list,' Greg said.

'Amber has run down alibis for her coven. So far they all check out, though she says one or two of them are shaky. I've suggested she gets Jess on board – at least then we'll know for sure if anyone is lying.'

'Good idea. I also heard back from Fritz.'

My mind went temporarily blank. What had we wanted with our computer wizard Fritz? Greg interpreted my vacant stare. 'We sent him one of the USBs Mark Oates had compiled on the council members.'

'Oh right, of course! Did he get anything useful from it?'

'He got a whole file. It was called Number 2, and it was about one council member in particular.'

'Who?'

'Scott Larsden.'

Scott was the council member who'd interviewed us after Ace's so-called disappearance. 'But he seemed so nice!' I objected.

'That should have been our first clue,' Greg said grimly. 'The council members aren't light and fluffy. He was entirely too agreeable.'

'You think he was checking that we were ignorant of his involvement?'

'Bingo. He was making sure he could tidy up any loose ends that Ace and Mark might have left.'

'He thinks we never found the blackmail material,' I speculated.

'Exactly.'

'What's in the file?'

'Sex, drugs—'

'And rock and roll?'

'No. Sex, drugs and cash. Fritz chased the money and found they were black tourney payments. Tracking the cash through shell corporations was what took him so long. He said they'd done a good job muddying the trail.'

'But not good enough to hide it from Fritz.'

Greg smiled proudly. 'Nah, there's not much that gets past him. From what Fritz found out, Larsden regularly received sizeable lump sums. He's already cross-referenced some of the references that came with the payments – and they always had two or three letters.'

'Initials?' I suggested, thinking of what I used on my spreadsheets to keep track of my clients.

'Exactly. Fritz cross-referenced them with the list of loners in the UK, and the initials matched up. I think Larsden handed over the loners to Ghost as contestants in the tourneys.'

Ghost is Bastion's daughter, Charlize, and she was the one who ran the black tourneys. Bastion had assured us that they'd been shut down for good, but Greg had heard rumours that they were starting up again, run by someone else this time. Bastion had sworn that Charlize was out of the game, and I believed him. I wondered if Larsden was the new organiser.

The monitor on Greg's desk flashed and the movement caught my eye. 'Looks like my family is here.' Wasn't that an absolute pleasure to say? *My family.*

They had come in convoy, three cars full of them, which made me smile. They'd gone all out for me. Some kids dream of ponies and horses, but for me there was no better gift than several cars full of battle-ready elementals.

Greg buzzed them in and told them to park on the drive. 'I'll sort them out with rooms and liaise with Maxwell to organise a mixed werewolf and elemental patrol. Tristan has been belly-aching since he found out about the transfer of the mansion to your name.'

'So Liam told me. Not that it matters, but how did he find out?'

'I've no idea.'

'Perhaps he saw the papers?'

'I don't see how – I don't think he's stepped in your office since you moved in here. But anyway, we need to shut him up. I think part of the problem is that he's feeling confined. His wolf is restless.'

'You think we should go on a hunt?'

'Yeah. Leave a strong crew here, and let the rest of the pack join you for a run in Black Park. It's late, it's dark, and I think it will release a lot of the tension that's been building.'

'Do you think now is a good time to go?' I asked dubiously. 'With the vampyr threat?'

Greg shrugged. 'The mansion has been vulnerable to vampyrs since the day we arrived – we just didn't know about it. Knowing about it now doesn't increase the likelihood of an attack. Besides, we have the fire elementals here to even things up. I think having het-up wolves is more of a danger. Fights will break out and bones will be broken. Going on a hunt gets out all that need for violence in a safe way.'

'Not so safe for the deer,' I commented. 'What about Beckett Frost?'

'What about Beckett Frost? It's weeks since he dumped that body on our lands, and since then there's been nothing. We can't put our lives on hold because of some nebulous threat. When he comes, we'll be ready. We have runes on the mansion, we have fire elementals, we have a surveillance system, metal shutters and blast doors. He can come, but we're good and ready to meet him.' He smiled confidently.

Something in me eased. 'Send out a message inviting everyone to a hunt at 7:30pm. We can get rid of some nervous energy and still be back here in time for Amber.'

Greg nodded. 'It's good that she's coming – everyone will be a bit steadier for a spot of curse breaking. If you're still feeling edgy, get the whole pack to have a sleepover tonight.'

I liked that solution. I liked even more that I could trust Greg to come up with such a good proposal. 'Good idea. Let's do a slumber party after the hunt, then everyone's on hand if the curse breaking gets complicated.' My phone beeped and I pulled it out. It was a message from Reynard: *I'll be there.*

I frowned. I'd asked him to bring some other gargoyles too, so I hoped he wasn't flying solo. I wasn't sure what breaking the curse on the gargoyles would entail, but it didn't seem right to do it unilaterally without consulting at least a few of them. This shit required a vote or something. Uncursing a whole species without discussing it with them first was nearly as bad as cursing them all in the first place. We all deserve to be masters of our own fate.

There was a brisk knock on the door and Mrs Dawes looked in. 'It appears that we have guests,' she said with a questioning smile.

'Yes,' I confirmed. 'A group of fire elementals will be staying for a while.' Until the vampyric threat is eliminated, anyway. 'And I'm going to call for a hunt later, if you can prepare some food for afterwards.'

Her smile grew strained. Rooms and food for so many people meant a whole lot more work for her. 'Sorry for the short notice,' I apologised quickly.

'Will the hunt be at Black Park?'

'Yeah, the usual stomping ground.'

'Right. That's fine.' Her tone suggested it was anything but. 'I'll work something out. Excuse me, I must ready the rooms for the elementals and put some food in the slow cookers.' She bustled out looking stressed.

'You're right,' I said to Greg. 'Even Mrs Dawes is tense. I think we all do need a hunt. It's been too long since the last one.'

'I've sent out an alert for the hunt and the sleepover. You've got half an hour before you need to leave.' He stood up. 'I'm going to co-ordinate with Maxwell.'

'Thanks, love.'

He stilled, before turning to me with a warm smile. 'I could get used to hearing that.' He winked as he closed the door, leaving me feeling a bit gooey.

Next order of business was to get out of the weird clothes I was wearing. I slipped into my living room where I always kept a spare outfit. When I went in, I paused. The room really did look much smaller than it had in the past. I looked at the bookshelves. Surely in the past they hadn't been so deep?

The room is much smaller, Esme agreed.

The furniture was still laid out in much the same way, focused on the fireplace. I walked to the wood-panelled back wall and looked down at the floor; one of the floorboards at the edge of the panelling was half exposed. Someone could have cut it very precisely to fit, but there was no edge to it, no beading.

I frowned and examined the bookshelves. One of them stood out. Most of the shelves were laden with texts on Other creatures, except this one, which appeared to be full of philosophy tomes. Suddenly I remembered something Lord Samuel had said to me.

'No, it's a "need-to-know" assignment. And they don't all need to know about it.' He tilted his head and looked at me. 'I'm partial to a bit of Kant, you know.'

He'd confused me; why was he talking about Kant? I didn't know much about the philosopher, other than he was into ethics in a big way. I remember that I'd wondered if Lord Samuel hinting that his new assignment wasn't ethical. Then he'd added, *'Never mind. Just ... remember that.'*

Kant. I scanned the shelves until I found an old book: *Kant's Foundation of Ethics.* I reached out to pull it down, but it didn't move. I pulled harder and, with our excellent hearing, Esme and I heard a faint click.

Oh! NO WAY!

What?

There's a secret fucking room! I'd never been more excited.

A secret sex room?

No. Sorry – poor use of swear words. Just a secret room. Probably. I'd be scarred for the rest of my life if I opened the door and there were whips, chains and dildos. Lord Samuel hadn't seemed like that kind of guy.

I pushed on Kant's *Foundation*s and the entire book-shelf swung back to reveal an opening. I gave a fist pump and barely held back the 'wahoo!' that wanted to escape.

Be wary, Esme cautioned.

It's not as if a sphinx can jump out of that tiny space, I pointed out, remembering my raid with Jess on Birken-head Town Hall.

A baby one could, she countered.

I snorted, pushed the opening wider and waited. Nothing rushed out to attack me.

They could be lulling you into a false sense of security, Esme muttered mutinously.

There's a 'they' now? I asked, only half-jokingly.

I crept forward and peered around the corner into a very ordinary looking room with a very fancy looking desk – and nothing else. *It could do with a few pictures and a potted plant,* I murmured. *Maybe a cushion or two.*

Is now the time to do interior designing? Esme asked, obviously proud that she'd remembered the correct term.

It's always the time.

I approached the desk cautiously. It had three drawers; one was locked, and I didn't have a key. I cursed myself for not learning lock picking like Jess, and added it to my skills-to-be-acquired list. I had superhuman strength but I didn't want to break such a beautiful piece of furniture, so I reluctantly left the locked drawer alone. For now.

Another drawer was open, but it contained only office supplies like highlighters and post-its. Nothing worth hiding. I bent to the final drawer. It was thin and long, and I held my breath as I pulled it open.

Inside was an ornate notebook. Its cover was actual leather, and it was tied up with twine; it looked *old*. I carefully unfastened and opened it. I could see immediately that it was a journal.

The first entry made my heart thud.

I commence this journal of my stewardship of the Home Counties Pack. Our alpha, Lucy Barrett, has left. Until such time as she returns, the Samuel line will continue to rule the pack in her stead.

I have consulted the rules extensively. Unlike alphas, stewards cannot be challenged for their authority; therefore we Samuels enjoy a place of continued security. It is a great advantage; it is my hope that this time will bring much prosperity to the Samuel line.

My eldest son has become a golden-eyed wolf; even now, his skin is turning pallid and grey, and I pray for the curse to be lifted soon. Therefore, I will entrust the knowledge of the stewardship to my second son.

There was an awful lot more, but I knew I didn't have much time so I reluctantly flipped through a few more pages until another entry caught my eye.

They have become known as gargoyles, and they do closely resemble the creatures depicted on gothic cathedrals. They are stout, twisted and winged – I think the witches' curse modelled them on the grotesques of Notre Dame.

I try and talk to my son now, but he spouts vile language in the same way that the gargoyles on the cathedrals spout water. It is atrocious, but I endure his insults to try and build our relationship anew.

Further on, Samuel had written: *Without their wolves, the gargoyles are bereft. They distance themselves from us. They have joined together, which is a relief, and taken up residence in the local churches. At least they are a pack once more, with cohesive thoughts. The madness has passed.*

Reports have come from all over Europe of more gargoyles being made. The witches' curse was extreme, and it has carried to the far reaches of the world.

My mouth was dry as I read on. What a horrible thing, to have your child made into a different creature and be unable to help them. I flipped on until the word 'miracle' caught my eye. We could all do with a miracle.

I have seen a miracle. In his gargoyle form, my son has been able to access a werewolf's lost powers. He can control the air! Something about the curse has once again released that power. If we can only work out how, then the wolves will once again be a force to be reckoned with. We will no longer be shown disrespect by the Others.

Lost powers? What the heck? I reached out to Esme. *What do you know about the werewolves' lost powers?*

We used to be able to control the air, to fling our foes to the ground with mighty force. Her tone was nostalgic. **But the how of it all was lost centuries ago.**

Control the air? Like an air elemental? I thought of Reynard and his wings. *Could we fly?*

Esme burst into laughter. **We are not birds, Lucy.** She got her laughter under control and snorted, **What an absurd thought.**

Reynard can fly, I pointed out sullenly.

He has wings.

The Other realm is weird, I pointed out. *It could happen.*

No, we could not fly, Esme said decisively.

So how could we use the air?

As I said, we have lost that ability. The old wolves in the Great Pack used to know, but they are gone.

So who is in charge of the Great Pack now?

New old wolves, she said, in a 'well-duh' tone of voice.

And they don't know about the air powers we used to have?

No.

I turned my attention back to the journal and looked at the final pages. I recognised the loopy cursive writing of a later Lord Samuel: Wilfred, the man who had made me a werewolf.

It is set in motion now. Jinx brought Lucy Barrett to me, and I knew what must be done. I have turned her and, in doing so, signed my own death warrant. She must be alpha. I look at her and wonder how and when it will be done.

She does not seem overly ambitious, or to be scheming for my death, but I have misjudged people before.

I felt sick. God, he'd turned me knowing I would kill him. He was even braver than I'd thought.

I flipped to the last entry. *You have just left my office, Lucy. We leave now together, just you and I. Something will happen and you will kill me. I know it in my bones. Someone in the werewolf council has set me up – I suspect Aitken or Ramsay. Elena and I have been investigating the black tourneys as quietly as we can, but perhaps not quietly enough. Someone wants to get rid of me.*

I attended a black tourney and caught scent of Aitken and Ramsay outside of the building, but I didn't see them. Once inside, the candles smothered my senses. I doubt their attendance was of an investigatory nature, though perhaps I am being unfair. Time will tell.

Be wary of Mark Oates, as well. I saw him at the tourney, although he didn't see me. Lucy, keep your friends close and your enemies closer. Draw Oates in until you can smother him. If you do fight him, know that he always lifts his paw a little before he pounds forward for an attack. Watch for that and you'll be ready for it.

The council have summoned me to investigate the Cheshire alpha, Jimmy Rain. It makes no sense; we are sworn enemies and no one would trust any report from me to be impartial. I assume he has been alerted to my presence and will be ready when I arrive. You must make sure he does not succeed me as alpha here; because of the temporal loop, I am certain that you will ensure this.

You will become alpha with all the responsibilities that entails. I have a pack of misfits here: Elena is grieving the loss of her brother; David is still trying to fit in; Mrs Dawes is still struggling to accept her wolf. Just know that there is much goodness to be found here. Marissa, with all of her snark, would help even her worst enemy if they were upset. Tristan has so much bark but no bite; he is gentle when you break down his barriers. And Archie, my son, is finally coming out of the drug haze that my separation with his mother wrought.

I could go on. I love these people, and one day you will, too. They'll make you work for it, but once they take you to their hearts, they'll never let you go again. Your position here is an honour and a privilege.

The Samuel line has served you steadfastly for decades; now it is time for you to serve us. Lift the curse, Lucy, like you promised my ancestor so long ago.

The next page was blank, but there was a small envelope with *Archie* written on it. I picked it up with shaking fingers. Man, that was heavy.

I swallowed past the lump in my throat and wiped my eyes. Lord Samuel's words had done the trick and put extra steel in my spine. I *would* break the curse. No matter what it took.

Chapter 16

I put the journal back in the drawer for now – it didn't seem respectful to lug it around the mansion. I could show it to Greg later. I carried the envelope for Archie in my hand; it didn't seem right to stuff it in my pocket.

I wanted to share the magnitude of the secret room and the journal with Greg right away, but I had to find Archie first. He deserved that letter. Lord Samuel had pointed me to the right room, but it had taken me entirely too long to find it. I quashed the guilt; it wasn't a helpful emotion, so I acknowledged it and set it aside. Now I needed to do right by Lord Samuel.

I went to Archie's room but he wasn't there. Then I went to the common room, but he wasn't there either. 'Have you seen Archie?' I asked Seren.

The Goth looked up from her magazine with a visible huff. 'He and Thea were making eyes at each other. Try her room.'

'Thanks, I appreciate that.' I gave her a friendly smile, and felt a burst of happiness when she returned it.

Actually, now was a great time to find Thea because I could speak to both Archie and Thea's wolf. Thea was still staying in the guest wing. I tracked her down and knocked firmly on the door. She answered it, looking faintly annoyed. 'Oh – Alpha. How can I help you?'

'I'm looking for Archie. Have you seen him?'

'I'm in here,' Archie called from inside the room. Thea reluctantly stepped back and allowed me in.

The room was sterile. There were no family photos, nothing personal, no homey touches. It looked exactly the same as it had done when Thea arrived weeks ago. She gestured for me to sit on the only chair whilst she perched awkwardly on the bed next to Archie.

'Thanks.' I took the chair, playing with the envelope in my hands. I had no idea what to say next. This was a letter from Archie's father, effectively a voice from the grave. He probably wouldn't want to read it in front of me, the woman who had murdered his father.

Hard and fast, Esme murmured. **Like we're pouncing.**

Like ripping off a plaster, I agreed.

I cleared my throat awkwardly. 'I found a book in my living room.' Technically, that was true. 'I found a note in it for you. From your father, I think.' I held out the envelope awkwardly.

As if in a daze, Archie stood and walked towards me. He hesitated before he took the envelope, as if he were reluctant to touch it. I pushed it into his hand. His Adam's apple bobbed up and down as he swallowed convulsively. 'Maybe take it somewhere private to read it,' I suggested.

He cradled the envelope reverently in his hands. 'Yes. Thank you, Alpha.' His voice cracked as he called me 'Alpha'. I was learning to hate that word; it was the word that kept me separate from the pack that I had to rule.

Archie went out of Thea's room without looking back. He left the door wide open, so I stood and closed it then turned back. Thea was right behind me, and she blinked as we stumbled into each other. 'Sorry,' she said. 'I thought you were leaving.'

'No, not yet. If I may?' I gestured to the chair again.

'Of course.' She recovered some of her aplomb and perched on the bed.

'I'd like to try and speak to your wolf again.'

'I'll try anything,' she admitted. 'I don't want to be this way – a werewolf that isn't.'

'Okay, I'll see if I can persuade her to talk to me. Just relax – for the next few minutes you'll be a bystander. If you can stay quiet whilst we converse, that would be great.'

I pulled my magic up from the well within me then thrust it towards her. I bypassed Thea herself and reached for the Other within her, her wolf.

Hello. My name is Lucy.

I know who you are, Alpha, Thea's wolf responded, her tone wary. **I have watched through her eyes.** Her tone was a mixture of grumpy and sulky: she was grulky. I got that; I'm grulky before my morning cup of coffee.

Yet you don't answer her call, I said as gently as I could. There was no point in alienating her.

Thea's wolf whined, **It would not help her if I did so.**

You keep yourself trapped for her. You must miss running free.

I do, she confessed. **It is making me less.**

What do you mean, less?

I am less able to protect her. I find myself sleeping when she is awake. I fear my time draws short.

You're dying?

What is death to a wolf? she replied indifferently.

But you'll stop existing.

Then it will not be so terribly different from what it is now.

My heart ached for her. She was saving Thea at the expense of her own life, and Thea didn't even know or care.

What is your name? I asked curiously.

What is a name to a wolf?

This was proving to be hard work. *It is a way to tell you apart from others,* I tried.

I am Thea's wolf.

You are more than that.

Am I? Her tone was cool, uninterested. She wasn't open or chatty, and she wasn't going to make small talk. I'd learnt through Esme that wolves were generally simple creatures: get to the point or get out of town.

Yes, I said firmly.

I'm not sure why it was so important to me that she had a name, but somehow it seemed essential that she did. She was more than Thea's wolf, more than a ride-along parasite. The wolf was her own being, just like Esme was.

Internally I reached for Esme and gave her a prod. I needed backup.

I am also alpha, she said firmly to the wolf. **I am Esme.**

As you choose. Total indifference.

Yes. I chose my name. What will you choose?

Silence stretched out. When I'd almost lost hope of getting a response, Thea's wolf spoke. **Sophie,** she said. **I've always liked the name Sophie. She was kind to us once.**

I looked straight at Thea. 'Sophie,' I said aloud.

Thea paled. 'What?'

'That's what your wolf has chosen to call herself, after someone who was once kind to you.'

'The cook for the Devon pack,' Thea said slowly. 'Sophie was the cook when we were little. She used to sneak us biscuits – until Father found out.'

'Then no more biscuits?'

'Then no more Sophie.'

Yikes.

Do you believe her? I asked Sophie. *Does Thea truly want to be on our side, or will she betray us to Beckett?*

She is sad, Alpha. Here in your pack, she can see a glimpse of happiness. Her offer of help is genuine, but she may recant if Beckett takes control of her again. Her fear of him is great.

And yours? I asked.

I do not fear him. I loathe him for making us what we are. We should have been honoured among the pack, but we were not treated as family. We were a disappointment.

Will you help her shift again?

It is not the best thing for her, Sophie said finally.

You're protecting her.

Protecting *us*, she corrected.

She is part of our pack now, and far away from Beckett Frost. She is safe. Will you not answer her call?

We will never be safe from Frost until he is dead. His wolf is mad, Sophie said firmly.

I will keep all the members of our pack safe from Frost – and Thea is one of them now.

He sees her as his, she argued. **He will come for her – for us. If she cannot shift then she is not a threat and he will not kill us.**

If she cannot shift, then she is of no use, I pointed out. *What does Frost do to useless things?*

He will not harm her. She is family.

He killed his own father!

Because he was alpha. Her tone indicated that she thought that was entirely reasonable.

I tried a different tactic. *How would Beckett learn of her recovery?*

He has spies in every pack. Nowhere is safe from him.

We will keep you safe, Esme interjected.

We will never be safe from him. Please, leave me. I'm tired.

I gently disentangled my mind from Sophie's and pulled myself back to my body, before letting out a frustrated sigh.

'It's not going so well, huh?' Thea asked in a small voice.

'Sophie is being stubborn,' I admitted. 'She says that she is protecting you. She thinks that if you can't shift, Frost will leave you alone.'

'Beckett will never leave me alone,' she whispered. A tear rolled down her cheek and she shook her head angrily before dashing it away and sitting up straighter. 'I'm sorry. I shouldn't have come here. I've put you all in danger, and I never intended to do that.' Her eyes, blazing with intensity, met mine.

'I believe you. You did the right thing by escaping and coming here, and I accepted you into this pack. I knew about your baggage and I accepted the risk. If Beckett comes calling, we'll be waiting.'

'Not if – when. *When* he comes calling.' Thea wrapped her arms around her slim body. I could see her determination leaching away.

'If he comes calling, you need to be able to defend yourself,' I pointed out as gently as I could.

'I know. He'll see me joining this pack as the ultimate betrayal – and he doesn't take kindly to betrayal.'

I stifled the urge to ask who did. A thought occurred to me. 'You know what? You're the person best placed to persuade Sophie. Let's see what I can do.'

I reached out again with my magic, and this time I reached for Thea as well as for Sophie. When I had tied Greg to his wolf, I'd had no idea what I was doing. This time it was all a little more familiar. I wrapped my power around the two females and tied a figurative knot, then severed the connection between me and them.

For a long, long moment, there was silence. 'Did it work?' I asked apprehensively. 'Can you speak to each other?'

Thea's eyes were wide and filled with wonder. 'Sophie,' she said aloud. 'My best friend. I can hear you! I can really hear you!' Tears welled up again in her eyes. She leapt off the bed and pulled me into her arms. 'Thank you! Thank you! We can hear each other! We've always *felt* each other, but we could never do more than send ... feelings. This is amazing. How long will it last?'

'I have no idea,' I admitted. 'But I can always make the connection again if we need to.' I stood up. 'I'll leave you two to get reacquainted.' I paused at the door. 'The pack are having a hunt, 7:30pm at Black Park, if you're interested.'

I left Thea and Sophie to talk it through. I'd seen the hope and yearning on Thea's face, and I knew Sophie would have felt it. I hoped she wasn't in the mood to crush dreams.

Chapter 17

After I left Thea, I had an almost overwhelming urge to find Greg. Fear was prickling at my spine, making me edgy. Thea's terror of Beckett was impossible to ignore, however much I tried to dismiss it.

Esme tried to reassure me. **We are not prey.**

I know. But something is coming, and I'm not sure we are ready.

We were whelped ready.

Born ready, I corrected.

That's what I said. She fluffed her tail at me; that was her equivalent of rolling her eyes. She wasn't fazed; in a dog-eat-dog realm, danger lurked everywhere. She was used to it nipping at her heels.

Greg and Liam were at the security console in my office. 'Can you give me and Manners a few minutes?' I asked Liam.

'Yes, Alpha.' Liam almost saluted before he trotted off to stand guard outside the door.

'Hey.' I sat on Greg's lap and rested my forehead against his.

'Hey.' He drew back. 'What's up, Peaches?'

'I don't know where to start. No, that's bullshit; I guess I do know where to start. I found a secret room behind my living room.'

'What?' he exclaimed.

'An honest-to-goodness secret room, hidden by a bookshelf.'

'That's awesome.'

'Isn't it? I've always wanted to find one of those. Anyway, there was a desk in it, and I found a journal in one of the drawers. It had been written by various Samuel stewards through the years. The final entry was addressed to me by Lord Samuel.'

'That's a bit...' Greg's voice tailed off.

'Creepy? Weird?' I supplied.

'I was going to go with "upsetting".'

'Yeah. Well, it *is* upsetting. There was a note for Archie, too.'

'What did it say?'

'I didn't read it. I gave it straight to Archie.' I paused. 'I hope it doesn't ask him to seek vengeance for his father's death. That would be a bummer.'

'That's not very likely.'

'No, probably not. Lord Samuel knew what was coming, and he went through with it. That's all kinds of brave.'

'Yeah, it is. The more I learn about him, the more I like the guy.'

'He was impulsive and ridiculous with his money. He gambled like a fish drinks water. But he was a good man.'

'I think his failings were a façade,' Greg said thoughtfully. 'Everyone knew about his gambling issues, and he made no secret about his drinking and womanising. But at the same time, he was investigating the black tourneys.'

'You think it was all an act? A smokescreen?' I asked, fascinated.

'Maybe not completely, but I think he played up his vices a whole lot.'

'You might be right.' I thought of the journal entries. 'There was something else in those old pages, a mention about a werewolf's "old powers". Like they could control the air, or something. Esme says it's true.'

Greg raised an eyebrow. 'Well now, I've always thought that wolves were pretty underpowered in terms of Other realm creatures. In the old tales we used to be feared, but nowadays we're not seen as much of a threat. We're fast and robust, but that's about all. Did the journal tell you how to access these old powers?'

'No, nothing so helpful. But remember when Hamlet died here? Reynard and the other gargoyles *flew*.'

'They used air power.'

'Right,' I said. 'I think something in the curse somehow released that old power in them.'

'I guess you'll have to add that to the list of things to talk to Reynard about.' He kissed me, hard and fast. 'You'd better go, love. It's time for the hunt.'

I gave him one last hug. 'Esme and I wish you were running with us.'

'Me too.' He kissed me again. 'Go, before I don't let you leave.' I rose reluctantly off his lap and called Liam back in. 'Stay safe,' Greg ordered.

Safety is for pups, Esme said in a derisory tone.

I quite like safety, I disagreed.

I went down to the gravel drive. A number of cars were already waiting, and I hopped into one with Seren and Marissa. On the way to the hunt, they told me that Greg had tasked them with watching my back. When they thought I wasn't looking, they exchanged catty glances; I had a feeling they would be trying to outdo each other in looking after me. I knew there was some gripe between them, but that was a problem for another day.

Tristan, Elena and Mrs Dawes were going to Black Park, too. Nearly half the pack had been summoned for the hunt; we all needed to blow off steam together. I'd left a handful of our battle core at the mansion. David's chest had puffed up with pride when I'd selected him to join the team tasked to keep the place safe. He and the other wolves who'd stayed behind would be backed up by a host of fire elementals.

Absently, I wondered what the collective term was for fire elementals? A crackling? An inferno? A blaze? All of those were so much cooler than a 'pack', which made us sound like a deck of cards.

I rang ahead to let the dryads know that we would be on a hunt. It was the courteous thing to do, and it didn't cost me anything to be polite. I didn't get through to the elder, so I left a voicemail and hoped it would be picked up quickly.

When we arrived at Black Park, we parked along the roadside. It was late, and the car park was already closed. We slipped out of our cars and made our way into the dense forest until we came to our cabin. 'Cabin' is a bit of a misnomer; it's little more than a shack, but it grants us some privacy and a place to store our clothes.

We took turns shifting until everyone was on four legs except me. A loud snap of a branch had every head swinging towards it.

'Just me,' Thea called out with a sheepish smile. 'Sorry I'm late.' She strode towards the cabin and entered it at my side. Together, we shimmied out of our clothes. I didn't question her presence; now wasn't the time. If she'd managed to persuade Sophie to answer her call, I was happy for her. She didn't need me asking her a dozen questions right now.

As I folded my clothes in a neat pile, I noticed that Thea's body had more than its fair share of scars. I started to understand why Sophie had stopped shifting.

To my surprise, Thea shifted in an instant. She was lightning fast, like me. Was it because of the close connection that I'd forged between them, like the one that existed between Esme and me? Whatever, I was just so grateful to Sophie for letting Thea be who she was supposed to be: a werewolf.

I reached out to her. *Thank you,* I said.

Do not thank me. I do not know if this is wise, but Thea and I are a team. As she said the last word, her pride was clear. For good or ill, they were in it together. **Do not let us be riven apart,** she begged.

I do not know how permanent the tie is between you, but I will do my best to keep it there.

I couldn't go back to being a silent watcher, unable to do anything, not even to warn Thea of danger! That would be hell. It is a wonder to be able to speak to each other.

It is very special, Thea murmured.

It is, I agreed.

Enough chitchat. Let's celebrate by spilling blood, Esme crowed. She nudged me, urging me to shift, and the change rippled over us. In an instant, we were on four and Esme threw back her head and howled. Let the hunt begin.

We poured into the woods, a pack of thirty strong. Esme yipped orders and the pack separated into three paws of ten. The cover of darkness would hide a lot, but thirty wolves together would raise eyebrows in the Common; ten was the most you'd ever see in a natural pack, so emulating that was our best option for slipping under the Common radar. Besides, ten wolves were a lot easier to hide than thirty. Tristan led one paw and Archie led the other, leaving Esme heading the remaining group.

We split off, and the game was afoot. Esme's joy at the hunt was infectious. She loved everything about it: the scents on the air, the rush of the race and, ultimately, the kill. She liked killing things, but I didn't hold it against her because it was her nature. I gave over to her wholly and embraced the feel of the breeze in our fur and the earth between our claws.

The first sign that something was wrong was an uneasiness in the trees. They whispered a warning, and worry skittered along my spine. I reached out to them, like I had done once before. The elder tree tugged me forwards and showed me a pack of wolves that lay in wait ahead. They weren't our wolves.

Bloody Beckett Frost.

I disentangled my mind from the elder tree and found myself back with a panting Esme. **You left me!** she accused, a shade hysterically.

No time now! We're being attacked. Wolves ahead!

It could just be Archie's or Tristan's paw...

No! It's Beckett's!

Esme trusted my knowledge, or perhaps my fear, so she threw back her head and howled a warning into the night. The rest of our paw pulled in tight, a hard formation with no stragglers.

Be ready! Esme called to our wolves.

We were braced when the attack came – and come it did. Beckett's pack came running at us with growls and teeth bared. We didn't wait for them to attack; instead we ran at them.

It soon became clear that we were horrendously outnumbered.

Esme threw her head back again and called Archie and Tristan to come to our aid. We were being attacked by at least twenty wolves, though it was hard to count as they flew at us. I tried not to panic; I had to trust Esme.

We fought with tooth and claw, slashing and biting. Seren was knocked off her feet and we flew at her attacker, giving her precious seconds to regain her footing. In the distance, Archie called out that help was coming – but how long would it take? We needed it now. Suddenly I had an idea. *I'll be back,* I said hastily to Esme, then I reached out to the trees around me. *Help me,* I entreated.

The trees grumbled and groaned, and I felt their distress, but then ... nothing. Nothing happened. I waited a moment, begging again for them to help us. When nothing happened, I sighed bitterly and turned my attention back to Esme.

I sank back into our body and felt her relief as I joined her again. I didn't know why she was so happy to see me because I brought no skills to the fight, but skills or not, I could pay attention and maybe give her an early warning.

The fight reached fever pitch. All around me, my wolves were bleeding. Then...

Stepping out of the trees themselves and armed with swords, came the dryads. That was enough to give the attacking wolves pause. There was a bark and they pulled back, slinking a few steps away although still clustered together, ready to attack again.

A man stepped out of the darkness. There could be no doubt as to who he was; he was a mirror image of Ace Frost. Beckett's eyes unerringly found ours. He knew who we were. 'You have something that belongs to me,' his human voice said.

It is his wolf that speaks, Esme said in alarm.

Where is his human? I asked, confused.

I do not know. The wolf has taken control of the human body.

That's possible?

I've never heard of it before. She admitted.

I shifted onto two legs and stood naked among my wolves. 'I have nothing that belongs to you,' I said defiantly.

'You have my sister, Thea.'

'She is not a possession to be owned or bought,' I scoffed. 'She chooses to be here of her own free will, and here she will remain until she chooses otherwise.'

'Not for long.' His smile held no warmth. 'This is only a taste of the battle to come. Hide behind your dryads if you will, but it won't save you. I will decimate your pack.'

I snorted. 'Why kill good wolves? It's not them you want, it's me.'

'I will kill as many wolves as I need to achieve my objective. You included.'

'And what is your objective?'

'Getting my sister home safely, of course.'

'You don't give a shit about your sister. This is an excuse to attack us and we all know it. You're trying to justify this attack for when the council comes knocking, but this crap isn't going to cut it.'

He laughed and looked at Thea, who was quivering by my side. 'Oh, she'll tell the council how you held her hostage. She'll even manage to squeeze out a few tears. Your pack is weak,' he sneered. He looked beyond me to the approaching wolves. It was Archie's paw – but where was Tristan's? Archie's wolves were heaving in gulps of oxygen. They'd run hard to get here.

'If my pack is so weak, why aren't you attacking us now?' I demanded.

'This is but a fracas. This is your moment of choice, *Alpha*.' He mocked my title. 'Give me Thea, or your wolves will die. You have two hours to decide.' He gestured to his pack and they melted into the trees and away.

I took stock. My body was littered with cuts and scrapes, but they were already fading. Adrenalin was surging through me and soon I'd feel it disappearing, but for now I rode that wave. I let his wolves go. We were under a time crunch.

We should chase them, Esme urged.

No. We need to get back home for the curse breaking. I want to get that sorted before Beckett Frost comes back. Let's tend our wounded.

Cuts and scrapes, Esme said dismissively. **They'll heal in the shift.**

Marissa's won't, I argued. She had taken her position as my protector seriously, and she was suffering for it. She'd taken a nasty cut to her side and was bleeding heavily. Amber was already on her way to the mansion to try and break the curse; we had to get Marissa home so the witch could heal her too.

As I thanked the dryads, emotion almost choked me. 'Thank you for coming to our aid.'

The elder stepped forward. She was dressed for battle, complete with a wicked curving blade with notches in it all the better to rip out your insides. 'He is an interloper. You have already proven yourself a worthy ally.' She gave me a slight bow.

'I had no idea you guys could—' I stopped myself from saying kick ass '—fight.' I blurted the first question that came to mind. 'Why didn't you rip into Mark when he pissed on the elder tree?' I remembered the offence my pack member had caused to the dryads; his disrespect had almost started a war.

'We are seen as one of the weaker creatures of the Other realm, and it suits our purposes to be perceived that way. Our children are taught to fight from a young age so we can defend ourselves. Some even chose to go down dark paths.' She frowned and my gut twisted. She was talking about the dryad assassin who had killed my parents. A dryad assassin had seemed incongruous at the time, an oxymoron. Now I knew differently.

The elder continued. 'If we had punished Mark appropriately, we risked sparking a war with the wolves and many would have died. Bringing issues to your attention works far better, does it not?'

'It sure does,' I agreed. She was making me do her dirty work for her; I could respect that. I was seeing the dryads in a whole new light. I had wondered how these peaceful creatures had survived so well in this cut-throat realm. Now I had my answer.

'Make haste and see to your injured,' the elder instructed. 'We will break bread together soon.'

'I would like that.' I bowed to her. The elder inclined her head and led her people back into their trees.

I turned back to my injured wolves, of whom Marissa was by far the worst. 'Let me pick you up,' I ordered. I saw a flash of gold in her eyes before her normal brown returned; she was losing control of her wolf, so I hoped her wolf would understand that I was trying to help. I didn't have time to muck about piping her wolf.

I slid my arms under her and lifted. I was still in human form and even I was surprised at how easily I lifted the injured wolf. 'Run,' I called to the wolves around me, and I broke into a jog.

We'd only been moving for a few minutes when we encountered a problem: two teenagers were lying beneath a tree, necking. They stared at us, wide-eyed. Fuck. The last thing we needed was the Connection coming down on us like a ton of bricks because we'd broken the Verdict.

Luckily Pinewood Studios was just around the corner. It was the first time I'd appreciated how useful it could be to live amid the movie industry. 'And CUT!' I yelled loudly.

I turned to the kids. 'Sorry, guys,' I said apologetically. 'You're in the shot. Do you mind moving back a few feet?'

'Are those wolves?' the girl asked, eyes wide.

'Yes – but don't worry, they're extremely well-trained. And, erm, excuse my lack of clothes. The scene requires it.'

The boy was looking around. 'I can't even see the crew.'

'Hidden cameras,' I bullshitted. 'We need them for this kind of action.'

'The blood is very realistic,' the girl commented.

'It's amazing what the makeup people can do,' I agreed. 'Now, if you'll excuse me, we need to get going. If you don't mind heading back to the main path so you don't disrupt anymore shots...'

'Of course,' they agreed. They stood up and brushed themselves down. The girl's cheeks were fuchsia.

'And ACTION!' I yelled and started running again.

Damn hormonal teenagers, and damn the Connection for forcing me to cover our tracks. I hoped the delay wouldn't cost Marissa her life.

Chapter 18

I hurried to the cabin to get dressed. When I arrived, Tristan's paw was already there, dressed, back on two and joking jovially. I saw red. 'Where the hell were you?' I exploded at Tristan. 'We called you.'

The smirk leached from his face as he saw Marissa, who was still in my arms. 'Mrs Dawes hurt her ankle,' he explained weakly. 'She could barely walk, so we came back here to shift. Her injury healed during the change.'

It needn't have taken the whole paw to help her, and Esme was rightly furious. **He ignored us, disobeyed us on purpose.** I'd rarely heard such anger in her voice.

I agree. His reckoning will come – but not now.

Not now, she agreed reluctantly. **But soon.**

I blanked Tristan and focused on getting Marissa to Amber as quickly as possible. 'Finley, you drive,' I ordered our newcomer.

He slid in behind the wheel whilst I stayed in the back to comfort Marissa as best I could. Casting an anxious glance back at us, Seren slid into the front passenger seat. Whatever the rivalry between them had been about, it was gone now.

The drive back was fraught. Marissa was letting out sad little whimpers. I rang Amber. 'Are you at the mansion?'

'Five minutes out.'

'Marissa is hurt. Get your healing supplies ready.'

'I'm always ready.' She rang off.

Next, I called Greg. 'Hey, love. How did the hunt go?' His voice was upbeat

'It was a raging disaster. We were attacked by Beckett Frost and some of his wolves. He said he's coming at us again in two hours, so expect him in one.'

Greg's tone changed immediately; now he was all business. 'Fuck. Is everyone okay?'

'Marissa is badly hurt. Amber is on her way, and we're not far behind. Get the fire elementals ready, but keep them out of sight. They can be our ace in the hole.'

'Got it.'

'And evacuate the pups,' I ordered. 'I want only the fighting fit in the mansion.'

'If we evacuate the pups, we have to split our forces and send someone to guard them,' he argued. 'They're safest here. They're having a sleepover in the basement.'

I rubbed my tired eyes. I knew shit all about military strategy but Greg did; I had to trust him and delegate, something that had never been my greatest strength. Reluctantly, I agreed. 'Fine, do what you think is best – but put an elemental down there with them, just in case.'

'Have we got any other allies we can call in?'

I couldn't think of anyone who was close enough to help. 'Maybe Bastion is about somewhere. I'll give him a call.'

'I don't know how much help he'll be,' Greg said. 'The witch's curse is still kicking his ass. I'll get things ready here.'

'See you in five.' I hung up and dialled Bastion. As usual, he answered with silence. 'I need your help. We're being attacked by Beckett Frost's pack.'

'Now? I'm in London,' Bastion protested.

'He said he's going to attack in two hours.'

'And you believe him?' he asked sardonically.

'No.' I sighed. 'But what can I do?'

'Call Jinx.'

'She's too far away.'

'She can fly down to you.'

'There isn't time for her to catch a plane,' I protested.

'Luckily, she has a dragon for a mate,' he pointed out flatly. 'I'm going to shift and start flying to you.' He hung up without even saying goodbye, and I mentally bitched about his lousy phone manners. Nevertheless, I did as he bade and rang Jess.

There was no answer, so I left a voicemail. 'Hey, hope you're okay. I'm being attacked by a rival werewolf pack. If you and Emory are about, I could use some back-up. This shit is going to get messy. If you get this too late, don't worry about it. I love you.'

We were back at the mansion – and I was all out of allies. The shit was about to get real.

As we pulled in, I saw that Amber's car was already on the drive and felt a surge of relief. She could tend Marissa. As I carried the injured wolf carefully inside, I saw how much blood she'd lost. Greg greeted me at the door. 'Amber's ready. She's set up in your living room.'

'Thanks. Check on Mrs Dawes – she hurt her ankle during the hunt. Find out if she needs to see Amber. If she's all right, ask her to feed the wolves. We're going to need all our energy. Get Finley to help.'

'Ten-four.' He followed me down the corridor and held open the living-room door. I carefully carried Marissa into the cheerful room that I knew and loved, pleased that the dark wood panelling of the past was gone. Imminent attack or not, I was glad to be home.

I laid Marissa on the carpet by the fireplace. Greg shut the door on his way out to give us some privacy.

'Make sure Marissa's wolf knows what I'm doing,' Amber instructed.

'Sure.' I reached out to the Other being residing within Marissa.

Hello? This is Amber. She is a witch, and she's here to help heal you.

It hurts, the wolf whimpered sadly in my head.

She'll make it better, I promised. *Will you let her help you?*

I will not bite her, she agreed.

'You can approach,' I confirmed to Amber. I decided it would be best to keep the skittish wolf busy; a promise not to bite wasn't the most all-encompassing guarantee I'd ever heard. I reached out again to Marissa's wolf as Amber started to pull out paintbrushes and jars of gloop. *What is your name?* I asked.

I am Wolfy.

Wolfy. That's ... nice.

Marissa named me when I first answered the call, she said proudly.

Have you spoken to her?

She cannot hear me, no matter how much I shout. But she stands in front of a mirror and talks to me often. A feeling of warm affection rolled over me.

If you like, I can make it so that she can hear you, I said.

I would love that more than going on a hunt, Wolfy replied wistfully. For a wolf, that was quite something.

Even after the change and the hunt, I still had all this extra energy fizzing through me; it felt like magic was bursting through my skin. Stupid Third realm. Expending some energy would hopefully ease the discomfort.

I pulled up from the well within and reached out to Wolfy and Marissa to tie them together. It was easier than when I'd done it for Thea and Sophie; maybe Marissa and her wolf were closer somehow.

Hello? Wolfy called out softly.

Wolfy? I heard Marissa say in astonishment.

Rissa! You can hear me!

I can hear you! I can really hear you! Oh my God – Grandad's stories were all true!

'There. She's all done,' Amber said with satisfaction. 'She needs to take it easy for the next day or two.'

'That didn't take long,' I said, impressed.

'She only had the one major wound, though she's still suffered blood loss. She'll need to rehydrate and rest.'

'Is she okay to shift back?'

'Of course, whenever she's ready.'

Wolfy stood back on four legs as I tied off the connection between her and Marissa, leaving a private wavelength just for them. A moment later, Marissa went through a lightning-fast shift and was standing before me on two feet. The evidence was beginning to stack up: the connections I was creating between humans and their wolves were enabling them to shift much faster.

There was a brief knock and Greg came in, automatically averting his eyes from Marissa's naked body. 'I'm glad you're okay,' he said gruffly.

I had a never-ending supply of dressing gowns for just such an occasion. 'Here.' I handed Marissa a white robe. No sooner had she tied the belt than she threw herself into my arms. 'Thank you!' She pulled back to kiss me on the cheek before hugging me again. 'This is amazing. I can never thank you enough. I can finally hear her, like Grandad's stories.'

I hugged her back. 'I'm so glad you're happy and you're all right. How do you feel?'

'Over the moon!' She laughed. 'A bit tired. But I'm so excited.'

'That'll wear off when Wolfy never stops talking,' I muttered.

Hey! Esme objected. **You talk enough for both of us,** she observed but her tone was affectionate.

'Can you tell me a little more about your grandad's stories?' I asked Marissa.

'I've got them all written down in his diary somewhere, but basically they say that werewolves used to be different. So his father told him, we used to be able to talk to our wolves rather than wrestling them for dominion during every shift. Now we have nothing more than a flare of emotion that we occasionally feel from our wolf, but in the past they had whole conversations. I always believed Grandad's stories, and that's why I chatted to Wolfy in the mirror even before my first call.'

She reddened. 'That's why her name is Wolfy – I named her when I was three or so. Anyway, according to the old stories, we all lived in packs. There was a leader, so pack disputes never went on too long, and all of the packs were linked, which made us stronger. If there was an issue, you took them to the ultimate Alpha and he adjudicated. Bob's your uncle.'

Why are you humans so obsessed with this Bob? Esme asked. **He must have been a mighty warrior.**

In my mind, I giggled. *It's just a saying. I've explained it before. There is no Bob really.*

You and your sayings, she grumped.

I gave her a mental hug. I was so grateful for having her with me, so grateful for the connection that we'd always shared courtesy of my piping magic. I couldn't imagine how it would feel to have an Other presence riding shotgun in your life and not be able to communicate with it.

'The Great Pack,' I said aloud to Marissa.

'Yes! That's what Grandad called it.'

I smiled. 'Not such tall tales, after all. You'd best go and get some rest.' I turned to Greg. 'Did Mrs Dawes manage to set up some food for everyone?'

'I couldn't find her, but Seren organised it.'

'I hope Mrs Dawes is okay. Did you check her room?'

'I knocked, but she didn't reply. I expect I just missed her.'

Marissa interrupted. 'If an attack is imminent, Wolfy and I want to fight.'

Amber snorted. 'No chance in hell. I haven't patched you up so you can immediately go out and die. If you try and shift, you'll use up magical reserves you can't afford to lose. You need to visit Rosie's first.'

Marissa looked deflated. 'I want to help.'

'Go to the basement and look after the pups. That would be a huge help,' Greg proposed.

She nodded reluctantly. 'I'll go now.'

'Perhaps get dressed first,' I suggested lightly.

She threw on some clothes and made for the door. As she pulled it open, there was Mrs Dawes with Reynard and a few other gargoyles. Marissa slipped away. 'The gargoyles are here,' Mrs Dawes announced, somewhat unnecessarily. She looked a tad flustered.

'Thank you, Mrs Dawes. Do show them in.' As she stood aside, I asked, 'Are you okay?'

She blinked. 'Fine, why do you ask?'

'Your ankle?'

'Oh. It's fine.' She waggled her foot. 'Thankfully, it healed during the shift.'

'Where were you before?' Greg demanded. 'I was looking for you.'

'I was in my room,' she said airily.

Greg frowned. 'You didn't answer when I knocked.'

'I was in the shower. I'm sorry I missed you – did you need something?'

'No, it's fine. Seren is preparing some food.'

'I'll go and help her and leave you to it.' Mrs Dawes backed out of the room and shut the door behind her.

Reynard watched her go. 'We've got a problem,' he said.

Didn't we always?

Chapter 19

'What kind of a problem are we talking about?' I sighed.

'The worst kind, my fine wench. Betrayal.'

Fuck. That *was* the worst kind. 'I don't want to be betrayed,' I said flatly, thinking of Tristan. 'Can we have another problem instead?'

'We don't get to choose our problems, bitey pup – though we can choose what we do about them.' His tone suggested doing nothing wasn't a great choice right now.

'Fine. Hit me. I'm ready.' I was not at all ready.

'Your Mrs Dawes was painting the house when we arrived.'

Relief washed over me. 'She's the housekeeper. She does maintenance.'

Reynard rolled his eyes. 'Not that kind of painting. She was painting runes.'

'But ... she doesn't know how to paint runes.' Even as I said the words, I remembered the bloody mess of Reynard being dumped on my door and how Mrs Dawes had helped me paint a stasis rune under Amber's direction. Then I remembered her painting a healing rune over Ares...

So maybe she knew runes. She'd said that a friendly witch had taught her some in case she ever got into trouble and needed them. Maybe Mrs Dawes had been painting a protection rune. Without telling anyone. Whilst a secret black witch was on the loose.

'I'm no expert, lovey,' Reynard offered, 'but she wasn't painting with Dulux.'

'She really does look a lot like... God, it can't be...' Amber trailed off, frowning. 'Let's go and look at the outside of the mansion. I'll be able to see any newly added runes.'

'Maybe they're protection runes,' I said out loud, trying to sound hopeful even though my gut was churning. 'We'll check in at my office on the way. The security cameras will show anything untoward. You guys stay here,' I said to the other gargoyles. 'Have a biscuit, grab a book. Get cosy. We'll be back.'

'Good idea,' Greg agreed. 'Liam is manning the security console. I'm sure he would have noticed anything amiss.'

We trooped down the hall to my office – which was empty. The security console was unmanned. Greg hauled his phone out and called Liam. 'Where are you?' he barked.

I made out Liam's reply, courtesy of my wolfish hearing. 'In the kitchen. Mrs Dawes said she'd spell me while I grabbed some food. I'll be back in five.'

'Be back NOW,' Greg ordered and hung up.

I swore aloud. 'You need to work on your cussing,' Reynard said. 'That's not going to make anyone blush.' I tried a bit harder. 'That's better,' he said approvingly.

Liam burst through the door, panting, with Maxwell close on his heels. 'What's up?' my cousin asked.

'Mrs Dawes has betrayed us,' Greg said grimly.

'We don't know that,' I protested weakly.

'Beckett knew exactly where to find you while you were on a hunt. She "injured" her ankle,' Greg said, using air quotes, 'keeping Tristan's paw away from the fight with Beckett. She lured Liam away from the security console, and she's painted runes on the mansion.'

I just couldn't believe it – not Mrs Dawes. There had to be an explanation.

'Bobby said the black witch felt familiar to him,' Greg continued. 'And Mrs Dawes paints her nails, just like Wren said.' It was all adding up to paint a picture I didn't want to see.

'Let's see these runes,' Amber repeated firmly and marched out.

'Liam, stay here – and for God's sake don't leave the console unmanned again. I'll go and see if I can find Mrs Dawes,' Greg ordered.

'I'll come with you,' Maxwell said grimly. 'And I'll make sure the Forge is ready.'

'The Forge?' I asked.

'The collective name for fire elementals,' Maxwell explained. Ah, so not a crackling, then. He gave me a quick hug. 'Stay sharp, cousin.'

'And you.'

Reynard and I followed Amber. The night air was crisp and cool. A shiver snaked down my back and my gut clenched as I searched the trees for something, some sign that we weren't alone. 'Quickly,' I said anxiously to Amber.

'Obviously,' she snapped back, already pulling out her trusty paintbrush and a jar of purple gloop. She swept on two quick runes and the runes on the mansion lit up. It was like a beautiful display of Christmas lights – but witchy. They shone into the night like beacons – but across each of them was a small wiggly line in a fluorescent-blue colour.

Amber swore and my gut clenched. Amber never swore. 'Cancelling runes. God, they've been painted on nearly all of the original ones,' she confirmed darkly.

'Can you fix it? Un-cancel them all?'

'That's not how it works. The runes have been nullified, so we need to cleanse the mansion before we can paint on more. Besides, I don't have the potions I need for a job like that. I brought stuff for healing and curse breaking.'

'The witch was here when we arrived.' Reynard pointed to the window next to my office door.

'Yes, you interrupted her before she could finish that one.'

'We flew in. She wasn't expecting us,' Reynard confirmed.

'Vampyrs,' I said suddenly. 'Are the runes that keep out vampyrs still working?'

Amber shook her head grimly. 'No, those ones have been cancelled out.'

I hauled out my phone and called Greg. We really needed to install an intercom system. 'It's as we feared,' I said carefully when he answered. I didn't want to blurt out something that other wolf ears might pick up. 'Get Maxwell and his family down to the basement to help protect the pups.'

'We're on it,' he responded grimly. 'We haven't found her. There's no sign of her in her room, and her stuff is gone.'

That was the final nail in the coffin. Until then I'd been holding out the tiniest hope that this was all some sort of misunderstanding, like maybe Mrs Dawes thought the cancelling rune was a protective one or something. But no; she'd packed her bag. She'd left us vulnerable by destroying our protection, exposing us to vampyric attack – and all in time for Beckett Frost's arrival. Why?

I felt sickened by her betrayal, but all that emotion had to wait. Now, we needed to act. 'Remember that little …

hiccup we had? Has the paperwork gone through for the solution?' I said carefully.

'No.' Greg sighed. 'Not as far as we know.'

'Fuck.'

'Yeah. I'll get the Forge ready for an attack.'

I thought suddenly of Voltaire. He had complained about missing vampyrs, and he'd suspected a black witch's involvement. Mrs Dawes' involvement. My God. 'An attack may be imminent,' I said grimly 'Remember what Voltaire said?'

'Vampyrs going missing?'

'Yeah. He suspected the black witch of kidnapping them. Rouse our whole damned pack. Get them shifted onto four.'

'If we get everyone ready and shifted now, they might use up all of their magical energy and get booted out of the Other before Beckett arrives,' Greg pointed out sensibly.

'We can't give them five minutes to shift if vampyrs are about to pop out of the shadows at any second. We'll be slaughtered,' I protested. Mrs Dawes' betrayal had scrambled my brains and I clearly wasn't operating at my best, because there was an obvious answer. 'Gather the wolves, every single one of them. Get them into the banquet hall. I'll be five minutes.'

'On it.' If Greg was curious about my plan, his voice didn't show it.

As I saw it, there were four ways forward: one, I could pipe and connect all my wolves to their human counterparts; two, we could break the curse; three, we could shift ready and risk being kicked out of the Other realm because we were out of time, or four, we could do nothing and hope we could shift in time. The second choice held a lot of appeal. If we could break the curse and restore the Great Pack, maybe I could get through to my wolves *and* Beckett's wolves and stop an attack before it started. It would also decrease our shift times in case of vampyr attack.

Amber frowned. 'Did you say vampyrs have been going missing?'

'Apparently.'

'And they suspect a witch's involvement?'

'Yes. So?'

She bit her lip nervously, an uncharacteristic look for her because she didn't do nerves. 'The truly blackest of witches slide into necromancy.'

'Necromancy?'

'Dabbling with the dead.'

My stomach lurched. Dead, like vampyrs. 'What does that mean for us?'

She shook her head. 'I honestly don't know. It's been decades since the last necromancer, so I'm not sure what she can do, though I expect she can control the vampyrs she's seized. They won't fight like normal vampyrs – they won't stop for fear of being hurt or killed.'

Bloody brilliant. I rang Greg back and relayed the information, telling him to warn the Forge that they would have to be ready to kill to frighten off the attacking vampyrs. Then I turned to Reynard; there was no time like the present. 'I think we can break the curse on the gargoyles.'

He stared at me. 'And what will happen to us when you do that, *ma petite* pup?'

I shrugged helplessly. I didn't know. I turned questioning eyes on our witchy expert. 'Amber?'

'You might just be restored to your human forms,' she said slowly to Reynard.

'Or?' he demanded.

'Or you might stay in your gargoyle forms, but no more gargoyles would be made. Or...'

'Or?'

'Or you might cease to exist. You're a couple of hundred years old now, and the curse granted you immortality. Breaking the curse might take it away.'

'So you don't know, either,' Reynard said flatly

'No. Nobody has broken a two-hundred-year-old curse in recent times.'

'If we're not sure of the outcome,' he stated, 'we must consult with the others.'

'The others?'

'The gargoyles that I brought with me. They head the gargoyle factions.' Reynard spun on his heel and headed back to my living room, where the others were cooling their heels. I winced; had I known they were so important, perhaps I wouldn't have chucked out the irreverent comment about getting cosy and having a snack.

It didn't seem like curse breaking was going to be a quick option, not if the gargoyles' lives hung in the balance. For now, it would have to be option one. 'I'll follow you in a minute,' I said to Amber. 'Start your preparations for breaking the curse. How long will it take?'

'An hour, maybe longer.'

'An hour?' I exclaimed. 'How can it take so long to paint a rune or two?'

'Because it's not *just* a rune or two,' she bitched back. 'You do your job and I'll do mine. Just get someone to keep me safe while I work.'

'Okay, get started. I'll send you a protector.'

Amber hurried inside. As she left, the lit-up runes faded from sight, leaving an ordinary building behind. I touched the walls. 'Get ready,' I murmured to the mansion. 'It's going to get hairy.'

There was a *whump* behind me and I whirled around, heart hammering and an inch from shifting. Bastion was regarding me calmly. He gave me a regal nod before shifting from griffin into human form. 'Talking to buildings is probably the first sign of insanity.'

'Bastion! You said you were in London.'

'I was. I flew. Where do you need me?'

Everywhere. I needed a hundred griffins, but I only had one. Right now, the most important task was breaking the curse. Amber wouldn't like it one bit because she'd despised Bastion ever since he'd killed her lover. Her hatred was understandable, but he was just a hired hand – except for the fact I hadn't actually *hired* him right now – so she was going to have to suck it up and deal with it. He was the only one I knew who could keep her safe. As capable as Greg was, Bastion had two hundred extra years of experience.

I studied him. In human form, it was clear that something was wrong. He had bags under his eyes and his skin looked pallid. 'Are you sick?' Part of me was genuinely concerned, but I also needed to know if he could handle what I was going to ask of him.

'I've been better,' he admitted. 'The witch's curse weighs on me.' His eyes flicked to the extra triangle on my head – a sure sign to anyone in the know that I'd done a spot of time travel.

'How is it affecting you?' I asked with concern.

'Exhaustion claws at me constantly and rest doesn't ease it.'

'Sleep doesn't make you feel better?'

'No. If anything, it makes it worse.'

'Have you spoken with a witch about breaking the curse?'

He gave me a flat look. 'I need the blood of the casting witch to break the curse.' He needed the blood of Mrs Dawes.

My stomach clenched. 'Or what?'

'Eventually, I will die of exhaustion.'

'But you're immortal!' I protested.

'Long-lived,' Bastion corrected me. 'Griffins are only long-lived. Perhaps my life has been lived out.'

'That's ridiculous. You'll be fine.'

'Not if we don't find the black witch,' he said drily.

'We know who it is,' I admitted unhappily. 'Mrs Dawes.'

He stilled. 'I always thought she bore a passing resemblance to a witch I once knew, but I dismissed it as a trick of my memory. It's difficult to remember everything clearly over so many years.'

'You think she's descended from a witch family?'

'Perhaps. The witch she looks like was one of those who cursed the gargoyles.'

I connected the dots. 'Was she the one you captured for Isiah Samuel?' So maybe we now had Mrs Dawes' motive: she was descended from one of the witches who'd cursed the werewolves, and now she was trying to finish her family's work – by finishing us.

Understanding shone in his eyes. 'You've been back.'

'Yes. I met young you – totally cute, by the way. Way less grim, and with a shittier poker face.'

Keeping his expression totally bland, he winked. The absurdity made me laugh, though I cut myself off quickly when I noticed my laugh had an edge of hysteria to it. All this drama, all this blood shedding – what did I know about battles?

You do not need to know, Esme reprimanded me. **I know. When the time comes, I will destroy our enemies.**

Talking casually of annihilating our enemies should have been upsetting, but it wasn't. If it was a choice between us or Beckett, it was going to be Beckett.

'You've got the blood to break the curse on the gargoyles?' Bastion asked.

'Yes. Stored in my safe.'

'Not the fridge?'

'Damn! Should I have put it in the fridge?'

'Well, I guess it's not being used for a transfusion so it might be all right. It might smell a bit, though.'

I hadn't thought of that. No use crying over spilt milk.

I don't know why you'd cry over milk anyway. Milk is for pups.

I ignored Esme's input. 'I need you to guard Amber whilst she tries to break the curse on the gargoyles. Are you well enough for that?'

'If it is the last thing I do,' he promised.

I hugged him. 'I don't want it to be the last thing you do.' My voice was muffled as I spoke into his neck.

His reciprocal hug was firm and fast. 'I do not intend to die this day, Lucy Barrett.'

'Okay.' I drew back. 'Go and protect Amber. Mrs Dawes has nullified our protective runes, and the mansion is owned by a company rather than a person.'

'That's only an issue if she or Frost have vampyr allies,' Bastion pointed out calmly.

'Remember Voltaire? He said vampyrs have been going missing, and he suspected our black witch...'

'You think she still has them?'

'It would make sense. Hope for the best, prepare for the worst.'

'If Mrs Dawes has learned to control the vampyrs, she's slid deeper into darkness than we'd thought.'

'What could be darker than planning to extinguish children?'

No pun intended, but Bastion's voice was grave. 'Necromancy. Raising the dead and controlling vampyrs is a necromantic art. As you can imagine, vampyrs hate necromancers for that reason and they kill them on sight.'

'So Amber explained.' I sighed and dragged a frustrated hand through the loose strands of my hair. 'Should I call Voltaire?' I asked.

'It's a risk. If he learns of your vulnerability, he could attack you.'

I brightened suddenly. 'No, he can't. He agreed that no vampyrs would attack the pack as long as I'm alive! All this time I've been panicking about the vampyrs and I'd forgotten about his oath.' For the first time, my gloom lifted a tad. 'We just have to worry about Beckett.'

'I hate to be the one to break it to you, but if Mrs Dawes is controlling the vampyrs as we fear, they won't be paying attention to the Red Guard's oath.'

My happiness fizzled and died. 'Fuck. Are you sure?'

'Quite. If she has control of them, they are little more than puppets. They won't be thinking of honour or the risk of being forsworn – they won't be thinking at all. That makes them even deadlier opponents. They won't care if they survive the encounter.'

'Then you'd better get to Amber now!' I ordered urgently.

I pulled out my phone to call Voltaire; I'd make a deal with the devil if it would keep us safe. Typically, his phone went to voicemail, I left him a detailed message and prayed he'd pick it up in time.

I hoped Bastion could keep Amber safe from the vampyric monstrosities that my gut said were coming. Breaking the curse was our best chance for surviving the waking nightmare in which we now seemed to be immersed.

Chapter 20

The assembled gathering of werewolves in the banqueting hall was nervous. I hadn't just summoned the battle core of the top fifteen, but the entire pack. Not all of them were ready to fight, but they would have to be.

As they focused their attention on me, I said. 'An attack is imminent. Beckett Frost is coming, with his wolves.'

Thea stood up immediately. 'I'll go back home. I must, to save you all.'

'You are part of our pack now; we will not turn our back on you just because the road ahead is rocky,' I promised. 'Besides, he's using you as an excuse, and you know it. Ace attacked our pack, and he was instrumental in Mark Oates' death and Archie's attack. We defended ourselves and put him down. Now his brother is seeking vengeance. If I can,

I'll try and fight him one on one and let that be the end of it.'

Archie spoke out. 'He is an honourless cur. If he kills you, it won't be the end of it, not for those that will be left. He cannot become our alpha.'

'Archie's right,' Tristan called. Even now, Tristan couldn't bring himself to say that *I* was right. 'Frost must be defeated. Giving Thea back won't halt his attack. He has an eye on this pack and its riches, and he won't stop until he has them.'

'I've heard his pack is poor,' Daniella agreed. 'Now that the Connection has largely stopped the black tourneys, he's all out of cash.'

'It was the Red Guard that stopped the tourneys,' Elena snorted. 'Not the Connection. The Connection did fuck all, as usual.'

Liam cleared his throat. 'Can we focus? An attack is coming, and our alpha is speaking.' The room fell silent, and all eyes turned to me.

'Our biggest vulnerability is the time that it takes us to shift, and the fact that we can't control our wolves.' I cleared my throat. 'I can solve both issues. Years ago, wolves and their human counterparts could talk with each other and make decisions together. There was none of the distrust that is apparent now, none of this wrestling for supremacy. Our wolves are sentient creatures, just like us. They are also fierce and battle-ready. They need to kill to survive, and they are ready to do so for you. I am not just a werewolf. I am a piper.'

The room exploded into noise. 'Quiet!' I shouted. 'We don't have time for this!'

BE SILENT! Esme roared.

'We don't have time to discuss the pros and cons of our every action. We've been betrayed. Mrs Dawes has painted cancelling runes over our protective ones, and we are vulnerable to attack because of her actions. Evidence suggests that she is the black witch behind Bobby's kidnapping.'

There were gasps, and several people started crying.

'How could she do that?' Sonia raged. 'I'll rip her limb from limb.'

'Take that anger and use it,' I instructed. 'But for now, you need to decide. I can make it so that you can hear your wolves. It's not a perfect solution, and it doesn't give us access to the Great Pack, but it's something.'

They all started talking at once.

'Talk to our wolves?'

'Impossible!'

'What's the Great Pack?'

'Enough!' I held up my hand. 'I've told you; we just don't have time for this. An attack could come at any second. Either you're in or you're out. If you're out, leave this room. Now.'

No one moved and I breathed a soft sigh of relief. 'Okay. I'm going to link you to your wolves. You'll be able to talk to them, and you'll be able to shift super-fast like me. Brace yourselves.'

I called up the magic from within me, pulling up more than I'd ever done before. I didn't know how long the tie I'd made between Greg, Marissa's and Thea's wolves and their human counterparts would last, but so far it appeared to be permanent. Maybe going to the Common would strip the bond away, though. Who knew? Not me. But even if the bond I made was temporary, it would do in a pinch.

I dredged the bottom of my magical well until I was holding so much magic that it felt as if my skin would burst. I reached the magic out to the nearest person, Tristan, tied him to his wolf and carefully disentangled myself from the loop. I watched as Tristan's eyes lit up with wonder.

I moved onto the next person, Seren. And then the next. I continued sweeping my magic through every person in the room. Finally, every human that stood before me had been linked tightly to their wolf within.

I'd used so much magic that I braced myself for the inevitable itching. Surely I'd be kicked out to the Common realm. But – nothing. There wasn't so much as an itch.

The dagger, Esme said suddenly. **It was the magical dagger that gave you the ability to pipe.**

Yeah, so?

Maybe when you use your piping skills, it doesn't drain you in the same way as normal pipers or werewolves. We've only once been sent back to the Common realm.

You may well be right, but we can't think about this now. We need to prepare the troops.

The wolves always stand ready, she reassured me. Pride hummed though her.

I'm not a bad public speaker, but I really wished I'd had time to prepare something rousing to say as I addressed the pack. 'Take this time that we have before we are attacked to speak to your wolf, and to set some boundaries for the coming fight. When I fight, I let my wolf have full control.'

The room exploded into noise as everyone started talking at once. I raised my voice. 'Listen! Your wolf can fight better than you can. We must work together with our wolves to maximise our chances of success. You've got maybe ten or fifteen minutes to get to know your wolf and make a plan. Use that time wisely.'

As quickly as I could, I left the room to give my pack time to adjust to the new status quo. Greg followed on my heels. 'Are the pups all protected?' I asked him when we were alone in the hallway. I took a moment to step closer and hug him, just a physical connection to steady us both. I was scared, not for myself but for my pack.

'As much as they can be,' Greg confirmed as he kissed my forehead. 'They're secure in the basement with plenty of snacks and a TV. There are five fire elementals positioned around the room, and the lights are on full blaze to prevent any shadows that vampyrs can slink in through.'

'Thank you.' Something in me eased. I brushed my lips against his and he deepened the kiss, sending my mind blank. Eventually I pulled back. We had things to do. 'Okay, great.' I said inanely, trying to collect my scrambled brains. 'Let's go and see Amber and the gargoyles.'

Greg threaded his fingers through mine, and we walked together to my living room. These snatched moments together meant everything – and at that moment they were keeping me sane.

Greg's phone beeped. He squeezed my hand before releasing it, then he pulled out his phone and checked our security systems remotely. 'We're out of time,' he said grimly. 'We've got intruders.' He held the screen towards me so that I could see the camera footage. Wolves were leaping over our fences.

'Next time, let's get bigger fences,' I suggested.

'A determined werewolf can jump pretty high. The fences are mostly there as a deterrent.'

'They don't seem deterred.'

'Sadly not. We'll have to teach them a lesson,' he said ominously.

'That we will. I guess our wolves won't get those ten minutes after all. Go and prepare our strongest fighters.

We'll approach and attempt to parlay. I'll speak with Amber and see how long she needs us to delay them.'

We split up. Moments later, I burst into my living room. 'Beckett and his wolves are here,' I said. 'We're out of time to debate.' I looked at the gargoyles, 'Will you let us try and break the curse?'

'You don't need our permission,' one of the female gargoyles pointed out. 'You could do it anyway.'

'I could,' I agreed, 'but making a decision like that about you and your species without consulting you would be plain wrong. I need to know what you want so that I can plan accordingly. I would like to break the curse, to free you from the constant pain that you're in, and prevent future wolves being twisted and turned into gargoyles against their will. But it's your lives that we're risking, so it must be your decision.'

'Break it,' said Reynard confidently. 'Not just for us, but for future generations. This life that we lead is no life at all. We're cursed to the shadows, and always in pain. End it. We are in agreement. End it,' he repeated vehemently.

I looked at the other gargoyles and they nodded.

'Bring it to an end,' the female gargoyle agreed. 'Come what may, we are ready.' But her tone was grim; she knew they were risking the lives of their people. It was the ultimate high-stakes decision; they would all live, or they would all die.

'You've got your marching orders,' I said firmly to Amber.

'I've been preparing in case that was the decision. I need the witch's blood.'

'I'll get it.'

I dashed from the living room to my office. My desk looked disturbed, and the code on the safe lock wasn't on the number where I always left it. Someone had been here trying to get into it. I guessed that's what Mrs Dawes had been doing when she sent Liam away from the security console, and I hoped she had failed.

My heart was in my mouth as I quickly keyed in the combination and the heavy metal door clunked open. I gave a sigh of relief as I saw the leather bag still inside, opened it up and found the stoppered flask of blood. Bastion was right: I probably should have refrigerated it. There again, Mrs Dawes had open access to the fridge.

We couldn't have known about her, Esme commented. She could tell I was beating myself up about it.

Surely there were clues that we missed.

Perhaps, but we are not perfect.

Sacrilege, I teased.

Even though technically I'd soon own the whole mansion, I still knocked on the door to the living room. It was a habit born of the politeness my mother had instilled in me. I went inside and held the blood out to Amber. She was glaring daggers once more at Bastion. 'Focus,' I told her. 'I need you to break this thing – and fast.'

'It's not something I can hurry. It will take as long as it takes.'

'How long do I need to delay Beckett for? Half an hour? An hour?'

'Yes.'

'Which?'

'How long is a piece of string?'

That's a stupid question, Esme said indignantly. **Obviously, it depends on the length of the string.**

That's kind of the point.

She sniffed. **It is foolish.**

I turned to Bastion and the assembled gargoyles. 'Keep her safe, all of you. We've reason to think an attack from some vampyrs may be imminent.'

'When it comes to vampyrs, we're more on the tasty morsel side of the food chain,' Reynard commented.

'Well, distract them then.'

'I shall extend my leg like a chicken drumstick for them to gnaw upon,' he said drily.

I rolled my eyes. 'Use your air magic or whatever.' I wished we could dig into the air-magic thing, but now wasn't the time. 'Just throw something at them,' I advised.

'Like what? Books?'

I shrugged. 'Whatever works.'

'Utilising books as a weapon is a crime of the highest magnitude,' Reynard drawled.

'Then throw vases or anything else you can get your hands on,' I snapped in frustration. 'All I want is for you to protect Amber so she can break the curse on you. Is that clear enough?'

'As clear as the Croatian sea.'

I paused. 'I've never been to Croatia. Is that a clear sea or a murky sea?'

'Clear, my bitey pup. You can see the little crabs walking on the seabed.'

'Fabulous. I'll book a holiday – if I survive being called out by the most brutal alpha in recent generations.'

'His father was equally foul.'

'So I gather.'

'You'll survive.' Reynard gave me a rare smile unlaced with sarcasm. 'You always do.'

'Until the one time that I don't,' I pointed out. 'All mushrooms are edible, but some can only be eaten once.'

He laughed. 'Are you sure you haven't been to Croatia?'

'What? No, I haven't.'

'That's a Croatian proverb.'

'Well, you live and learn.'

'Except if you nibble poisonous fungi,' he quipped.

'I have to go. Stay safe,' I said to the room in general. 'Break the curse,' I ordered Amber.

'I'm on it, but I need more time. Go. You're distract-ing me with your chitchat about mushrooms. Who cares about a portobello in a time like this?'

I opened my mouth to reply then closed it. Sometimes silence is golden, and this was one of those times. I needed to find myself a violent alpha werewolf to fight. Luckily, there was one on my doorstep.

Chapter 21

I couldn't fight Frost alone, so I jogged back to the banqueting hall where my wolves were still gathered. I was just
about to enter the room when something slid out of the
shadows. 'VAMPYRS!' I shouted the warning as loudly as
I could. Werewolf hearing would hopefully pick it up.

The vampyr before me moved jerkily, like each limb had
to be commanded to move. That gave me the split second
I needed to shift.

Pleasure rolled over us and Esme took the driving seat.
Her sensitive nose picked up the faint trace of decay that all
vampyrs carry before a feed. Although this one was hungry
and it needed blood to sustain it, it wasn't having ours. As
Esme leapt towards it, it phased back into the shadows.
It was repeating the same moves; I guessed the vampyrs
hadn't needed a new strategy for a century or two.

They're predictable. Watch them, they repeat their attacks, I warned Esme. I felt her acknowledgment, but she was focused on our enemy.

Once again, its scent was the beat of warning we needed as it reappeared behind us. Esme whirled around, ready to face it. Vampyrs are fairly slow movers, a blessing we sorely needed in a fight against them. Esme leapt towards it and raked her claws down its chest. The vampyr let out a gurgling noise – but it still didn't utter a sound. It was eerie.

It stepped back into the shadows, then re-emerged from the first place from which it had attacked. This time we were ready, and Esme jumped even as he was stepping out. Her mighty jaws closed over the vampyr's jugular and ripped it.

As its body convulsed, it met our eyes. For a moment I saw a flicker of intelligence there, then the light died. The vampyr disintegrated into a cloud of dust, causing Esme's sensitive nose to sneeze.

We shifted back onto two. Dammit: I'd lost yet another good pair of jeans.

'Vampyrs!' I shouted again, in case anyone hadn't heard me the first time.

I opened the door of the banqueting hall onto total chaos, though not onto the carnage that I'd feared. The wolves were working in small teams, and the vampyrs were slower and far fewer. Our ace in the hole, the fire elementals, were also there with flames springing from their hands.

The wolves harried the vampyrs and kept them in the centre of the room, away from the shadows, then the fire elementals threw flames at them. I watched, trying to stay clinical and detached, as Alyssa threw a fireball at a vampyr who ignited faster than dry kindling. The burning corpse remained creepily silent until the end.

The evidence was undeniable: Beckett and Mrs Dawes were working together, using the vampyrs to soften us up. However, if they thought they would find a tired, weary pack when Beckett finally attacked, they were mistaken. We had an advantage that Mrs Dawes didn't know about: with our fast shift, no one was in their vulnerable human form when the vampyrs phased in.

The elementals were dealing with our attackers with impressive speed and efficiency. There's a reason why vampyrs don't tangle with elementals; they like to hit weaker targets like werewolves and gargoyles. Well, they'd find nothing weak at the mansion. Our pups were heavily guarded by the Forge, and I was confident that I could turn my attention to Beckett and his wolves.

When Maxwell sent the last vampyr up into flames, my wolves threw back their heads and howled their victory.

I crossed the room to the window and looked out onto the lawns. Frost's wolves lined the grounds, standing in neat rows like soldiers. It was spooky and wrong – wolves don't act that way. We cluster in groups of five or six; we don't stand in long lines of ten like a neat little regiment. Unease stirred in my stomach.

Greg joined me. He didn't speak but handed me a robe, which I slipped on. He waited until I'd tied it up before passing my phone. I slid it into my pocket and turned to him. 'Thank you.' I gestured through the window at Frost. 'He's waiting for something.'

He snorted. 'He thinks that the vampyrs are going to destroy us.' Pride coloured his tone.

'He'll have a bit of a shock then, won't he?' I smirked back.

At that moment, Voltaire stepped out of the shadows next to me. 'HOLD!' I barked hastily, instructing the fire elementals and wolves alike. 'He's friendly.' I grimaced. 'Kind of.' I glared at the vampyr. 'You're late,' I said flatly.

'Bad traffic,' he lied blandly. He'd been hoping that the puppet vampyrs had done their work before he arrived, but no such luck. The puppet vampyrs were shish kebabs, thanks to the Forge.

'You gave your oath that no vampyrs would attack the pack.'

'And I meant it.'

'And yet here I am being attacked by vampyrs. You are dangerously close to being forsworn.'

'These vampyrs do not act of their own accord, so I cannot be held responsible for their actions. But my team and I will clear the mansion of any of them that remain.' He flashed a dark grin. 'Then we will hunt for the necromancer,' he said with relish.

'Leave her alive,' I demanded. 'I need her blood.'

'I do not answer to you. What I do with her is clan business.' With that, he stepped back into a narrow shadow and slunk away.

'Well, that's the vampyrs dealt with,' I said optimistically. 'Now we just have to sort out the rival werewolf pack camped on our lawn.'

'Easy,' Greg quipped.

'People are going to die if we meet them on the field.'

'What do you suggest?'

'That I challenge Frost one on one. Winner takes all.'

'And if you lose?'

'I die. But I don't intend to lose.'

He pulled me into his arms. 'I can't lose you. Fight hard, Esme.'

I always fight hard, she retorted.

'She'll kick ass,' I promised.

'Beckett might not agree,' Greg warned. 'He's got numbers on his side, and his wolves are trained to be fighters almost from the cradle. If we do have to face them on the field, it won't end well for us.'

'Our wolves are connected to their humans now. We're far stronger than we've ever been. Voltaire has dealt with the vampyrs, so we can use the Forge on the battlefield. That levels things up a bit.'

'You know Beckett's not going to fight fair,' Greg argued. 'Even if he agrees to a one-on-one challenge, he'll break the rules.'

'I expect so – it's in his character. But what can I do? If he accepts one-on-one combat, it would save lives.'

'You are entirely too honourable.'

'It is what it is. Can you gather all the wolves that want to fight into the hall? I'll check on Amber, and make sure she's okay after the vampyr attack.'

I popped my head into my living room. 'Everyone alright in here?'

My room looked like a tornado had hit it. Reynard was bleeding from a cut on his leg, and. there were three piles of ash. Lovely. 'I'm glad you recruited an assassin,' the gargoyle admitted.

'Me too,' I agreed, looking at the destruction. In the centre of it all, in the middle of a large pentagram, was Amber. She was painting runes as intricate as Indian henna paintings in each triangle. Only three of the five wings of the pentagram were filled. 'You're not ready, huh?' I asked.

She glared at me. 'Obviously not.'

'Right you are. I'll go and stall for a bit.' I needed to get us some time, and if that meant fighting Beckett Frost then so be it.

'I need twenty minutes at least.'

'Roger,' I said.

Her name is Amber, Esme reminded me.

I giggled, and Amber raised a questioning eyebrow. 'It's just Esme being Esme. I'll leave you to it.'

'Do you need me on the field?' Bastion asked. He looked loose and limber; killing the vampyrs had re-invigorated him and chased away the shadows on his face.

I considered. To be honest, I wanted him by my side; I was far less likely to die with Bastion next to me. But the greater good said... 'No. Keep Amber safe.'

'I'll come with you,' Reynard offered.

I smiled at him. He was a gargoyle, not a warrior, but he'd stand with me against the coming horde. 'Thank you. I'd like that.'

'I'll come too,' the female gargoyle said abruptly. The remaining gargoyles exchanged glances and sighed. As one, they stood; at least it looked like I'd got some gargoyles on my side.

I pulled out my phone and sent a quick text to my mum to say I loved her; if this was going to be the end, I wanted her to know that. Then I pocketed the phone again and fixed the redheaded witch with a smile. 'You can do it. I'll see you on the other side.'

'Stay alive, so we can get that drink,' Amber retorted.

'Deal.'

I walked out with the gargoyles on my heels. Clustering in the hallway were the members of my pack that felt ready to fight, forty in total. The others were in the basement ready to protect the pups, a last defence that I prayed we wouldn't need.

I manoeuvred my way through my people – my pack – to the front door and turned to address them. I felt the need to say something rousing but I hadn't got any speeches prepared for a hostile invasion. I tried my best anyway and channelled my inner Winston Churchill for the second time recently – well, I cinched the white robe around me – Winston Churchill on a spa day maybe. I made sure to meet the wolves' eyes as I spoke. Archie, Noah, Elena, David, Seren, hell – even Tristan was there – were going to risk their lives for me. It had better be a damned good speech.

'Beckett Frost comes here with his pack under false pretences. They say they're here to help retrieve Thea, but Thea doesn't want to be retrieved. She isn't a hostage here; she's a member of our pack and our community. Frost is talking shit, lying about his reasons for his invasion. He's coming with violence in mind, planning to use us as an example to instil fear in other packs and to take our wealth. For all he can shout at the top of his lungs about his altruistic motives, we know that he has none. He comes here to bring death and destruction – but he will not find the quiet little pack he is expecting. We will fight him, we will harry him, we will resist him with every fibre of our being until he is dead or gone.'

The pack erupted into cheers and shouting. Energy sizzled in the hallway.

'We are stronger and far faster than he knows,' I concluded. 'We are bound to our wolves. Trust your wolf and let's end this. Shift on my command and not before. Let's go!'

Chapter 22

I turned to open the huge door, but Greg reached out a hand to stop me. 'Watch Beckett's eyes,' he murmured. 'Even in wolf form, most people betray where they're going next with their eyes. Let him attack and hold your energy in reserve.'

Tell him this isn't our first rodeo, Esme said dismissively.

I smiled at her vernacular; she was learning. *He is scared for us,* I said softly.

What use is fear? We will fight, and we will win.

Or we'll die.

At which point we won't care, she pointed out philosophically.

True enough. I bucked up my ideas. Esme was kick-ass, we trusted each other, we would win. Probably. And if we lost, Greg would surely avenge me and kill Beckett, so ultimately I'd win anyway. One way or another. Though frankly, I had a preference.

'We'll be okay. I love you.' I gave Greg a long kiss and prayed it wouldn't be our last.

We had no more time. No more delays. It was showtime.

I pulled open the heavy door and marched my people out to meet the intruders. We walked out human, but on the other side only Frost was still human. He smirked, malicious joy shining in his eyes as he took us all in. He thought he'd slaughter us before we could even turn.

Fuck you, Frost. Let him see what we could do. 'Shift!' I ordered.

Forty humans shifted as one to become forty wolves. Beckett's smile slid from his face, and his pack was visibly shaken. They exchanged glances and some of them even stepped back.

Ha! Not such an easy target now, were we?

Voltaire phased out of the shadows. 'All of the vampyrs are dead,' he announced loudly. He may not have been on my side per se, but it seemed he was throwing me a bone.

The rival wolves shrank back further, slinking lower. We were not the beaten-up targets they'd been expecting.

Voltaire gave me a nod then phased into a shadow and disappeared off to hunt Mrs Dawes.

My front door opened and this time my family, the fire elementals, came out. Pride roared in my heart that they were here, standing with me. Of course, they were all dressed in black; what else would anyone wear in this realm? They marched out with military precision and formed a line behind us. One by one, they called fireballs into their hands in an impressive pyrotechnic Mexican wave. They knew all about intimidation.

'The Forge stands ready,' Maxwell announced in a hard voice.

'Scrounging around for allies?' Beckett Frost mocked with a hard smile, but his wolves around him shifted uneasily.

'Not just allies,' I said calmly. 'Family. I'm Luciana Alessandro.'

The smile vanished from his face. 'Impossible,' he snarled. 'Luciana died. They all died. Father ordered it, and I made sure of it. We're not having a queen bitch rule us.'

The world slowed and stopped. The Frosts? The Frosts were behind my parent's murder?

I saw red and reason fled. 'I'm going to kill you,' I announced. I didn't recognise my own voice. It was harsh and low; it was a promise of violence that I meant with all my heart.

For the first time, I truly let Esme have carte blanche. No qualifiers, no 'please don't maim or kill'; I gave her the freedom to destroy him any way she thought fit, any way we could.

We shifted and she took front and centre, but I stayed as present as I could. A dim part of me recalled that I was supposed to challenge Beckett one on one, but that moment was gone. We wanted blood to spill.

Esme charged towards him on four legs. The scents of enemy wolves filled the air and she growled, then howled to our pack, ordering them to bring pain to the interlopers. Answering howls rang out and we attacked – but we didn't attack alone. A whinny rang in the air as Ares waded in, white mane gleaming, clawed feet ready for death and destruction. His eyes gleamed with the thrill of battle.

The Forge had lost their battle line; perhaps that had been Beckett's purpose all along. They were acting emotionally, out of grief for Luca and Maria. A part of me knew that I should try and rein them in, but I was lost too. I was riding a wave of sadness and rage so strong that it took my breath away. A lifetime of resentment had bubbled up and destroyed any clarity I might have had.

Frost had destroyed my family. He had ruined my chance to be raised with a father who taught me to ride my bike, with a mother who had my smile. My adoptive parents were wonderful and I loved them with all my heart, but that didn't diminish the pain I felt at the loss of my birth family.

As Esme and I ran towards Beckett, everything faded away but our objective. His wolves leapt in the way, stalling for him as he took precious time to shift, but Esme howled our fury and ripped into those that dared to stand between us and justice.

Another day I would have begged her to be careful as we fought, but today I egged her on. I felt nothing as she ripped away an attacker's throat. Moments later the body shifted to human and a woman lay on the ground, her eyes hard and glassy. I didn't feel anything. There was no time or inclination for regret. We waded on.

Ares reared up, slamming into the invaders with his wickedly sharp claws. He disembowelled a wolf that was attacking us and cleared the way to Frost. The bastard was already on four. Although Esme is a large wolf, he was huge and he dwarfed us with his solid muscle mass. But that meant he was heavy, too, and he would tire faster than us.

Esme slammed into him and bounced off like she'd hit rock. He snarled, and in our mind's eye we could see his human smirking over us. I needed him to know what I thought of him.

I reached out with my piping magic and connected my mind to his. Unlike every other werewolf I had met, the dominant voice was the wolf. The human felt – supressed, somehow. It didn't matter. Human or wolf, he'd been responsible for my parents' deaths.

You killed my parents! I screamed into his mind. He lost his footing for a second, surprised by the mental screech. Esme used her advantage to slam into him and force him to the ground, but he was back on all fours before she could rip into him.

I did, he gloated. **With my own claws.**

You're lying. You hired a dryad assassin.

Oh, that too. Father's orders were clear. There was a prophecy in the works, announcing a girl – you – as a future ruler of the werewolves. It was an absurdity, of course, because back then you were a fire elemental. It was clearly bullshit but, bullshit or not, Father said it was best to act. He wanted to hire someone to give us a layer of deniability – but why let an assassin have all the fun? The dryad used the trees around it to capture your parents and hold them still while I ripped their stomachs out. I had to move quickly – I couldn't risk them using their fire against me. But they struggled to concentrate with their guts pouring on the ground.

Whether it was real or in my imagination, a picture rose in my mind of my mother weeping and my dad roaring with futile anger, both of them held against a tree by its branches. The blood, oh God the blood, gushing out of them...

Such a slow way to die, Beckett gloated, as we circled each other.

Everything faded away but me and Frost. *And yet I lived. Not so smart there, were you?* I flung out.

The dryad was supposed to finish the job. He told me you were dead and presented me with your death certificate. I will punish him for his failings, he growled.

Presumably the dryad had accepted my grandfather's forged death certificate at face value. Great-great-etc-grandfather truly *had* saved my life that day.

A flash nearby distracted me momentarily. Greg had shifted into human form right next to me. 'We need you, Lucy! We can't fight them *and* the dead. Pipe his wolves!' he shouted. The dead? What was he talking about?

Just like that, my tunnel vision ended and noise was restored like a switch had been flipped. Growls and whimpers rang out, and death carried on the air. The battlefield was a bloody mess.

And the dead were rising.

Chapter 23

Mrs Dawes! I gasped to Esme. *What has she done?*

All around us, dead bodies were being re-animated; it seemed that her necromantic arts weren't restricted just to vampyrs. The dead moved with the same jerky movements of the possessed vampyrs. The werewolves' dead bodies were twisted, their hands partially shifted back to wolf form so that they had deadly claws for arms. And the other thing was that they were dead. No matter how much my wolves ripped into them, they would keep on coming.

How could I have missed that possibility? God, what was *wrong* with me?

She's a helpful lady, your housekeeper, Frost mocked. **She's been trying to capture the essence of immortality for years by playing with those vampyr pricks, and she's going to grant my pack immortality.**

We will finally be a force to be reckoned with. My pack will be elevated above all others, and yours will be so much dust. It turns out Mrs Dawes has got a real beef with you.

Me? What did I do, except be friendly? Did I demand too many tubs of Ben and Jerry's? Because that was *not* a reason to go raising freaking zombies.

She's toying with you, I argued. *She can't grant you immortality. She's a necromancer – she works with the dead, not the living.*

She is nearly two hundred years old. She's been under your nose this whole time, and you still don't know what she is capable of. She was one of the original witches to curse the golden-eyed wolves. She even persuaded weak Lord Samuel to turn her wolf, even though it was against the rules. She thought it would give her access to the Great Pack, but she didn't realise that the curse had silenced them. He laughed. **And she worked with Ace when he was here. She drugged little Archie so he could be sliced and diced. And now she's working with *me*.**

He was trying to goad me, and it was working. He was diverting my attention from the real matter at hand – the zombies. But if what he said about what she'd done to Archie was true, the knowledge would kill him. Mrs Dawes had pretty much raised him since his own mother had absconded to France. That she had deliberately tried to harm him was almost unthinkable. What kind of monster was she? And how had she hidden her true nature for so long?

I heard a *whump-whump* sound and I looked up. My heart leapt. On the horizon was a red dragon with magnificent golden wings. Emory? Jess? Help was coming. I just needed to keep going, and focus.

FOCUS, Esme yelled at me.

Beckett was trying to distract me, and he'd been succeeding nicely. I was failing my pack, but not any more.

I let Esme take full control once again; I hadn't even realised that I'd wrestled control from her. I dropped to the backseat where I wouldn't distract her as much. *Sorry,* I breathed to her.

I felt her acknowledgment but all of her energies were concentrated elsewhere – on Beckett Frost.

I reached out with my piping magic to the wolves around me that weren't mine. *This is not the way,* I said firmly. It was hard to influence so many at once; if I'd been touching them, I had no doubt I could control them, but controlling only one or two of the enemy would solve nothing. I needed all of Beckett's pack to withdraw. *We are all wolves. We should be together, as one. We should be part of the Great Pack.*

I felt a ripple go through the attacking wolves' minds like a shocked gasp, and they paused. I pressed my advantage. *Beckett is not a true alpha. He should not lead you with fear*

*and violence. Pack is family. He is supposed to be your leader,
not your tormentor. Remember the tales of the Great Pack?
He has twisted what you should be. Stand down.*

They hesitated and paused, and the lull in the battle gave
me a surge of victory.

ATTACK! Beckett barked fiercely, his teeth bared in
threat. A lifetime of fear galvanised his pack and snapped
my tenuous link. Once again, they leapt forward at his
command.

I was struggling to reach out to them again when a
shockwave radiated out from the mansion. Pain exploded
between my eyes, and then Esme and I felt it: a presence,
huge and overwhelming. It was not Emory but something
else – not a one but many.

I stretched out with my piping sense, and for the first
time I connected to the Great Pack.

Welcome, Lucy, they greeted me. ***It is time to end
this. This is not the way of the Pack.***

How do I end it?

Command it to be done.

And why should they listen?

Because we order it. The voice was one and many, and
the weight of all those minds pressing down nearly made
me faint. Then, just as I was at breaking point, the presence
was gone and I was back battling for my life.

The curse had started to lift; the wolves were reconnect-
ed to the Great Pack, and now *all* the human counterparts

were connected to their wolves, not just my pack. It was a shame that our advantage had been so fleeting.

STOP! I ordered Frost's wolves again, this time reaching out to the human minds around me. *This is not the way. Speak with your wolves.*

Around me, the invading wolves did exactly that and one by one they froze. In a blink, they shifted back to human. Naked and confused, they huddled together and pulled away from the fight. My wolves let them withdraw.

There was still a danger left: the dead. The broken curse had not affected them a jot. The dead still came. The Forge were doing their best, but exhaustion was setting in and the flames were growing weaker. The dead were flambéed, but they still weren't stopping. We needed a cremation, not a sauté.

'Get out of the way!' Jess shouted from above.

I realised her intention straight away, as did Esme. Canine or not, she was a smart cookie.

Fall back to the mansion! Esme ordered our wolves. **Now!**

Our wolves turned and ran to the mansion, leaving the stumbling dead to chase them. Emory's great wings stirred up the air around us, and then he roared. It was like he was breathing a giant flamethrower. He directed his breath at the handful of undead still on the field, and in moments they were so much burnt ash.

Beckett Frost was a lot of things, but a realist wasn't one of them. He refused to accept defeat. **Attack!** he roared again at his now-human wolves. No one moved towards him; if anything, they stepped back.

You have lost the way. Stand down or die. The Great Pack addressed Frost, or rather his wolf.

Fuck you! he snarled.

Die then, the Great Pack said indifferently. It reached out and wrenched Frost's wolf from him, extinguishing it and forcing him to shift to human.

'No!' he shouted, eyes mad and feverish. 'You can't stop me! I'm a Frost! I will be the alpha that conquers all.' He picked up one of the clawed limbs of the dead and ran toward us, using it to swipe at us, but in human form he didn't stand a chance.

Esme leapt at him and threw him to the ground. With his footing lost, Frost's eyes flashed with fear at what he knew was coming. For once, I didn't care. He had killed my parents, and I bet they'd been scared at the end, too.

Esme didn't hesitate and I didn't try to stop her. She clamped our jaws around the soft underside of Beckett's throat and, with one harsh movement, she ripped it out. Hot, coppery blood filled our mouth and Esme's satisfaction rolled over us. Our victory was complete. Revenge tasted just fine to me.

Esme threw our head back and howled our triumph to the assembled wolves.

All the werewolves, in human and in wolf form, bowed to us.

Chapter 24

Something was happening to the gargoyles. The shock-wave that had ripped through us was still riding through them, and they rose in the air, wings extended.

I bypassed Esme and reached out directly to the Great Pack. *Can they be saved?*

The curse is being leached from them. A great magic is being torn from them. Without something to replace it, they will die.

What can we replace it with?

There was only silence and regret. The Great Pack was not *all* knowing, it seemed.

Emory was in human form, and it gave me an idea. I shifted into human. 'You're the Prime Elite, yes? King of a bunch of creatures, including the gargoyles?'

'Yes,' he admitted, watching the gargoyles in the air sadly.

'Then command them. Give them an order, a geas or something! They need some great magic to replace the curse that's being ripped away or they'll die. All of them. Do something...'

'There is one magic ... but it is forbidden,' he said slowly.

'You can't let them all die. Please, Emory, there are hundreds of them in the world. You can't let them all die. Please, if there's something you can do, do it.'

He turned to Jess with his eyebrows raised. 'There'll be consequences,' he said softly to her.

'Can you save them?' she asked.

'I think so. I've never tried this magic, but I've heard tales.'

'If you can, then you've got to try,' she said. 'They're your people. They bowed to you in order to have a protector from the vampyrs, but you are more than that to them now – you're their Prime Elite. It is your duty to save them, whatever the cost.' Jess has always had a strong moral compass and I held my breath, praying she could persuade him to do the right thing.

He nodded decisively. 'Then so mote it be.' He shifted again into dragon form. With a couple of flaps of his mighty wings, he was level with the gargoyles. He breathed upon them, not with flames but something else that swirled around them like a kaleidoscope of stars.

Suddenly the lights struck the suspended gargoyles, and as one they cried out – but it wasn't the sound of a few voices but of hundreds. The stars whirled faster and faster until they sank into the gargoyles' very beings.

With one final flash of light, it was done. The gargoyles gently fluttered down, the night sky still contained within their skin. Their wings were changed; no longer grey and scaley, they were feathered black. As we watched, their skin lost its grey pallor and their forms became humanoid again.

Reynard landed softly on the ground, looking like the French alpha I had met when I'd travelled back in time. There was no trace of the two hundred years he had lived since then, save for the addition of his newly feathered wings.

Emory's emerald eyes rolled back into his great head, and he fell from the skies.

'Emory!' Jess screamed, her hands extended. 'Slow,' she barked out, using the IR to command the air around him to slow his descent. He still landed hard upon the ground, but hopefully no bones had been crushed.

Jess ran to him and knelt next to him. She checked him over anxiously. 'He's okay,' she called to me. 'Just passed out.'

Amber and Bastion ran out of the house, the witch carrying her black bag over one shoulder. Hopefully it was full of healing supplies because God knows, we needed them. She took one look at the stars whirling under the gargoyles' human skin and paled. 'What did you do?' she demanded harshly of the unconscious dragon.

Greg was back on two legs, naked and unabashed. 'He made them brethren,' he breathed.

'I thought brethren were born – offspring from dragons that didn't become dragons themselves?' I queried.

'That's one way to become brethren. Making brethren like this has been outlawed for centuries.'

'Why?'

'This way, it makes the brethren almost fanatically loyal, or so the old stories say. The dragon council decided it was wrong because that was in the days where free will was particularly in vogue with the philosophers. They argued that this level of brethren creation took away free will because it creates such devotion to the dragon who makes them. It's been outlawed for centuries.'

'Will he get in trouble for this?' I asked. 'I mean, he's the Prime Elite, right? He should be able to get away with murder.'

'Murder maybe, but this?' Greg shook his head slowly. 'The elders are not going to be happy. When brethren-making was outlawed, the elders had to sacrifice the brethrens that they'd made. It's going to cause waves.'

'He knows how to ride them,' Jess murmured. 'We'll deal with what comes. We always do.'

'Enough. This isn't urgent,' Amber snapped. 'Where are the most badly wounded?'

The field was a mess. The dead had been burnt to a cinder, courtesy of Emory, but blood and ash was sprayed across my lawn. David's roses were blackened and dead. Each side had pulled back its wounded, and a wide distance separated us.

'Who's hurt?' I shouted loudly to the gathered assembly. No one moved. 'Don't be coy! Who is hurt?' I repeated.

'My leg's hurt pretty badly,' David admitted. He had an arm around Daniella and he was leaning on her heavily. She helped him sit down, then started bandaging the gaping wound using the first-aid kit that always sat in the entrance hall. It seemed like a waste of time to me: a good shift or a handy rune from Amber, and he'd be right as rain, but I guessed Daniella's nurse's instincts were too strong to ignore.

'My arm,' Seren called out. 'But it's starting to heal.'

'Noah!' Noah's mum, Sally, screamed. 'Over here! Noah! Oh my God. He's not healing. Quickly!'

As Amber bolted over, she pulled out her paintbrush. I saw her smile reassuringly at Noah, and that scared me more than anything. I joined her, an eyebrow raised in question, and she gave the barest shake of her head.

Sally saw the shake too. 'George,' she called, her voice cracking. 'Get over here.' She sank down next to Noah and took his hand in hers. 'There now, the witch will make it all better. A few runes and you'll be right as rain.'

'Hurts.'

'This will help,' Amber said briskly, painting a rune on his hand.

The lines eased from his face. 'Better,' he agreed. He looked strange to me, and that's when I realised his forehead was unmarked. He had expended too much magical energy and had been sent back to the Common realm. It was shitty timing; without the Other, he couldn't shift and heal.

George ran over, and I saw the query in his eyes as he looked at Sally. She shook her head as Amber had. George's nostrils flared and his jaw tightened, then he also sank to the ground next to his son. He held Noah's hand. 'All right, son. You'll be all right soon,' he lied gently.

I jerked my head at Amber, and she followed me a few paces away. 'Is there nothing that we can do?' I whispered.

'Only a shift would save him now,' she murmured. 'Runes rely on his innate magic to kickstart his healing. If you look at his forehead, you can see he's been booted into Common. He can't shift.'

'Maybe I can force a shift.' I returned hastily to Noah's side. I'd done it once before with Archie – but Archie hadn't been in Common.

I reached out to Noah's wolf with my piping skills but there was an impregnable wall that my magic couldn't get around or through. In desperation, I reached out to the Great Pack again. *He's in Common, but he's dying. He needs to shift. Can you reach his wolf?*

If we were to reach his wolf, it would die in the shift. It cannot survive in Common.

But if we do nothing, he will die anyway.

No, the human will die. The wolf will return to the Great Pack.

He won't return if he does this?

No. He will be lost forever. You ask too much. There was a sound like a murmur of a hundred voices whispering. Finally it stopped. **We will give him the choice.**

There was a long and painful moment's silence whilst I watched Noah's chest rise and fall. Sally was looking at me, hope in her eyes. I closed my eyes so I couldn't see it.

I felt another mind touch mine; I was being pulled forward by the Great Pack, by Noah's wolf. **I will do as you bid, Alpha,** he said firmly.

You will die, I admitted softly.

Yes, but Noah will not. He is a kind person, far gentler than me. The realms are better for his presence. He is young and he deserves to have time.

What is your name?

We named me Roan in the short time that we were truly as one.

I had a lump in my throat. I'd had Esme for months to talk to, to laugh with, and Noah and Roan had had so little time together. It wasn't fair. Yet still Roan would sacrifice himself for Noah. *We will remember you, Roan, and your sacrifice.*

What is fame to a wolf? he asked indifferently.

It is all I can offer.

No. You can offer to protect Noah, to see that he flourishes.

I will do all that I can to ensure that he does, I promised.

Then it is done. My honour to meet you, Alpha.

My honour to meet you, Roan. His quiet dignity touched me. I felt awful for asking him to sacrifice his life for Noah's. Why did a human life have more value?

But it was too late. I opened my eyes to see Noah snap into wolf form. Roan opened his eyes. 'Quickly!' I said to Amber. 'Heal him!'

'How is that possible?'

'It doesn't matter how, just hurry. The shift will help, but Noah will need more than that to see him safe. I won't let Roan's sacrifice be in vain.'

Amber pulled a jar out of her bag and opened it, then hastily dabbed her brush in it and started painting runes on any bit of fur she could reach. There wasn't much; Noah's body – Roan's body – had been ripped and rent in a truly horrific way. But as we all watched with bated breath, the wounds began to close and heal.

Sally started to sob; George had tears in his eyes. It felt like the whole pack were holding their breath.

Another beat passed and for a second Roan's coat was luminescent, then the light faded. When it was gone, Noah was there: human, whole and safe. George started to sob too as the small family clung to each other. Noah accepted their hugs, but his face was ashen. 'Roan,' he breathed in a heartbroken whisper.

I hugged Esme to me fiercely, frantically. *Nothing will separate us,* I vowed.

Nothing, she agreed, clinging to me just as desperately.

Greg touched my shoulder lightly. 'We have a problem.'

I blinked away my own tears and the overwhelming guilt. I couldn't help but feel like I'd made the wrong choice but if we had a problem, now wasn't the time to deal with my churning grief. I stifled a sigh and Greg and I stepped away from the emotional family. 'What?'

'Do you remember that when Ares was hurt, Mrs Dawes helped him?'

Now I sighed aloud. 'Yes. She said her witchy friend had taught her some runes.' Mrs Dawes' deception was all too obvious now. Hindsight is such a bitch.

'For witches, unicorn blood and horn are vital ingredients.'

'Yeah? So?'

'Ares is missing.'

'What do you mean, he's missing? He was just here.' I looked around frantically for those familiar blood-red eyes.

'Exactly,' Greg said grimly. 'I've been doing a quick roll call to see who's fallen in the battle. Ares was here and now he's not. But he was just by me, and he definitely didn't die.'

'Who did we lose?' I asked. I should have asked that question sooner but I'd dreaded the answer.

'Most of the dead were Beckett's. Their hearts weren't in the battle like ours. But we did lose a couple.'

'Who?'

'Brian and Cassie.'

'Dammit.' My heart clenched. They were dead because of me. Cassie had been vibrant and vivacious, a real force of nature. She wasn't an easy person to get on with, but she'd been through the mill. She'd lost her ex-husband, whom she'd never really gotten over, and she'd never had the children that she dreamed of. Now she never would.

Brian had never liked me, but that didn't mean I didn't feel awful at his passing. I was responsible for it; I would never forget that, or the sense of heavy responsibility. Never before had calling myself alpha meant so much, but it was a hard lesson to learn.

'We need to find Ares,' Greg said, ruining my moment of introspection. There was no time for regret. We weren't done.

'You think Mrs Dawes has him,' I said flatly.

'Yes, I do. She had to be close to reanimate the dead like that. She's on our grounds somewhere.'

Fuck.

Chapter 25

'Try and locate Ares,' I said briskly. 'Check the security footage. I need to speak to Frost's wolves, then I'll be right with you.'

Greg hesitated. 'I'll come with you first.'

'No, find Ares. Beckett's pack won't give me any trouble.' I hoped I was right. They were sitting on the other side of our huge lawn, but they'd made no effort to leave. I grabbed a robe from inside the house and strode across the ground to meet them.

'Hello,' I said as I neared them.

I was greeted with a chorus: 'Alpha.' My mind went blank, then cleared. Of course I was their alpha: I'd killed Frost, though I hadn't thought of that in the moment, I'd thought only of revenge. Not the worthiest of motives.

'I'm Lucy,' I said. 'Nice to meet you all. Is anyone badly injured?'

There was murmuring amongst them, then a young lad was shoved forward. 'We have a few that are hurt.'

'Okay. Well, welcome to my pack. Let's get you all sorted. Take the injured to that witch over there. That's Amber DeLea, and she's going to help you.'

They stood slowly and started to follow me back across the grass, looking at me cautiously like they expected me to explode.

Thea pelted towards me. 'Xander!' she shouted.

'Thea!' A young man ran across the remaining space between them and pulled her into his arms, nudity be damned. 'Baby girl, don't you run off in the dead of night like that ever again!'

'It wasn't exactly my choice,' she grumped. 'Beckett grabbed me out of my bed.' Xander gave a low growl. 'It's okay! He didn't hurt me – and he sent me to Lucy. Come and meet her.' She pulled him over, smiling, her body relaxed for the first time since I'd met her.

I gave a finger wave and a smile. 'Hi.'

He touched his hand to his heart, dropped to one knee and bowed his head. 'My honour to meet you, Alpha.'

Thea grabbed him by his elbow and pulled him up. 'Get up, she's not like that. She doesn't want any grovelling.' She turned to me. 'Do you?'

I smiled. 'No. This is a grovel-free zone.'

I quite like the grovelling, Esme objected.

Shush, you. We're being welcoming.

Ah. Is that what we're being? She sounded amused.

'My honour to meet you Xander. You're a friend of Thea's?'

Xander hesitated as he stood up. 'As much as I could be,' he admitted unhappily.

'Beckett didn't like anyone talking to me,' Thea explained. 'Xander would sneak down to see me sometimes. We've been friends since we were pups, and he never abandoned me even when I lost my wolf.'

Xander shot her an alarmed look, like she shouldn't be talking about her inability to shift.

'It's good,' Thea reassured him loudly. 'Lucy fixed it. I can shift again.' Murmurs and gasps ran through the Devon pack. Thea swallowed. 'Actually, my wolf named herself Sophie.'

Xander's eyes softened. 'Sophie?' He took a sharp breath and tears sparkled in his eyes before he blinked them away. 'That's nice. She would have loved that.' He saw my questioning look. 'Sophie was my mother. Frost killed her when we were young.'

'I'm so sorry.'

'Yeah, me too. You can see why I'm not shedding any tears over you killing him.'

'Indeed. Will there be tears from anyone present?' I asked softly for his and Thea's ears alone.

'A few,' Xander murmured, equally softly. His eyes lingered on a couple of muscley-looking men towards the front.

'Keep your eyes on them,' I instructed Xander. 'There are other matters that require my attention just now, but I'll need a full debrief when we have time.' Me, using words like 'debrief'? Spending time with Greg had rubbed off on me.

'Yes, Alpha.' He bristled to attention.

I bit back a sigh; I suspected it would take a long while for the new wolves to stop looking at me without fear. But I'd got there with Thea, and I could do it again.

I looked at the throng of people behind Xander. There were thirty people joining me, and probably more waiting for me in Devon. Life was never boring since I'd become a werewolf. I decided I needed to address the new group before starting the hunt for Ares, so I strode over to them.

'Hi, everyone. My name is Lucy, and I killed Beckett Frost. This makes me your new alpha. I'm much nicer than he was.' I smiled and met the eyes of a couple of the wolves that Xander had pegged as Beckett's supporters.

'He could be charming,' an older woman called out from the back.

'No doubt,' I agreed. I'd heard that Hitler was charismatic.

'Charming, but deadly. You're charming, too,' the woman continued. The rest of the sentence hung in the air, so I said it for her.

'And deadly too.' My smile faded and I gave the whole pack a long stare. I let the moment draw out so that they felt the threat. Coming from an environment like Beckett Frost's, I couldn't allow them to think that I was weak. I would adjust their attitudes towards pack life, but it had to be done delicately.

I smiled again. 'But mostly, I'm nice. I really only kill people that threaten my pack, so I'm sure we'll all get along famously.' My eyes lingered on the two men that Xander had picked out; they knew that I had their measure. 'My pack recently completed a tourney, so for now you will join unranked. We'll get to know each other a little better and then, when the time is right, I'll call another tourney.'

There were a few disgruntled looks but nobody spoke out against my pronouncement. Nobody likes to remain unranked in a pack where rank determines your role, pride and position, but I wasn't going to risk some of the new pack wolves entering my battle core before I knew who they were and if they could be trusted.

I raised my voice and looked at my own pack to make sure they knew that they were included in what I said next. 'Today we broke the curse that has lingered over the werewolves for centuries. You will feel your wolf in a way that you've never felt before. Talk to your wolf, get to know each other. Through them, you now have access to the Great Pack, and through the Great Pack you can communicate with any other werewolf. If you find yourself alone and under attack, your wolf can send an alert to any other wolf close by. With our link to our wolves restored, and through them our link to the Great Pack, times are going to change for the werewolves. We are no longer going to be second-class citizens in the Other realm, half on the human side, half on the creature side, embraced by no one. With the curse lifted, we are once more a force to be reckoned with.'

My pack broke into whoops and cheers. Frost's wolves looked encouraged, but none of them visibly celebrated the changes that I proposed. It would take time to amalgamate the two packs – but I had time, and I would use it wisely.

As I looked at my pack, I noted that Greg must have released the pups from the basement. Marissa was sitting next to Seren, her arm around her, her gaze defiant, daring anyone to comment on the clear affection between them. Seren looked decidedly smug. Bobby ran out to stand by a tired and mucky Sonia. Elena was handing out jogging bottoms to our pack. I met her eyes and tilted my head towards the other pack. She grimaced a little, but nodded and started passing them clothes as well.

As soon as they were clothed, the two men who'd been glaring at me started to walk off the grounds. **We should**

kill them, Esme advised, but there was a sigh in her voice. She knew I wouldn't go for it; time was pressing and our priority had to be to find Ares and Mrs Dawes.

We need to find Mrs Dawes. Let them go lone.

They'll be back.

And we'll be ready for them, I said confidently.

David's leg was healed and Amber had moved on to her next patient. 'Are you okay?' I asked him.

He beamed at me. 'I'll be just fine, Alpha, thank you,' he said, polishing his glasses on his top. I wondered how many spare sets of glasses he had squirreled away. It was even funnier when you considered that his eyesight was perfect as a result of the change, and his glasses were made with plain lenses.

'Can you help with food?' I asked the former loner Finley as my tummy gave a vicious growl.

'Of course,' the chef agreed. 'I'll get right on it.' He straightened and strode off purposefully. There was another man who was beginning to find his way in our pack.

Normally, I wouldn't have to ask someone to sort out food because Mrs Dawes would have been there handing out biscuits before I even thought of it. Damn it. How could she be the black witch?

I realised that I was stalling. A part of me – a large part of me – didn't want to find her, to believe that her betrayal was real. Time to put on my big girl panties. I was in charge of even more people now and I couldn't hide because I didn't like something. It was time to face the music – even if it was loud, screamy, rock music.

Heart pounding and feeling sick, I stretched my senses out to search for the duplicitous necromancer.

Chapter 26

You must stop the witch. NOW! the Great Pack's choral voice called urgently. I could feel their fear, and it scared me shitless.

I'm trying, I responded shortly, continuing to stretch out my piping magic. I sent it wide, hoping to collide with Mrs Dawes' familiar mind, but I encountered nothing. It was hard skimming over all the new packmates, all of whom were unfamiliar to my magic, and I struggled to discern who was who. But no one felt like Mrs Dawes.

In frustration – and desperation – I sent my senses out to the woods. I didn't find Mrs Dawes, but I did find the trees, and they were anxious, upset. A feeling of abhorrence was rising in them, like their bark was crawling. Something unspeakable was occurring in the woods, and my money was on a spot of necromancy.

The black witch – Mrs Dawes – had made it so that Bobby and the other kids couldn't be scried. I guess she had a few other tricks up her sleeve after two centuries that would make my magic skim over her like a pebble on a still lake. Too bad she didn't know I could commune with trees.

I thanked them for their insight and snapped back to my body. When I'd been searching, I'd felt Greg in my office, so I ran in to him. I didn't bother dressing because I knew I'd be shifting again soon.

'You got anything?' I asked.

He ran a hand through his hair in frustration. 'Nothing. She's not anywhere on camera.'

'She knows where the cameras are,' I pointed out. 'She's not stupid.'

'No. She's not stupid,' he admitted grudgingly.

'I think I know where she is – and the Great Pack says we need to hurry.'

He didn't question me, he simply stood up from his desk. 'Then let's go.' He was dressed, not just in clothes, but with weapons. He had two guns – that I could see – and a few knives.

'Let's take some back-up,' I suggested.

He flashed me a grin. 'You're learning.'

'Even the most hard-headed of us get the idea eventually.'

'It's not about being hard-headed, it's about learning to trust the team around you. Who are we taking?'

'Archie, Liam and Maxwell?' I suggested. Jess was still tending to an unconscious Emory, and I didn't want to take her away from him. I hesitated a moment. 'Tristan, too.' Tristan was my third; my continued failure to treat him as such would cause an issue if I didn't make a conscious effort to get over my mistrust of him.

'Not bad,' he said about my proposed line-up. 'But let's take Amber and Bastion as well.'

'I'm not sure if Amber is done healing people.'

'Most of the wounds were either deadly or flesh wounds. The flesh wounds will heal by themselves.'

I grimaced. 'And the deadly wounds have done their job,' I said balefully.

'Exactly. Let's see what she's up to.'

Noah was looking pale and haunted. Sally hovered behind him, touching him frequently like she was afraid her son would disappear. Noah was ignoring her, determinedly helping David to distribute biscuits and crisps to the assembled wolves, including Frost's pack. My new pack, I corrected. It would take some major adjustments for all of us.

Amber looked tired. She was packing her supplies back into her trusty bag.

'You good to come witch hunting with us?' I asked her.

She rubbed a hand across her green eyes. 'Sure. Who needs rest?'

'Rest is for the wicked.'

'Then let's hope we catch Mrs Dawes napping,' she said darkly. She grabbed my wrist. 'Listen, I know this is going to sound crazy, but when I joined this coven there was an older witch who went by the name of Jane Dorey. When Mrs Dawes tied her hair back, she looked like Jane Dorey's twin who'd not aged a day since the last time I'd seen her. Jane disappeared and was presumed dead – there was a thing with a local vampyr clan. Anyway, none of that matters. What's important is that Jane was very anti-werewolf. I remember because she was fanatical about it. I think that Janice Dawes is Jane Dorey, and she's been using her magic to extend her life force. That's what all of this has been about. That's my theory, anyway – I know it sounds crazy.'

I shook my head. 'Not really, Frost more or less confirmed it. He said she was one of the original witches to cast the curse on the golden-eyes werewolves. He said she was more than two hundred years old.'

Amber's expression was horrified as she stared at Greg and me. 'She must have killed so many people to survive that long, Lucy. She must be stopped. At any cost.'

We exchanged grim glances, united in our dark purpose. Mrs Dawes or Mrs Dorey – whatever or whoever she was – wasn't walking out of our woods.

'Let's go,' Greg called, collaring Liam, Tristan and Archie to join us. Tristan looked at us in surprise when he got the tag, but he gave a willing nod. Whatever our differences, he was still on Team Home Counties Pack. The boys shucked off their clothes and shifted back onto four and into fur.

'To the woods.' I led the way. Tristan quickly swept ahead, and Archie and Liam brought up the rear. I caught Bastion's eye and he gave me a weary nod, tiredness wracking him once more. The boost that he'd gotten from fighting and killing the vampyrs was gone; if anything he looked worse. That was another urgent reason to catch Mrs Dawes; I was honestly not sure how long Bastion had left.

I grimaced with worry as I watched him take nearly a minute to shift; in the past, his change had always been instantaneous. Bastion didn't look at me as he took to the skies.

I shifted, too, and let Esme take control. As I reached outwards with my magic, I felt the trees' unease and let them tug us forward and guide our steps. My communion with the elder tree felt like it had happened years ago, but really it was only a matter of a few weeks. It had done something to me, given me an affinity with the trees around me and my piping magic an extra depth. Esme followed the tug of my magic, and we plunged deeper into the woods.

The woods around the mansion aren't vast, and it didn't take long for us to find Mrs Dawes – and Ares.

He was tied to the floor, trapped under ropes that were secured with wooden stakes. It was entirely too reminiscent of a certain scene with Aslan in *The Chronicles of Narnia*. My unicorn's eyes were wide with fear and rage, but his body was eerily still. I suspected the rune painted on his back was keeping him immobile.

Outrage welled up within me. I shifted onto two and darted forward. 'You bitch!' I yelled. 'Leave him alone.'

Mrs Dawes was dressed in a black cloak, straight from Victorian times. Her hair was swept back and her smile was cold, cold, cold.

'Hello, Lucy,' she crowed. 'How kind of you to join me. And thank you for giving me access to the Great Pack.' She smirked. 'Our curse all those years ago didn't go far enough. It *shielded* the Great Pack from their humans, but it didn't destroy the bloody thing. Now I can go that bit further and fix that oversight. I'm grateful to you for restoring them. I never dreamt I'd have a second chance to destroy the wolves utterly.' She smiled happily.

I stepped towards her. 'You do realise you're talking about yourself? *You're* a wolf.'

'Tisch, nonsense! My wolf is wrapped up tighter than a mummy. Now, Alpha, step back if you don't want your dear Ares to die.'

She was kneeling by his side, and she lifted her hand a little so I could see the wicked serrated knife in her hands. It was long and curved with a hook at the end, designed to pull out insides. She'd drawn a pentagram around her more complex than the one that Amber had been painstakingly painting only an hour earlier. Ares lay frozen across its centre, obscuring a good chunk of the runes.

I sent Amber a querying look. She was studying the visible runes, deciphering their meaning. 'She's going to destroy the Great Pack,' she said, aghast. 'She's trying to draw them all into the daemon realm.'

'Yes,' Janice Dawes said cheerfully. 'Let the monsters fight amongst themselves.'

Amber tried to reason with her. 'This might not just pull the Great Pack – it could drag *all* wolves *and* their human counterparts into the daemon realm. They're not monsters, they're just wolves.'

'Tell that to my mother and my father, my sister and my brother,' Mrs Dawes snapped. 'They were slaughtered by the golden-eyed ones before the curse could be wrought.'

'How old *are* you?' I asked nosily. 'Are you really two hundred years old?'

'It's rude to ask a lady's age, Lucy. Your mother raised you better than that. Suffice to say I'm older than your dear dragon, Emory. For years I've ... borrowed a little extra life force.'

'It's not borrowing,' Amber said furiously. 'It's murder. Their life for yours. It is forbidden.'

'There is power, and there are those who are too weak to seize power. And there is nothing weak about me.'

'Are you quoting Lord Voldemort? Because you know he was the bad guy, right?' I pointed out helpfully.

'You're a monster,' Amber accused Mrs Dawes, ignoring my attempt at levity.

'Grow up, Amber. I'm not the monster here, they are.' She pointed to Archie and Liam, who were still in wolf form. 'They're the ones that can turn feral in a blink and kill hundreds of innocents.'

'And how many innocents have you killed?' Amber retorted.

Mrs Dawes waved away her words. 'A handful – and they were reprobates, the lot of them. They didn't deserve life, not like I do. Look how much good I've done already. I'm a genius. I've nearly perfected the art of transferring magical energies, not extinguishing them but passing them on. I call it *ascendence.* A few more sessions with those children and I'd have had the powers of a dryad and a fire elemental.'

'And Bobby? You didn't need the powers of a werewolf because you already had them.'

'But what if I had the power of *two* werewolves? To be able to heal in a blink rather than having to shift each time to kick-start the healing powers? It was worth a try. Besides, it was so easy to take him. Poor little Bobby. With a bit of insider knowledge from me, I had James pretend to be his dad and he came nice and docilely.'

'You're evil.'

'Don't be ridiculous. I'm no more evil than you are. I'm a hero. I'm saving the Other realm, for the greater good of all. The werewolves will be crippled properly this time, the way we should have done it the first time.'

'You're a werewolf,' I pointed out desperately again. 'You'll be crippling yourself.'

She snorted. 'I'm a witch. First and foremost, I'll always be a witch. I keep my wolf tightly shackled, and she knows what will happen to her if she disobeys me. It was necessary to get myself turned – revolting, of course, but necessary. How better to acquire first-hand knowledge of the enemy than to reside in its very heart?

'I worked hard all those years as Wilfred's housekeeper, but he never let me see anything important. Finally, I took a hefty dose of iron and, when I was dying, he turned me to save me. I had deferoxamine ready in case he didn't turn me because I wasn't sure that he would. It was totally against the rules and he didn't have council permission, but he *liked* me. Everyone likes me because I'm so kind.' She winked, making my stomach turn. Every hug or kind touch had been an act.

'After my shift, Wilf never looked at me in the same way, and I think he sensed how tightly I controlled my wolf. It was a nuisance, but I couldn't have him suspect me so he had to go. It didn't take much pressure on Mark Oates to get him to start Wilfred's confrontation with Jimmy Rain.'

She looked at me proudly. 'I sent Rain a nice little poison that I'd concocted to coat his claws. I wanted to bring Rain closer to me because he's a wicked alpha, and his whole pack deserves death. I could have sprinkled a little poison in their food and they'd have been gone. But no, little Lucy had to step in and slaughter Wilfred instead.'

'I didn't slaughter him!' I objected. 'I mercy-killed him, like he asked.'

'Poh-tay-toe, poh-tah-toe. You killed him and ruined my plans. Luckily, I always have a Plan B, and Beckett Frost was such an obedient little puppet.' She laughed. 'Better than Rain – he was so easy to toy with. It's a shame you killed him because I was very close to getting him to slaughter the whole council.'

'Why didn't you kill us all with your "little sprinkling of poison"?' I asked, genuinely curious.

'I've extended my life dozens of times, not just to live on but to finish off the wolves. Killing one pack wasn't my aim – I want to destroy you all. Besides, if everyone except me died, questions would have been asked. That's the downside of this modern era. The council have photographs of us all and it makes it harder for Janice Dawes to disappear.'

'Harder than it was for Jane Dorey,' Amber added.

'Ah, you made the connection! It was silly of me to tie back my hair, but I'd forgotten that Jane always styled hers like that.' She sighed. 'It gets harder and harder to keep all these identities straight.'

'And dabbling with necromancy?' Amber accused. 'Even you must know how wrong that is.'

'A necessary evil,' Janice Dawes said dismissively. 'I'd hoped that the vampyrs had the key to immortal life, but so far the crucial rune has remained elusive. No matter, I have time. I don't need immortality, I can just keep extending my life, one ruffian at a time.'

I edged a step closer and she raised her blade. 'Now, now, Alpha. Step back, or Ares gets it.'

She suddenly looked into the distance, then laughed aloud. 'Finally,' she called out. 'You took your time. I had to keep talking until you arrived. Now, stop fighting me and embrace it.'

There was I thinking she was just being chatty, and she'd been stalling the whole time.

Voltaire and four other vampyrs stepped out of the shadows. Fuck. They moved with jerky, puppet-like movements, but Voltaire's eyes were furious unlike the blank, slack look in the eyes of the vampyrs we'd killed in the mansion. Damn it: I should have brought the Forge with me, but it had seemed like overkill for a single witch. After all, it was just nice little Mrs Dawes. I'd underestimated her and I was furious with myself.

I resisted the urge to look up to where Bastion was no doubt hiding. I hoped he could keep us alive, even in his exhausted state.

'Kill them,' Mrs Dawes ordered. She raised her knife and stabbed Ares in the stomach, pulling her blade swiftly across his belly. He screamed as his guts poured out onto the pentagram. His blood sizzled as it hit the runic drawing and, as if directed, started to run along the markings.

'Stop it from completing!' Amber screamed. 'Break the design! It's warded against anything living entering the ward. Throw stones or sticks – anything! Mar the lines!'

A vampyr ran towards her but Bastion plummeted down and the vampyr's blood sprayed across the ground before he disintegrated into dust. One down, four to go. But now the vampyrs knew about our ace in the hole.

I shifted onto four again and ran towards the design but Voltaire was already there. He phased out of the shadows and grabbed Esme's body, throwing us off course. Instinctively she leapt back at him, claws ready.

Don't kill him! I pleaded hastily. *Pin him down.*

Esme didn't ask questions, she just did as I asked and held Voltaire down with her body weight. He was fighting against Mrs Dawes' control with all his might; if he hadn't been, he would have simply phased away from us. I had to save him – and I had an idea how. It wasn't going to be a popular move, but it would do the job.

I reached out with my piping magic, not to talk to him but to control him. This was the reason why pipers were so disliked and distrusted; we could talk to animals and control them too, whether they were sentient or not. Pipers were raised with strong moral foundations; if anyone broke the rules, the piping community would wield justice heavily and swiftly. But the pipers couldn't afford to have the Other realm turn on them, so mostly they kept their heads down.

I hoped what I was about to do wasn't enough for the pipers to kill me, but it was a risk I'd have to take. Mrs Dawes *had* to be stopped.

I reached out with my magic; whilst Esme's paws were still touching Voltaire's skin we had four points of contact and it was easier to control. I could see Mrs Dawes' tenuous hold over him, like a black hook in his heart. I took hold of Voltaire, snapped her weak bond and replaced it with my own.

Mrs Dawes screamed.

Esme relegated control and I shifted onto two. Unfortunately, I ended up lying naked on top of Voltaire. I rolled off him and carefully removed my controlling hold over him at the same time. 'Please destroy the pentagram!' I entreated. I was careful not to order him.

If his eyes were angry before, they were furious now. He sent me a soundless snarl, but nevertheless he phased into the pentagram's circle and scuffed the design with his shoe.

Mrs Dawes continued to screech furiously as it started to lose its power.

As Ares' blood stopped its relentless flow around the morbid diagram, she pulled out a paintbrush; she was intent on fixing the damage. With a snarl, Voltaire punched her in the face so hard that she flew out of the warded area.

She got to her feet and scrambled up and away, plunging deep into the woods. I hesitated. Ares' chest was slowing, and he was letting out slow, snuffling breaths. 'Amber! Help Ares!' I shouted, then ran after Mrs Dawes.

Voltaire continued to scrub out the rest of the pentagram with his feet, his eyes lit with malicious joy at foiling the necromancer.

Amber tried to get to Ares but the three other vampyrs zeroed in on her. Greg fired at one of them, but the bullets were no more than an irritating distraction. They continued towards Amber; Mrs Dawes' last order endured, even though the pentagram had been destroyed. Luckily, Bastion was there with his deadly claws and a beak that could rip the head off a man – or apparently a vampyr.

I left them behind and focused on chasing down Mrs Dawes. 'Stop running and fight!' I snarled at her.

She turned to face me, her smile warm and oh-so-treacherously familiar. 'Lucy, you've got to understand. I did it all for the good of the Other realm.'

'Kidnapping Bobby wasn't for the Other, was it? It was for you.'

'I made sure he was treated well. Unlike me, when I was held captive by the wolves.' She drew back a sleeve and pointed to the horrific scar I'd seen on her arm before. 'I got this when Isiah Samuel stole my blood.'

'You were the witch that Bastion captured.'

'Captured and doomed to imprisonment. They held me for five years until they grew complacent. I promise you, I treated Bobby a darned sight nicer than they treated me.'

'Oh well, that makes it alright then, doesn't it?'

Her smile slipped at my sarcasm. 'Now, Lucy, don't be like that. Just let me go and I'll move on to another pack.'

'You've got to be nuts if you think I'll let you go anywhere.'

'Call the Connection then.' She folded her arms and looked at me pugnaciously.

I shook my head. 'I've underestimated you for long enough. You'd escape from them. You're a black witch, a necromancer.'

'I've been playing nice,' she sighed, 'but I guess now it's time to play dirty.' With that, she shifted and leapt at us – but we were quicker. Esme and I shifted as we ran, controlling our motions together; we moved as one, in complete accord.

Mrs Dawes had never fully accepted her wolf and they still hadn't reached any kind of unity. And ultimately, Mrs Dawes' wolf answered to the Great Pack. Her eyes flashed gold as her wolf took control of her body, then she stood, frozen and immobile. She lifted up her head and offered Esme her throat.

Esme and I were agreed that this was no time for mercy. We stalked forward, intent on the execution in which Mrs Dawes' wolf was complicit, then moved in close and leapt at her. As our jaws clamped around her tender neck, her eyes flashed blue as she struggled to regain control of her wolf. It was too little, too late, and Esme shook off her futile struggles with hardly any effort.

We did not hesitate. For the second time that day, we ripped a throat and stole a life.

Chapter 27

We shifted onto two and ran back to the others carrying Mrs Dawes' body. I had no idea what to do with it, but Bastion needed her blood to break the curse that was torturing him. As I entered the glade, I saw that the other three vampyrs were dead or gone. The fury on Voltaire's face suggested the former.

Amber was by Ares' side. She looked up as I approached; her eyes shining with unshed tears. A huge lump took up residence in my throat. God, no: not Ares. We'd already had so much death today, I couldn't handle another.

Greg was sawing at Ares' restraints, freeing him even if it was just for his last moments. I laid Mrs Dawes' body down none too gently and stared at my unicorn. I wasn't feeling charitable. 'Bastion,' I called to the griffin. 'Get the blood you need to break the curse on you.'

'Do you have something I could use?' he asked Amber politely.

She glared but rummaged in her bag for a glass vial. 'It's all I've got,' she said curtly.

'Thank you. It'll do just fine.'

Esme's sorrow and regret were profound, and she wanted to say her goodbyes to Ares. We shifted so she could say farewell first. She padded forward and gave Ares a nuzzle and a lick, then let me take over so I could say goodbye too.

I shifted back onto two legs and knelt by his head. His blood-red eyes met mine. How had I ever thought them malevolent? They were full of affection for me; after all, we'd been together through the centuries.

'Hey, Ares, you're home now. You're okay,' I said aloud. I reached out with my piping magic to forge the link between us one last time. He sent me an image of the rose garden and the mansion, and I felt his love wash over me. I struggled to hold back my tears; crying wasn't fair on him, not when he was dying. I managed a cracked smile and stroked his soft fur.

We're all safe, thanks to you. You can rest. Just let go. It's okay. Everything is okay.

He met my eyes and his chest rose one last time. I waited for the exhale, but it didn't come. He was gone, and now I could cry. I wept brokenly and Esme howled with me.

Greg bundled me into his arms and rocked us back and forth. When the tears finally eased, I pushed back a little out of his arms. 'Thank you,' I murmured, swiping tears from my face.

'I've got you,' he promised.

'You have.'

Amber was scrubbing at her face. 'I'm just tired,' she said finally. 'I'm so tired.'

I pulled her into my arms. 'Me too. But it's alright to be sad.'

'He was just a unicorn.'

'There was nothing *just* about him.'

She looked up at me. 'He always came and said hi when I arrived at the mansion,' she said abruptly. 'I always carried Polos with me. He loved Polos.'

'He had a soft spot for mints.' I smiled. 'He liked you.'

'I liked him,' she admitted, then she sighed. 'I don't know how much more grief I can take.'

'A little more,' I said softly. 'We can always take a little more, because what's the alternative?'

'To stop caring.'

'You could sooner stop the sun. For all your brusque exterior, you're gooey sweet on the inside.'

She sighed again. 'Don't tell anyone. It's kind of a secret.'

'Your secret is safe with me,' I promised. I looked around the small glade. No sign of the vampyr. 'Voltaire?' I asked Bastion.

'He split. He wasn't happy that we killed his men.'

'His men were controlled by a necromancer and had been ordered to kill us.'

'His view was that you should have piped them, as you did him,' Bastion admitted.

'I didn't have time for that. I couldn't let Mrs Dawes get away.'

'What happened between you?' he asked.

'She didn't get away,' I said grimly.

Bastion gave me a one-armed hug. 'You did the right thing.'

'Then why does it feel so damn wrong?'

'Leadership comes with a price.'

I closed my eyes. 'I don't want to pay it anymore.'

'You don't have a choice. You can't resign from being alpha.'

'I can retire,' I pointed out.

'When you're old, but you're not even thirty. You've a way to go yet.'

I didn't want to think about it, not just now. What I wanted was food, a shower and rest, in that order.

The sun was creeping up on what had been the longest night of my life. I looked at Ares lying so unnaturally still; he didn't even look like my unicorn. Now he was only fur and flesh; whatever had made him uniquely Ares was gone.

'We'll see to him,' Greg offered, nodding to Archie and Liam. 'You go and get some rest.'

I wanted to argue but I also wanted to obey. Exhaustion and hunger were calling the shots, so I turned and started the trek back to the mansion. I'd just reached the field when Jess and Emory came running towards us. 'Luce! What happened? You should have got me!' Jess protested.

'You were looking after Emory.'

'I'm fine,' Emory reassured me. 'I just passed out. We were coming to help – I'm sorry we were too late.'

'I appreciate the thought, but thankfully I think we're all done.' I bit my lip, 'Actually, maybe you could help Greg? Mrs Dawes killed Ares and we could use some help sorting out the body.'

'Of course,' Emory said. 'Do you want me to help bury him or cremate him?'

'Cremate him. I don't want any of his body parts being used in a potion. Just – yeah. Cremate him. We'll scatter him in the roses. He'd like that.'

'Sure.' He paused. 'Are you sure he's dead?'

'His chest stopped moving,' I said flatly.

'Yes, but unicorns do that catatonic thing, you know?'

My heart started to race. I wanted to quash the tiny hope that flared because it was going to hurt so damned badly when it was snuffed out. 'No, I don't know. What do you mean?'

'They go into some sort of stasis when they're threatened. They can survive truly horrific things – that's another reason they're used for potion ingredients. They can be kept alive for a long time and that keeps the ingredients fresh.'

I didn't bother speaking again; I just turned on my heels and ran back the way we'd come on.

Come on, miracle.

We'll give up feeding on fish food for a miracle, Esme agreed.

Phish-food ice cream, I corrected, close to hysteria.

I stumbled back through the woods. Bastion was gone, presumably with the vial to get the curse broken, but Amber and Greg were still there with Liam and Archie. 'Catatonic,' I blurted. 'Could Ares be catatonic? Emory says unicorns go into a coma to preserve themselves.'

Amber blinked. 'I don't know. I've never seen a unicorn coma. It seemed a lot like he died.'

'I know – but can you heal him? Try painting some runes on him.'

She bit her lip. 'I'm itching pretty badly, but I might have one rune left in me. I'll try.' She shook her head. 'But manage your expectations, because I don't think this is going to work. I think he's already dead.'

'Then why try?' I demanded.

'Even I have been known to be wrong on occasion,' she said drily.

She got out a paintbrush, drew a nullifying squiggle across Mrs Dawes' rune and started to paint a new one. We waited with bated breath until it was complete.

Amber slumped, and the triangle tattoos disappeared from her forehead as she fainted into the Common realm. I heard the *whump* of Bastion's wings, which was all the warning we had before he landed next to her. 'I thought you'd gone already!' I said.

'Not yet. She wasn't safe yet, and you told me to keep her safe. I'll carry her to the mansion.' It was the oddest thing to see his golden beak move and human words come rolling out.

Bastion gently cradled Amber's unconscious form in his huge claws and rose up. All eyes turned back to Ares. As we watched his wounds began to close. 'What does that mean?' I asked Greg frantically, pointing at the healing. 'Does it mean anything?'

'I don't know,' he admitted, threading his fingers between mine. 'Watch,' he breathed.

We stared as more of the skin drew together, but still Ares didn't move. My heart began to sink: we'd healed a corpse. I turned to Greg, and he pulled me into his arms.

'Sorry,' Emory said faintly. 'False hope is the worst.'

'Wait!' Jess shouted. 'He moved! Look, his chest!'

I whirled out of Greg's arms and ran to Ares' side, grabbed my magic and reached out to him with my hand and my magic. *Ares?* An image of a huge pile of raw burger patties came back, and I burst into tears. 'You can have all the burgers you want,' I promised, throwing my arms around his neck. He gave a soft whicker and lay back down. He was tired, he needed sleep. I let him rest and disentangled my magic.

'He's going to be okay,' I said in disbelief. 'It's a freaking Christmas miracle.'

'It's April,' Greg pointed out.

'So? Santa delivered early this year.'

'Or really late.' Greg was grinning, happy to be chatting shit with me. He gestured to Archie and Liam. 'We'll stay here and guard him until he can move.'

'Shall we?' I said to Jess and Emory and nodded towards the mansion. I wanted to stay with Ares but duty called, loudly and incessantly. She's a real bitch.

Jess and I strolled arm in arm until we reached the lawns. I stepped away from her and she moved to hug me but I shook my head, conscious of the watching eyes. Hurt shone in her eyes.

'If you hug me, I'm going to fall apart,' I told her. 'Today has been rough as hell. We've ended on a high, but I've killed people. I'm hanging by a thread, and I can't break down now. Later. Hug me later, when we're alone.'

The hurt vanished, replaced by understanding. 'Of course. What can I do?'

'Can you help mobilise the pack? Let's get everyone in, fed and then to bed. We could all do with some rest.'

'You got it.' She walked briskly to the nearest group of people and started corralling them inside.

'You're a good person Lucy,' Emory observed. 'And a good alpha.'

I smiled tightly. 'It sucks being the boss.'

'Yeah, but someone's got to do it.'

'And it's us mugs.'

He smiled. 'Indeed. But as bosses, there are some benefits. Let's get someone to find us some food.' He barked out an order to Elena; that man could even deliver an order with panache.

We went to my sitting room. 'Where are the gargoyles?' I asked Elena when she brought me a bacon sandwich and some tea.

'They left just before sunrise.'

'Are they still at risk of turning to stone?'

'They weren't in a hurry to test it. Apparently, it's quite an uncomfortable experience for them,' Elena explained.

'Fair enough.'

'Alpha, can I ask... Ares?'

I beamed. 'He's going to make it. Please tell the pack – I know they were all anxious.' Ares was more than a pet or a mascot, he was family. He was pack.

She grinned with relief. 'Yes, Alpha. I'll spread the word.' She excused herself, leaving Emory and I alone. Amber had been laid on one of the sofas and was sleeping the slumber of the truly weary, deep and unmoving.

Emory and I ate in companionable silence. After a while, Maxwell and Alyssa and Niccolo joined us. Maxwell explained that the rest of the Forge were being sent back to the portal to re-charge. I couldn't blame them; I'd need a visit, too, and soon.

Maxwell hugged me; it was indescribably nice to know he was family. Eventually we were joined by Greg, Archie and Liam. They had moved Ares to the back courtyard, and David was standing guard over him.

Jess came in. 'Everyone's settled in either the bunkrooms, the pack lounge or the banquet hall.'

'Thanks, Jess. You're the best.'

Finley and Noah came in with trays of tea and coffee, and enough biscuits to revive a hypoglycaemic army. After they withdrew, exhaustion set in. A shower seemed like a really good idea.

'No Gato?' I asked Jess.

'He wasn't so keen on riding here on a dragon.'

'Was it fun?' I asked my adrenalin-junkie friend.

'It was amazing!' she admitted, grinning. 'Like a cross between being in a plane and skydiving.'

'I'll stick to aeroplanes, thank you.'

'Skydiving is great fun,' Greg interjected. 'You should give it a try.'

Fuck, no. The expletive from Esme took me completely by surprise. A laugh rolled out of me before I could stop it.

Greg raised an eyebrow in question. 'Esme is not keen on that idea,' I explained with a grin. I checked the time.

'It's late. Or rather, it's very early. Can I suggest we all hit the hay? We could use a few hours' sleep.'

Hitting hay would be ineffectual, Esme commented. **If you wished to get rid of it, it would be best to eat it, or set it on fire.**

It means go to bed, I explained.

She huffed. **Ridiculous.**

'Sounds like a good idea,' Maxwell agreed, a yawn splitting his face.

'Everybody grab four and then reconvene here,' Greg ordered. 'We're going to have one helluva of a clean-up job after this, but it'll keep for a few hours longer.'

I tangled my fingers in Greg's rough-hewn hands, and we headed towards my rooms. As Archie trailed behind us, I took a moment to check on him. He looked like shit. 'Are you alright?' I asked.

'I've been better,' he admitted. 'Mrs Dawes... It just doesn't seem real. She drugged me.' His voice was bewildered. That woman had half-raised him.

'She could have poisoned you loads of times, but she didn't,' I pointed out, trying to offer some sort of twisted comfort.

'She enabled our enemies to tie me to a chair and torture me,' he pointed out bitterly. I had nothing to say in response to that.

Archie cleared his throat and looked at a space behind my left shoulder. 'I wanted to say thanks. For the letter from my dad.'

'Of course! Was it ... nice?'

'Yeah. It really was. He knew what was coming, he planned it all. Sometimes that feels worse, because he knowingly left me. But still, the note – it's closure. So, thanks. I just wanted to say thanks.' He shrugged awkwardly. 'Sleep well, guys.' He turned abruptly on his heel and left for his own room.

I was too tired to process all of that, but I was glad Archie had closure. Greg and I continued to my penthouse suite. Sleep was screaming my name, and I'd never been happier to see my bed. 'I'd love to jump your bones,' I said, 'but the truth is I'm so damn tired.'

'Me too,' he admitted. 'We can cuddle.'

I grinned. 'I never imagined you'd be the type of guy who loves cuddling.'

'Of course I love cuddling. Smushed up against the sexiest woman alive, what's not to love?'

That made me laugh. 'I'm no Angelina Jolie.'

He kissed me. 'You're better.'

'Now I know you're deranged.'

'Not deranged, just in love.'

'Same thing.'

We peeled off our clothes and slumped onto the super-king-sized bed. Greg pulled the covers over us and we huddled together; I was little spoon to his big spoon. As we cuddled, I felt something stir against my back. 'I thought you were too tired?' I laughed.

'Me too, but it turns out I'm not.' He kissed my neck. 'How about you?'

I turned in his arms. 'It turns out I've got a second wind.'

'Hallelujah.'

My alarm beeped to say we'd had our four hours down time. Unfortunately, Greg and I had used a fair portion of that *not* sleeping and I didn't quite feel as daisy fresh as I'd planned. I hoped a fast shower would beat some life into my weary limbs and make my eyes a little less red and bleary.

Greg joined me in the shower and for once there was no hanky-panky; instead, he helped me wash my back as the hot water sluiced down our bodies. I sighed against him. There was so much pleasure in such a simple action.

It was hard to step out and dry off. I didn't want to face the day; I wanted to sleep for a week. But there were charred remains on my lawn and forty of Frost's uncertain werewolves in the mansion.

I took the time to cleanse, tone and moisturise. A moment of small luxury. I moisturised my elbows too. Even the burlap of the skin world deserves moisturising. We dressed in clean clothes and went to my living room to concoct an action plan. Everyone else had already arrived and we were the last to the party. 'Another restorative shower?' Jess teased me.

'This one really was! It was the bedtime that wasn't so restorative,' I admitted with a wink.

Amber, Bastion and Emory were sitting on one sofa, with my family opposite. Most of them looked a little more vibrant for having a decent rest – though Bastion still looked like hell.

There was a gentle knock at the door and Finley came in bearing food. The scent of freshly baked pastries made my mouth water, and my stomach gave an audible growl. He had barely laid down the massive tray of croissants and Danishes before we all piled in. 'These are amazing,' I said around a *pain au chocolat*.

'Thank you.' He looked pleased. 'I made them myself.'

I blinked. 'Wow. Well, we need a new chef...' I thought of the hole that had been left by Mrs Dawes' death. She may have been a homicidal necromancer, but boy, she could cook up a storm.

'I'd be honoured to feed the pack,' Finley said proudly.

'Then you're hired. Can you make more of these? We have a lot of mouths to feed,' I said, thinking of Frost's pack. *My* pack. Holy hell.

'I'm already on it. Noah and Elena have been helping me in the kitchen.'

'Brilliant, thank you. Keep up the good work.'

'Yes, Alpha.' He left the room and closed the door behind him.

'You're a natural,' Emory commented.

'A natural blonde?'

He grinned. 'A natural leader.'

'Oh. Thanks. I try.'

'You're doing a great job.'

'That's what I keep saying,' Greg said with a huff. 'But she never takes it from me.'

'That's not what I hear,' Jess mumbled under her breath. I shot her a glare that made her laugh.

There was a knock on the living-room door. It swung open and David tucked his head around the edge. 'I'm sorry to intrude, Alpha, but we have company drawing up to our gate. Lots of company.'

I let out a sigh. 'Of course we do. Who are they?'

'They say that they're the council.'

'The werewolf council?'

'Yes. Shall I open the gates?'

I nodded and stood. 'Yes, we'd better not keep them waiting. I'll meet them at the front door.'

Emory stood. 'I'll come with you – a show of political strength, in case you need it.'

'You think I'll get in trouble?'

'You killed an alpha and subsumed his pack, so trouble is a possibility. A few obvious allies won't hurt.'

'I'll come too,' Maxwell offered. 'They'll think twice before crossing the Forge.'

'I'm grateful for your help,' I said to my cousin, 'but what will Roscoe think of all of this? I don't want to drive a wedge between you.'

'Family comes first – Roscoe knows that. You're an Alessandro, so I stand with you.'

'We all do,' Alyssa confirmed. 'I'll come too.'

I was still bone tired. The short sleep hadn't stopped my eyes feeling sore, and that was probably why they were full of tears. I swallowed hard and waited until I was certain that I could speak. Their support meant everything to me. 'Thank you, all of you. It's been the longest night, and it seems like it's going to be a long day. I'm so grateful.'

Jess squeezed my shoulder. 'We've got you.'

Greg smiled proudly at me. 'Let's show them what we've got.'

From the couch, Amber let out a loud sigh. 'You're going to owe me the biggest drink ever.'

I grinned at her. 'Strawberry daiquiri?' I suggested.

She looked horrified. 'Champagne,' she corrected. 'Obviously.'

I looked around the room and felt content. I'd struggled my whole life with being adopted; now I felt so grateful that I'd found my birth family – and so much more. I knew that whatever was coming my way, I could face it.

We are strong, Esme said.

And lucky, I whispered back, amused.

Both are helpful. Let us face this council. I do not fear their judgement.

I'm not feeling warm and fuzzy about it.

She snorted. **If you want warmth, start a fire. There is no time to delay. We should be waiting for them in a show of strength when they arrive.**

'Let's rock 'n' roll,' I said aloud. 'Let's show this council what we've got.'

'Damn right,' Greg called.

We filed out and stood on the mansion steps. We could hear the gravel crunching as cars drove up our long drive with ceremonial slowness. Four black Range Rovers drew up, full of the country's most deadly and powerful werewolves. If I ignored the butterflies in my tummy, perhaps they would go away.

They'd have a fight on their hands if they were coming for my head, but exhaustion was weighing on me, and I really needed time in Common to recharge. I wasn't sure how much magic I had left, and I'd be screwed if I got dropkicked back into Common before I was ready.

The cars parked neatly in rows. As if they were synchronised, the doors opened and the black-clad passengers filed out. On my left, Maxwell, Alyssa and Niccolo blatantly called flames to their hands. On my right, Greg, Liam and Archie were ready to shift at a moment's notice. Behind me stood a wan Amber, Emory, Jess and Bastion.

The potential for violence hung in the air.

One of the men stepped forward. 'Lucy Barrett, alpha of the Home Counties Pack. You have killed Beckett Frost and taken control of his pack.'

He said it as a statement but nevertheless I answered. 'I have.' Maybe killing Frost had automatically given me his seat on the council. Was that what this visit was about? If so, it was one hell of a welcome wagon.

'You have broken the curse over the werewolves and gargoyles and freed the Great Pack.'

'Well, to be honest Amber was the one who broke the curse. I gave her the blood and everything, but she's the one with the witchy powers.'

'You ordered it,' the spokesman argued.

I straightened my shoulders. Own it. 'I did.'

'You bring in a new age.'

I didn't know what to say about that, because I didn't know much about the old age, so I said nothing.

The assembled crowd of council werewolves bent their knee as one. 'My Queen,' the spokesman intoned.

Fuck.

Coming Soon

What's Next?

Whether I write more stories from Lucy is up to you! If you want to see more of Lucy, please review and let me know! To keep you going I have an extra treat coming your way, *Defender of the Pack,* a Lucy prequel novella.

After that, next up on the schedule is more from Jinx and Emory! Jinx has to get to grips with Emory's dragon court in *Challenge of the Court,* coming 2023 – the exact date is yet to be decided, after I've written the series, but I've put up a little pre-order now if you want to grab that so you don't go forgetting all about little old me.

I have been working hard on a bunch of cool things, including a new and shiny website which you'll love. Check it out at www.heathergharris.com.

Hear about all my latest releases – subscribe to my Newsletter at my website www.heathergharris.com/subscribe.

Heather G. Harris' Other works:-

The Other Realm

0.5. Glimmer of Dragons, a prequel novella.
1. Glimmer of The Other,

2. Glimmer of Hope,

3. Glimmer of Death, and

4. Glimmer of Deception.

The Other Wolf

0.5 Defender of The Pack, a prequel novella.
1. Protection of the Pack,

2. Guardian of the Pack, and

3. Saviour of The Pack

About Heather

Heather is an urban fantasy writer and mum. She was born and raised near Windsor, which gave her the misguided impression that she was close to royalty in some way. She is not, though she once got a letter from Queen Elizabeth II's lady-in-waiting.

Heather went to university in Liverpool, where she took up skydiving and met her future husband. When she's not running around after her children, she's plotting her next book and daydreaming about vampires, dragons and kick-ass heroines.

Heather is a book lover who grew up reading Brian Jacques and Anne McCaffrey. She loves to travel and once spent a month in Thailand. She vows to return.

Want to learn more about Heather? Subscribe to her newsletter for behind-the-scenes scoops, free bonus material and a cheeky peek into her world. Her subscribers will always get the heads up about the best deals on her books.

Subscribe to her Newsletter at her website www.heatherg harris.com/subscribe.

Contact Info: www.heathergharris.com
Email: HeatherGHarrisAuthor@gmail.com

Social Media

Heather can also be found on a host of social medias:

Facebook Page

Facebook Reader Group

Goodreads

Bookbub

Instagram

Tiktok

Reviews

Reviews feed Heather's soul. She'd really appreciate it if you could take a few moments to review her books on Amazon or Goodreads and say hello.

Made in the USA
Las Vegas, NV
05 August 2023

75696470R00187